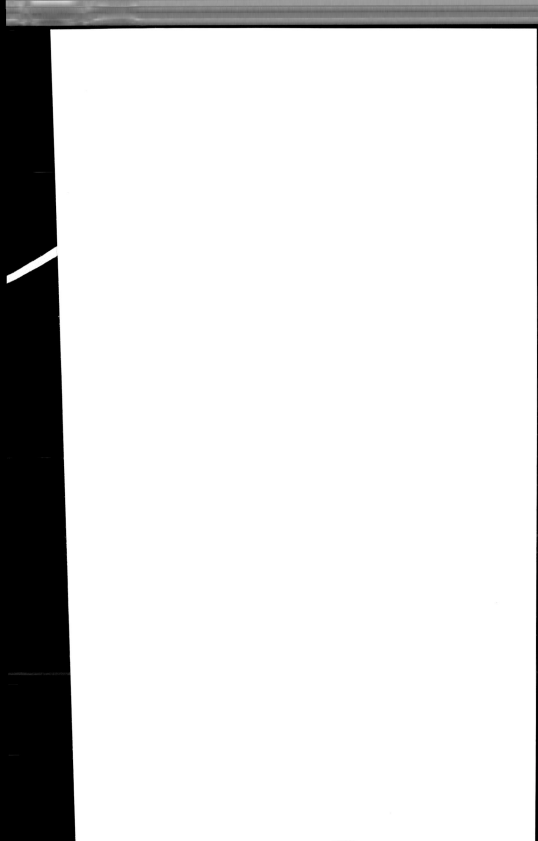

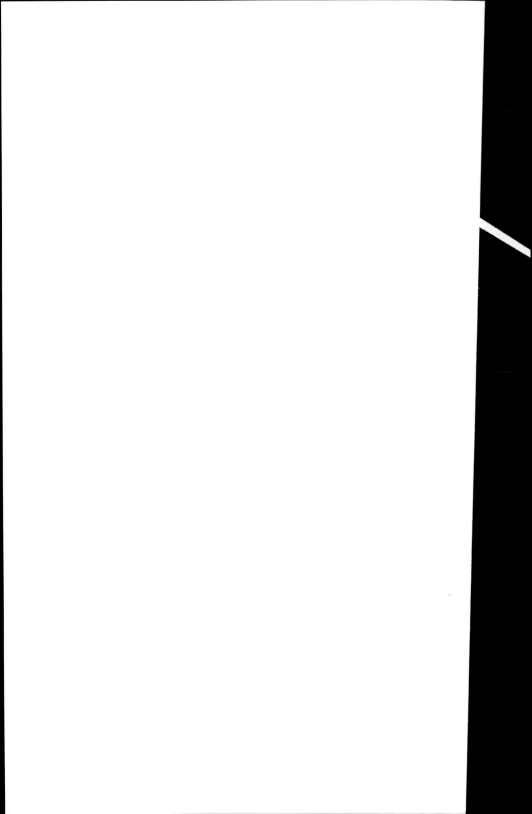

FEISTY FAMILY VALUES

To Gayle,
Best Wishes!
Bill Sharp

FEISTY FAMILY VALUES

B. D. THARP

FIVE STAR
A part of Gale, Cengage Learning

Detroit • New York • San Francisco • New Haven, Conn • Waterville, Maine • London

GALE
CENGAGE Learning

Set in 11 pt. Plantin.

Printed on permanent paper.

LIBRARY OF CONGRESS CATALOGING-IN-PUBLICATION DATA

Tharp, B. D.
  Feisty family values / B. D. Tharp. — 1st ed.
    p. cm.
  ISBN-13: 978-1-59414-849-1 (hardcover alk. paper)
  ISBN-10: 1-59414-849-X (hardcover : alk. paper)
    1. Older women—Fiction. 2. Cousins—Fiction. 3. Family secrets—Fiction. 4. Families—Fiction. 5. Domestic fiction. I. Title.
  PS3620.H35F45 2010
  813'.6—dc22   2009041464

First Edition. First Printing: February 2010.
Published in 2010 in conjunction with Tekno Books.

Printed in the United States of America
1 2 3 4 5 6 7 14 13 12 11 10

This story is dedicated to my father, my husband, my son,
and all of the Feisty Families out there
that we know and love.

ACKNOWLEDGMENTS

I'd like to acknowledge the many people who helped me on the journey to write this novel. I'd like to thank Alice Duncan for sharing her editing expertise. To Sandy, Peggy, Sheila, and Staci, thank you for your critiques. Thanks go to Maxine for being my dearest friend, first reader and stalwart supporter, provider of company, a willing ear, and the hot tub when I needed it most. To my friends Karen, Kim, Brenda, and writing buddies Stephanie, Judy, Peg, Cindy, Colleen, and Lu who inspired me, encouraged me, and hung with me through all the rejections, you know who you are and how much I love and appreciate you. I want to thank my teachers Carol Konek and Emily Hanlon for guiding me down the writing path. To Jim for ignoring the dust and poor cuisine while I labored over the pages, thank you. To my son Matt, thank you for believing in me. I also want to thank Maureen and the others at the Women's Crisis Center, Carolyn who shared her own breast cancer experience, and the folks at the American Cancer Society for providing information about the many who struggle with abuse and disease respectively. Your assistance was invaluable. If I have forgotten anyone, please forgive me and know that your help was appreciated.
—B. D.

PREFACE

The grinding of the brakes jolted her back to the present and the smell of dirty socks and stale cigarette smoke.

"Is this the place, ma'am?" the driver asked.

She looked at the three-story house; pristine white paint glowed in the sun. "Yes," she said.

"That'll be five seventy-five," he said and hung his open palm over his shoulder into the back seat. His knuckles bulged, and his fingers were crooked, and the skin cracked.

"I'm sorry, how much?" She held her breath for a moment, hoping she had enough for the fare.

"Five seventy-five," he flipped the meter handle down and put the car in park. Turning, he looked over the seat with his grizzled chin and rheumy eyes. "You okay?"

"Yes, fine . . . sorry . . ." Annabelle stuffed her handkerchief back up the sleeve of her cardigan and opened her cracked vinyl pocketbook. She pulled out four crumpled ones, two quarters, and an assortment of dimes and pennies from her coin purse. She dropped the wadded bills in his palm and proceeded to count the coins. "Ninety, ninety-one, ninety-two . . ."

"It's five seventy-five, lady," he said. The radio squawked, but he didn't answer.

"That makes five, forty-two," she said. "Just a minute, I always have coins in the bottom of my bag. They fall out sometimes . . ." She found another thirty cents in change and dropped it in his palm. The money she'd placed there had already disappeared into his pocket.

"You're three cents short," he said, and she jumped at the growl in his voice. "Why'd you call a cab if you didn't have the money? Geez, short and no tip besides . . ."

"I'm sorry, I'll go up to the house and see if my cousin has some change." Her eyes filled with tears and her throat constricted.

He snorted, wiping his nose on the back of his hand. The microphone squawked, so he picked it up and spoke. "I got that one. I'm in Riverside now."

He had no idea how hard it had been to come here. She didn't mean to cheat him, but it was all she had. A lone tear escaped down her wrinkled cheek. Annabelle lowered her head and pulled the threadbare hankie from her sleeve.

As she dabbed her eye she noticed two pennies on the floorboard. Reaching down she picked up the coins. "Here you go," she said, a stiff smile on her face. "I found two more."

"Good enough, I got to go, lady," he said. "Got another fare a couple blocks from here."

"Oh, okay. Well, thank you. If you'll give me your name, I'll send you the tip and the penny." She opened the door. The sidewalk appeared a mile long to the porch.

"Forget it," he said and revved the engine. "I suppose you want help with your bag now, too," he spoke to the rearview mirror.

"No, I can . . . manage," she said. She scooted the battered Pullman across the seat and stepped onto the walk. Bracing her hand on the rim of the door she pulled it onto the curb with a thud, then dragged it upright.

He leaned over the back of the seat, eager to close the door, but she beat him to it.

"Thanks," she said, coughing from the exhaust fumes. She

watched him zip around the corner, feeling her courage go with him.

Straightening her shoulders she faced the house and an uncertain welcome. It didn't appear to have changed a bit since she'd last seen it. But she had. Oh, how Annabelle Hubbard had changed.

CHAPTER 1

A dusting mitt lay abandoned on the coffee table. The luscious scent of baking bread wafted through the house, causing Regina's stomach to rumble. She listened to the sounds of her housemate, Tillie, crooning an old Motown tune from the kitchen.

Tillie sauntered into the parlor, still wiping her hands on a dishtowel. "Hey girl, I'm off. I'll see you later."

"Have a nice dinner," Regina said to the air, hearing the back door bang against the frame.

Quiet, at last, she thought and settled onto the window cushion to catch the ebbing light.

A car door slammed, sending a mass of barn swallows into the dusky sky heading northwest of the river, drawing Regina's attention from the tawdry romance that had only just captured her attention. From her seat, she had to look twice before she realized it was her cousin Annabelle who stumbled from the cab dragging a huge tattered suitcase toward the house.

"What the . . . ?"

She stared at what she hoped was an apparition wearing a pink flowered cardigan draped over a faded gunnysack dress, two shades lighter than the blue hair. A white vinyl belt cinched the ample waist of her older cousin.

"Good Lord," Regina muttered. The paperback slipped to the floor, unnoticed. She smoothed her skirt before gliding into the foyer, where she took a deep breath and flung open the massive oak doors before the bell.

"Why, Annabelle, what brings you here?" Her eyes bore a hole into the older woman's brown eyes.

For a moment Regina detected defiance, but it soon disappeared as Annabelle's shoulders rounded. She sniffed back fresh tears, her nose red and chins quivering with the effort. "Hello, Regina. May I come in?"

Regina narrowed her eyes, then scanned Annabelle from head to foot, noting the swollen purple smudge barely concealed by make-up beneath her right eye. "What's wrong with your face?"

A shaking hand quickly covered the swollen bottom lip nearly split in half. "I fell."

With a raise of her eyebrows, Regina made no comment.

"Can I come in?" Annabelle righted her posture, her breasts leading.

Rolling her eyes heavenward, Regina said, "Well, come in off the stoop. I'll get us some refreshments, and then we'll sort out your troubles." She turned to lead her cousin into the cozy parlor.

"It's just . . ." Catching the toe of her shoe on the rug, Annabelle stumbled over the threshold.

Klutz, Regina thought. "Tell me inside, over a cup of tea."

This better be good or I swear to god she's out of here.

Annabelle sank down onto the rich brocade of the carved settee, pulled a crumpled handkerchief from her sleeve, dabbed her lip, then wiped her drippy nose.

"Wait here," Regina said. "And don't break anything."

"Okay. Thanks." Annabelle tugged at the laddered stockings, sniffled, and replaced her nail-bitten fingers in her lap.

From the darkened doorway, Regina paused to watch her cousin scan the room, no doubt taking inventory of the antique furniture, shelves of leather bound books, and crystal vases perched on the fireplace mantel.

With shock, Regina heard her dead mother's voice.

"Poor relatives and baggage is not a good sign."

Swallowing bile, Regina straightened her own shoulders.

I'll handle it, Mother. Good Lord, where did that come from? She shook her head and continued to the kitchen.

The smell of warm pastries accompanied Regina's return to the sitting room. With grace born of privilege, she placed on the coffee table a china tray supporting a matching teapot, plate of scones, and two gold-rimmed cups.

"Always use the best china for guests, even the unwelcome kind," her mother drilled into her head.

Her cousin's face creased with a crooked frown that matched the uneven part in her tinted hair. "How lovely, but why so formal?"

"I don't suppose you know this, but . . . tea tastes better when served from fine china."

She saw Annabelle's mouth tighten as she watched Regina arrange the folds of her silky skirt, then pat her long black and silver braid.

"Where's Matilda? Does she still live here with you?"

"Almost ten years now. She's just left to go shopping and then to dinner with friends."

"Oh, well, I guess I'll see her when she gets back." Annabelle bent down and retrieved the novel from the floor. "Since when did you read heaving bosom books? I thought it was high brow all the way for you."

Regina snatched the book from her. "At least I read," she said, then gave Annabelle a poke on the arm. "Get on with your story. I'm sure it's gripping."

Were the woman's brains stuck in neutral?

With a flinch, Annabelle cradled her arm under the protection of her bosom. "I've been staying with my daughter Liddy, and she's had a hard time since her husband left. She just can't afford another mouth to feed."

"I remember Lydia. Overbearing, judgmental, and self-centered . . . a veritable clone of her late father. So unlike . . ." Regina's foot began to tap.

Puzzled by her cousin's nastiness, Annabelle continued, "I tried not to be a burden. She's got three kids, you know, but I'm always in the way, although I tried to be helpful . . ."

Here we go.

"For instance?" Regina fidgeted, dreading the unavoidable details of yet another of her cousin's woeful sagas.

"Well, I always forgot to thaw out supper. Never got the fabric softener in. I tended to drop things. You know, that sort of thing." Annabelle wiped her nose.

"Somewhat inconvenient, definitely annoying, but hardly catastrophic," Regina said.

"Sometimes I forget my doctor appointments, and I'm a mess in the kitchen." She stared at her shoes.

"I have no problem believing that," Regina said.

Annabelle appeared to be unable to face her. "Everybody burns things sometimes."

"Only inattentive, incompetent . . . oh, never mind, that's still no reason to get the boot. I assume she kicked you out."

The older woman turned toward Regina, twisting her hankie. "Not exactly. A couple of weeks ago the bacon grease caught fire and smoked up the kitchen."

"Tillie does the cooking around here, thank God," Regina said.

"I had to paint and have the curtains cleaned."

"Naturally."

"It took a huge bite out of my Social Security, so I was short on food money. She really can't afford . . ." Annabelle folded her hands over what used to be her waist. "Heavens, it probably wouldn't hurt me to lose a few pounds."

Regina didn't attempt to stifle a yawn, caught in her cousin's web. *Why do I feel like we're kids again?*

I know I'll live to regret it, but she does look pitiful, sagging on mother's settee. Father did say to be kind to those less fortunate, but he never said it again after Mother threw a snit.

Maybe it won't be so bad. Tillie and I can clean her up and find her a new home. Lord help us, we're definitely going to need it.

"The fact is, Annabelle, you could be a Rubens model. He liked to paint fleshy women."

Rising from the chair Regina shivered.

Whoever's keeping track, angel or minion, do me a favor and don't tell my mother.

"For now you may stay. I'll show you to the guest room. It overlooks the garden." She gestured toward the stairs.

"Is there something I can do to help out around the house?" Annabelle asked. "I don't want to be an inconvenience."

Looking away, Regina mumbled, "It's a bit late for that."

"Pardon?" Annabelle said.

"Never mind," Regina said, turning slowly on the toe of her leather slipper to face her cousin. She scanned Annabelle's disheveled outfit from uneven hem to frayed collar.

"As I recall, you used to be pretty good with a needle and thread."

"Oh, yes." Annabelle smiled. "I've taken in sewing for years."

"Good. I don't care to learn, not after all these years, and Tillie has ten thumbs outside of the kitchen. You can help with the mending." Regina tossed her salt-and-pepper braid over her shoulder. "Come along."

Hesitating, Annabelle scanned the parlor again. "I can't believe this place. It's like I stepped back in time. Even though the house is nearly a hundred years old, it's still in beautiful shape. Your mother would be proud."

"I'm sure she is, and I manage very well, thank you."

Standing with the slowness of a Centurion, rather than the sixty-five-year-old she was, Annabelle straightened.

"With Tillie's help, of course."

"Quite." Regina turned on her heel and headed for the staircase in the entryway.

Lifting her bag with effort, Annabelle followed, pausing at the bottom of the stairs to touch the satiny walls. "Do you paint walls as well as landscapes? Oh, no, that would be much too messy. I recall you were never allowed to get dirty when we were kids. You missed out on some great fun."

With a practiced smile, Regina turned to watch her intrusive cousin.

"I've learned to do all kinds of things since we were children. There's no point in paying someone to do simple things, Annabelle, and I've never been afraid of hard work—or soap and water."

"Surely you had plenty to pay contractors after inheriting from your parents and Grandma Morgan?" Annabelle stopped short.

"That's none of your business, and you mean *Grandmere*, don't you?" Regina said.

Ignoring the comment, Annabelle followed Regina to the stairs. "With the animals and garden to tend to, I never seemed to get anything done inside my home."

"It showed."

Her knuckles were white where Annabelle gripped the railing.

Regina's smile thinned. "I just adore Mother's diamonds and the Cadillac. Oh, and of course, the house."

On the way up the stairs, Regina waved her manicured hand, conducting her cousin's attention toward an oil painting of an ancient farmhouse. A wooden fence led to a weathered barn nestled amongst a stand of sycamore trees.

Annabelle gasped. "I remember that painting. It hung in the dining room when Grandma Morgan was alive. You painted it, didn't you? It's always been my favorite."

Regina winced. "*Grandmere*. And you're correct, that painting is one of my earlier works."

"I always dreamed of living in a place like that."

Annabelle followed Regina to the back of the house.

With perverse satisfaction, Regina smiled. "Dreams have a way of turning into nightmares, don't they, Cousin?" With a flourish, she flipped on the light.

"How could you possibly know?" Annabelle said, and then gasped at the sight before her.

Climbing Peace roses blossomed on the walls. Billowing ecru lace hung over an elegant queen-sized four-poster with carved vines that twisted their way up to the finial. Lace runners adorned the vanity and chest that flanked the bed. An imposing wardrobe with fiddle-back inlays stood alone on the opposite wall.

"Oh, my." Annabelle said, sniffing the air. "I can almost smell them." Tears filled her eyes. "For once I'll get to live amongst the roses. But not without the thorns, eh Cousin?" She chuckled. "Thank you, anyway. I do appreciate your helping me out like this."

"I know you'll be comfortable for the short time you'll be staying." Regina took the suitcase and placed it on the bottom of the bed. "Here, let me help you put away your things. It's easier to keep the room clean if it's uncluttered."

Perched on the edge of the bed, Annabelle closed her eyes. "Thank you, no, I can manage unpacking by myself. I am a grown up, Regina."

"Well . . ." Regina studied the wretched blue hair surrounding her cousin's wrinkled face. For a moment it cast a forlorn aspect on her skin. Taking a deep breath, Regina swished out of the room, just catching her cousin's comment.

"I'm a Morgan, too."

"*I warned you,*" her mother's grave voice whispered in her ear.

Too often to count, Regina thought, knowing her mother would hear in whatever level of hell the woman dwelled.

Once downstairs, Regina strode to the kitchen and yanked open the junk drawer. Finding a crinkled pack of cigarettes, she tapped out one, smoothed it between her fingers and lit up. Her thoughts followed the smoke patterns to the ceiling.

"*Nasty habit.*" That pesky voice had followed.

"Convulsing in your grave, Mother? I can't believe I'm talking to myself."

The diaphanous spirit of her mother seemed to appear in the smoke. "*I thought you'd quit.*"

"I only smoke when I'm upset." Feeling an army of invisible bugs crawl up her arms, she rubbed them.

"*The house will stink for a week.*"

Resigned to the fact that she was going insane she sighed. "Yes, Your Majesty, I know."

"*Cigarettes and poor relations were never tolerated in my house.*"

Regina walked through the smoke of her mother's ethereal form, whispering, "Sometimes you're a royal bitch, Victoria Morgan. Oh, how I wish I could've said that when you were alive."

Her hands shook as Regina stubbed out the offensive butt. She tried to muffle the reflexive cough that would mar her controlled demeanor.

Her mother was right about one thing. Annabelle was still whining after all these years.

Sinking into the kitchen chair, Regina resumed the rigid posture drummed into her from earliest childhood. She concentrated on the scarred birch tabletop and waited for the oppressive weight in her chest to recede and her hands to steady.

The grocery bills would definitely increase. Maybe Annabelle could coax something edible out of the garden. When she was eight or nine, she loved to follow her older cousin around in the vegetables, enjoying the aroma of growing things and sunshine, afraid her mother would catch her and switch her back for getting her Mary Jane's dirty. But that was before.

Pushing away from the table, Regina hurried to the door as a chill tickled her spine. Escaping into the parlor, she perched on the window seat to watch the autumn wind blow through the rust and orange leaves. The bird chatter usually lifted her spirits, but not today.

The next morning, the brightness of the sun belied the distinct nip in the air. While the Howard Miller clock struck seven, the new guest slept.

Pursing her lips, Regina blew on the scalding liquid and scanned the newspaper headlines—tension on the Wichita school board and continuing road construction in Central Riverside Park. Nothing new.

Sipping her coffee, childhood memories drifted through her mind. As far back as Regina could remember, Annabelle had whined and cajoled to get her way, especially with Annabelle's father. He'd scared Regina to her bones.

His huge paws would fist at his sides when Frank and Victoria Morgan weren't looking. Anger vibrated off his body in waves, but only Regina and his wife, her beloved Aunt Rose, seemed to notice. She wasn't afraid of him, not like Regina.

When nine-year-old Regina refused to share her fragile china dolls, Bossy Belle would stomp and cry. "My papa says you're a spoiled brat and don't appreciate what you've got because you don't have to work for it. I'm older, I should be allowed to play with anything I want to."

21

Regina relished one particularly scathing retort she'd given to the then twelve-year-old Annabelle. "I appreciate my things. That's what keeps me from sharing them with someone as dirty as you," Regina said, mimicking her stringent mother.

But Annabelle's childish taunts still hurt. "Papa says you're ugly, like the old dead hickory in the north pasture, and just as tough as its nut."

Annabelle's father had been a jackass while alive, and no doubt continued to be one even after his death. Why her delicate Aunt Rose married such a man remained a mystery. Whereas Victoria, Regina's mother, had been like a flawless, beautiful statue, her sister Rose had been as elemental and interesting as her flowering namesake. Clearly, Victoria had once said, Rose had married beneath her.

Regina could picture Annabelle back then, her limp hair, the color of depleted soil, and too thin for barrettes to grip. She was thin back then, made in her father's physical image, complete with dirty nails bitten to the quick.

While a younger Regina, who was always clean and starched, could still hear the echo of her mother's words: "You have an obligation to conduct yourself well, Regina, especially with the lesser branch of our family. Class will tell. Annabelle is poisoned by her family's misfortunes. She cannot appreciate your finery, thus covets everything you are and own."

Closing her eyes, Regina willed herself back to the present. "Mother and her speeches. Annabelle will drive me into the rafters with her incessant mewling. And why has Mother chosen now to haunt me?"

The sound of slippers slapped the stairs, mingling with the creaks from the floorboards, creating a disgruntled symphony.

"I think I'm allergic to mornings," Tillie said, shuffling to the coffee pot.

Regina eyed the embroidered slogan "Under Pressure" issuing from the openmouthed face on the front of her housemate's enormous purple sleep shirt. Her gaze moved up to Tillie's curly white hair lying flat on one side and sticking out on the other. The woman resembled a sea urchin with slits for eyes.

Slopping coffee into a mug Tillie flopped into the chair. "I thought you were in the bath."

"Excuse me?" Regina kept her face composed. "Where are your eyes?"

"Hopefully, in this coffee cup." She squinted at the dark liquid.

"How are you feeling this morning?" Regina struggled to keep from grinning.

"Not worth a shit," Tillie said and sneezed.

"Bless you. And did we party a little too hearty last night?" Regina didn't bother to hide her smile.

"No, we didn't party at all. Just dinner with the bistro bunch." Tillie sipped from the steaming cup and sighed.

"Well, perhaps you realize now that you aren't as young as you used to be."

Tillie's nose hovered above the rim of the cup. "Never. I'm just a little tired, that's all. Working with a great bunch of college kids keeps me young."

They sipped in silence.

Regina watched Tillie's face for a reaction to her next words. "Annabelle's visiting."

"Really? So that's who's in the bath. I was too fogged to give it much thought. We could use some new blood around here. We've become positively stale." Tillie spoke over the rim of her steaming cup.

Regina's earlier humor evaporated. "Since when does a relic over the age of sixty-five qualify as new?"

"As I recall, she's always been a healthy woman," Tillie said.

"That wasn't how she appeared yesterday with her suitcase and rumpled hankie. She looked a lot like you do now, disheveled and ancient."

"These bones may feel like they've been around more than fifty years, but my mind's a youngster. You might try not acting your age and see if it doesn't spice up your personality." Tillie closed her eyes and sipped.

"You're younger than I am," Regina said.

"Less than a year doesn't count," Tillie said. "We'll both be sliding into sixty before we know it."

"Humph."

Three cups later, Tillie headed for the shower. She tapped on the bathroom door, but heard no response, so she stepped into the room and found Annabelle's still form lolling in the water. A snore issued from parted lips. Her cheeks were ruddy and her hair fuzzy from the humidity in the tiny room. The sight of her black eye and pink fleshy arms covered with yellow, green, and purple smudges made Tillie gasp.

"Annabelle?"

Blushing, Belle lurched, sloshing water on the wall and the floor.

"Oh, my, I must've dozed off." She grabbed the face cloth. It was too small to hide behind, so she began a frantic lathering. "Sorry. I'll be out in a minute."

Grabbing a folded towel out of the cabinet Tillie tossed it under the tub as more water slopped over the slide.

"What the hell happened?"

"It's just a little water, I'll clean it up," Annabelle said.

Tillie could feel her teeth clench. She put her hands on her hips with feet braced apart. "Who did that to you?"

"What are you talking about?" Slouching forward, Annabelle's face and ears turned cherry red. She attempted to cover the limbs in question with the pitifully small rag. "Oh. I'm very clumsy. The slightest bump bruises me."

Leaning forward for a closer examination Tillie snorted. "Those look like handprints, and who hit you in the eye?"

"Don't be ridiculous, I fell into a doorknob. They're nothing. Really." Annabelle cupped her hands with water to rinse the soap from her bare form. "I'll only be a minute. Now, Tillie, please leave."

"I'll give you five minutes, then we talk," Tillie said, slamming the door closed behind her.

Storming back into the kitchen, Tillie clobbered the countertop with her mug and slopped coffee over the rim. Grabbing for a paper towel, she unrolled five before they tore free. "Dammit."

"What are you growling about now, Matilda Jean? Didn't get enough caffeine?"

"Don't use that schoolmarm tone with me, Regina Louise. Someone's been beating the hell out of Annabelle." She sopped at the mess then tossed the towels in the trash bin.

"Really?" Regina sipped her coffee. "I've felt like throttling her a time or two myself."

"I'm serious, and I don't care if she is a pain in your backside. She doesn't deserve to be beaten."

Regina shrugged. "She's not exactly graceful."

With a sputter, Tillie stared at her friend. "Graceful? What planet are you on?"

"You don't know that she has been beaten. Besides, what can I do about it?" Regina followed the rim of her cup with her finger.

"We can report it. We can protect her." Tillie's black eyes blazed.

"To whom? How? We don't even know what happened. Unless you want to pad her already padded body with pillows, my guess is she's going to stumble into the furniture and bruise herself more."

"I'm not buying it. No one is that clumsy." Tillie crossed her arms over her chest.

"You don't know my cousin. Settle down. You act like she needs rescuing." Regina pushed Tillie's coffee cup closer. "What are you going to do, don tights and a cape? Be Wonder Woman, perhaps? Halloween will be here in a couple of weeks."

Her arms dropped as Tillie clenched her fists. "It isn't funny. She's your family."

"Unfortunately, you're correct, but I don't want her here. She'll drive me insane." Regina pushed back from the table and rummaged in the drawer for a cigarette, muttering, "I'm halfway there already."

Annabelle hesitated in the doorway, wrapped from neck to ankle in frayed pink chenille. "Excuse me. Could I have some coffee?"

"Of course." Regina forced a smile.

Whispering her thanks, Annabelle pulled up a chair.

Returning to her seat, Tillie spoke to Annabelle's bowed head. "Now, what about the bruises?"

Annabelle sputtered, dribbling coffee down her chin. "What about them?"

Handing her a napkin, Regina said, "Tillie wants to know who's been smacking you around."

"No one. I fall down a lot. You know that. And I bruise easily."

"There you are, Matilda Jean," Regina said, taking another sip of coffee.

"Bullshit," Tillie said.

"It's just my old skin. When you get to be my age, you'll understand." Annabelle clasped her hands on top of the table. "Don't worry about it."

"Whatever you say, Annabelle," Tillie said, narrowing her eyes.

"Don't glare at me," Regina said. "I told her she could stay. For a while, anyway." She leaned over and slipped the sleeve up on Annabelle's left arm. Dark stains marred the pale skin from wrist to elbow.

With a lift of her nose, Tillie said, "It's criminal. If it ever happens again, I'm calling the cops."

"It's no one's fault—but my own," Annabelle said.

Finding it hard to swallow, Regina cleared her throat. There were times growing up that she'd felt sorry for Annabelle. She'd hated Annabelle's father and husband, both torn from the same damaged cloth. They had no right to do what she suspected they had done to their women. But both were dead. Was Annabelle hurting herself on purpose? For attention?

"To be honest, no one has the right to injure anyone."

"Gee, Regina, I'll bet that hurt," Tillie said.

"Do what?" Annabelle said, keeping her eyes averted. "You can't protect me from myself, ladies. Face it, I'm a menace."

Regina stared at the discolorations. "Yes, it would appear that you are. Just stay out of the kitchen. There are sharp objects in there."

The sunlight caressed the space between them, and the quiet room became safe, comfortable.

"I always hated purple," Annabelle said, breaking the strained silence.

Regina nodded. "It never was your color."

CHAPTER 2

"Well, hell," Tillie pushed away from the table. "On that note, I'm heading to the shower."

"Annabelle, you really should lie down. You look positively haggard." Regina tucked an errant strand of hair behind her ear.

"Nice, Reggie," Tillie snapped. "I guess it's easier to be a bitch than to admit you care." She knew differently and had a twelve-year friendship to prove it. "Come on, Belle, let's go upstairs where it's quiet."

Ignoring them both, Regina took another sip of her cold coffee.

Tillie opened the door to Belle's room and smiled at the climbing rose wallpaper. "Cozy. Have a nice snooze and don't mind her. You're a Morgan, too, Annabelle. You have as much right to stay in this house as she does. We won't let her kick you out."

"Grandma willed the house to her, not me." Turning toward the bed, Annabelle sighed. "This used to be one of grandma's favorite places. It makes me feel like I'm living in a garden." She sat on the edge of the pale pink comforter.

"All you need is a batch of fresh roses." Tillie wrinkled her nose. "Regina furnishes plenty of fertilizer."

For the first time that day, Annabelle smiled. "Grandma Morgan always had a vase of fresh flowers in her room."

"I'll bet it smelled nice."

Annabelle closed her eyes for just a moment. "Oh, yes."

Giving her an affectionate pat, Tillie headed down the hall.

Of all the rooms in this old house Tillie liked hers the best. It had become her sanctuary, a secluded spot to dream and draw strength, in subtle green tones. So what if there were a few thorns and the occasional pile of manure.

Testing the air as Belle had done, Tillie shook her head in dismay. A stale odor wafted to her nostrils. "Shower time, old girl."

A few minutes later she relished the steaming water and drew circles of bubbles around the divot in her right breast.

A tape from more than ten years ago replayed in her memory, and she was once again standing facing the hospital elevator, her head drooped. She hadn't noticed the woman inside the tiny box when the doors opened. She was too busy watching her feet shuffling over the lip, wondering if she could liquefy and slide down the crack and disappear into the darkness.

"Matilda?"

Her neck wasn't doing its job properly, but then nothing else was either. Struggling, Tillie lifted her chin far enough to see a teal floral broomstick skirt. Recognition gave her the strength to scan up to the silver hoop earrings of Regina Morgan-Smith, more than an acquaintance, but not quite a friend. "Hi."

"Are you all right, dear?"

"That's kind of a dumb question, considering our present location."

"Don't be flip. Why are you here?"

"I don't know, I thought maybe I'd come in and see if I had the big C. Guess what? I do."

Regina stepped back against the wall with a time-lapsed blink. "Have you sought a second opinion?"

"What's the point?" Tillie said with a shrug of her narrow shoulders.

Slipping her hand under Tillie's arm Regina reached out to press a number. "Floor?"

"Eighth floor, room eight-eleven. Aces and eights, the dead woman's hand."

"I'll accompany you."

Watching the numbers glow orange, Tillie felt gravity drag her bones as they ascended. "What're you in for?"

With tight lips Regina responded, "Testing."

"Oh? Did you pass?"

"The therapist says so," Regina sniffed. "In fact, they told me to go home, disregard the ignorant praises sung on Devlin's behalf, and go forth into volunteer work."

Tillie's eyes popped. "Wow, you've never been this open with personal stuff before. You must really be in a funk."

They arrived at Tillie's room, where she promptly collapsed on the hospital bed. "In other words, they're telling you to move on?"

"Precisely." The corners of Regina's mouth were pinched.

"Medical morons. I could've told you that, and at no charge." Tillie closed her eyes.

"Well, why didn't you?"

"You never asked." They sat in companionable silence for a few minutes.

After clearing her throat, Regina spoke. "Will you have to have surgery?"

"A lumpectomy."

"And what sort of treatment regimen?"

Tillie turned her black gaze towards her companion. "Your basic intravenous poison, outpatient, a couple days a week."

"But how will you manage?"

"Oh, I'll manage just fine. It's called independence, Regina. Try it sometime."

Raising her eyes to the ceiling, Regina cleared her throat.

"You're not normally such a termagant, Tillie."

"I'm not normally a card-carrying member of the cancer club, either. I think I'm entitled to be a bit pissed off."

"Very well, but I'm asking a serious question. How will you get around?"

Taking a deep breath, Tillie answered, "There's a shuttle that comes for us victims every few hours. You know, one of those spouses of former patients-volunteer driver things."

Regina's mouth paled and slashed the bottom of her face. "I see." She seemed to have a problem swallowing. "What if you get sick?"

"Pretty likely, I imagine. That shit's toxic."

Tillie watched Regina grip her braid and wondered what had happened to that normally cool behavior. A war appeared to be waging hot and heavy in the woman. "Why do you care what's happening to me?"

"Maybe we could help each other," Regina said.

"How so?" Tillie pushed up onto her elbows, her eyebrows raised.

Pulling the chair closer to the bedside, Regina spoke in a monotone. "The doctors think I need someone else to focus on besides myself. You're alone now and may need someone to look after you for a while. I was just, I thought maybe . . ."

Hmm. Second time today Regina had opened the locked door to vulnerability. And Tillie had never seen her at a loss for words. "Thanks, but no thanks. We'd kill each other, and you know it."

Stoic as ever, Regina sat back in the chair and studied the tiny woman. "I don't know any such thing."

"I don't need charity."

"I'm not suggesting anything of that ilk, but if that's the way you feel about it, fine." Regina flipped her braid over her shoulder. "I was offering a limited partnership. Friend to friend."

Tillie's smile sagged. "I do appreciate the offer."

"Fine." With renewed military stiffness Regina rose from her chair. "Take care of yourself."

"Wait." Tillie studied the imperious woman as she paused before the exit and wondered who was the more desperate.

"Let's talk . . ." This suggestion led into the present time, where Tillie discovered she was freezing. "Damned ancient water heater."

After toweling off, she pulled her favorite wild woman t-shirt over her head. Neither of them had given in easily, but the limited arrangement had lengthened into permanence. Now, they might add another member to their clan. She only had to convince prissy Regina to do the right thing.

CHAPTER 3

It had been fifty years since she'd slept in this house, and Annabelle still felt as unwanted as a bug in the pantry.

She tossed off the covers and stretched her stiff back. Time to check out the garden. It would be good to smell the fragrant earth again. She missed the early days with her husband David on her daddy's farm. The time before he had shown her the power of his fist. Annabelle buttoned up a blue cotton housedress while she pushed her thoughts away from those images.

"Tillie's right. I'm a Morgan, too," she said aloud. Exiting the room, Annabelle passed the farm painting over the stairs. She sighed. Regina got the house, the paintings, the car, and the diamond earrings, while all she'd gotten were Grandma's string of pearls and bruises. Proof again just how low on the food chain she lived.

Walking through the kitchen, she grabbed a handful of cookies and headed out the back door, stuffing them into her mouth. Her fingers flexed with the urge to dig in the dirt.

A bakery rack stood sentinel on the porch, holding small gardening tools, clay pots, and a crumpled straw hat. Smiling at the dusty bonnet, she tucked a pair of gloves and a spade into her pocket and headed toward an impressive collection of weeds.

"I'll stand up straight and tall, by damned, strong as those thistles, however undesirable we both might be," she said.

The roses needed the least attention, so Annabelle crossed the grass to the once productive vegetable garden. She started on the corner nearest the stepping-stones.

Sinking to her knees, she wondered if Liddy would water the plants she had nursed back to health. Probably not; her daughter only soaked herself, with eighty proof. Peggy might take care of them. She's such a budding young lady at thirteen.

Resuming her role of doing the dirty work, Annabelle found she enjoyed it.

What a waste, to let good dirt go unused. She loved to create pretty things from the dark loam.

With both hands, Annabelle yanked on a particularly stubborn clump of weeds, only to discover a matted gray fur ball hidden behind it.

"What in the world?" Reaching for it, she was startled when it hissed and two bright green eyes popped open.

Leaning closer, Annabelle could see that the kitten was sorely mangled and missing a back leg. Its eyes never blinked when Annabelle scooped it into her arms.

"Poor little thing," she said, cradling it close. Annabelle stroked the tiny, velvet ear and watched the eyes slowly close. She smiled as the cat's motor began to rumble.

Struggling to rise without disturbing her charge, the old woman creaked onto one knee, and then managed to stand.

"Whew, now, let's see if we can get some help."

When she started toward the back porch, the light snapped on over the sink. Tillie's mop of white hair popped into view. "Psst, come here."

Tillie emerged through the back door with two cups of steaming coffee. "What've you got there? Someone's gray muff?"

"No. It's a three-legged cat."

As if on cue, the kitten lifted its feeble head and mewed.

"Only three? Well, it looks awful. Don't let Regina see it, or she'll have a fit. She doesn't approve of pets."

"I can barely feel its heartbeat, and it's all bones. Is there a vet close by?"

Tillie set down the mugs so she could hold the door open. "There sure is, honey. Let's give him a call."

A few moments later, Tillie hung up the phone. "Dr. Kincaid is waiting for us."

"What about a car?"

"We'll borrow Regina's."

"Oh, Lordy," Annabelle said, crossing herself.

"You'll borrow my what?" Regina sailed into the room under full steam. "Is the coffee ready?"

Spinning around in an attempt to hide the cat and Annabelle behind her, Tillie smiled. "We need to borrow the Caddy."

"For what purpose?"

"We have an errand to run."

Annabelle stood mute, watching the interplay. She could clearly see Regina's expression had turned suspicious.

"May I ask where?"

"You can ask, but I'd advise you not to. It'll just piss you off."

"Matilda Jean, what is going on here? Quit trying to hide Annabelle behind you. It's an impossibility."

Straightening her shoulders, Tillie stepped closer, pointing a finger at her friend's sternum. "We found an injured kitten outside, and we're taking it to the vet."

Grabbing Tillie's thin shoulders, Regina moved her aside and gasped. "That disgusting bundle can't be a cat. It's a stinking rodent. Annabelle, throw it back outside."

"I will not." She cradled the kitten to her bosom. "It's hurt, and I'm going to see that it's cared for, even if I have to walk."

Tillie held out her cupped palm. "Hand over the keys, Regina."

"Over my dead body," Regina said, crossing her arms over her chest.

"Don't tempt me." Tillie pushed her out of the way.

"I will not have that filthy animal touching the leather seats, do you hear?"

"Don't be such a priss. It can't ride in the trunk," Tillie said.

Regina snatched her keys out of Tillie's hand. "Fine. Annabelle can hold it in her lap, and I will drive my Cadillac, if you don't mind."

With a wide grin and a wink, Tillie signaled Annabelle to follow.

Annabelle cuddled the animal now safely wrapped in her apron, humming softly in time with its purring. "I'm surprised you didn't make us both ride in the trunk, Regina," Annabelle said.

Emitting a very unladylike snort, Regina pulled the car into the animal clinic lot.

Tillie held the door for Annabelle and her charge, and then bumped into her as she stopped in the doorway. She was gazing with her mouth open at the young Dr. Kincaid, the very image of Cary Grant. Certain he could read her thoughts, Annabelle blushed.

"Ms. Tillie, is this the little baby you called me about?" the doctor asked.

Pushing the frozen Annabelle forward, Tillie replied, "I'm afraid so. See what you can do for the wee thing, will you, doc?"

Without a word Annabelle handed the foundling over.

When he shut the door to the exam room, Tillie fanned her face with her hand. "He is so hot. Oh, to be ten years younger."

"Better make that twenty, my dear," Regina said.

"Whatever."

Feeling anxious, Annabelle paced outside the door.

Regina muffled a cough behind her long fingers. "I swear I'm suffocating on pet dander."

When Dr. Kincaid opened the door he came face-to-face

with Annabelle and Tillie.

"Ladies." He smiled.

"Well, spill it," Tillie said.

"I'd say this little girl is about a year old."

Clutching her hankie to her chest, Annabelle asked, "Will she be okay?"

"Fine. Her tail is broken, and she's lost her right hind leg. Whatever she tangled with removed it with a surgeon's skill. It was probably a mower or weed eater. Will you be keeping her, or shall I put her down?"

"I'll take her," Annabelle said.

Tillie nodded.

"Then I'd like to take some x-rays and clean her up."

Startled by Regina's cold grasp on her arm, Annabelle didn't protest when she turned them away for a private conversation.

"Excuse us for just a moment, Doctor," Regina said over her shoulder.

"Fine, I'll have my assistant get started, and you can pick her up in the morning," he said.

The connecting door opened and shut with a click.

Hissing in Annabelle's face, Regina spat, "What in the name of heaven do you think you're doing? And who's going to pay for all this?"

"Oh." Annabelle's hand flew to her throat. "I hadn't thought. You know I don't have . . . anything."

"Don't worry, Belle," Tillie said, "I'll take up donations."

"Thank you, Tillie," Annabelle said.

Straightening her shoulders Regina said, "It's my house, and you're a temporary guest. Neither you or that creature are welcome."

Tillie stepped between them. "Hold on, girlfriend. That poor thing won't be any trouble. You know how much I love animals. Come on, let her stay."

Throwing up her hands, Regina turned on her heel and sat on the sagging sofa cushions. "There'll be hair and fleas all over the place," she said, brushing at her skirt.

Smiling, Tillie said, "Get over it, Scroogette."

"Mother will haunt us all if a pet resides on the family estate."

"Aunt Victoria is dead, so it shouldn't matter anymore." Annabelle sighed. *Aunt Victoria hated pets—and me, too, for that matter.*

Stiffening her spine, Regina stared at her cousin. "Ah, but it does matter."

"What matters more? That your mother's gone or a cat's coming to live with us?" Tillie said.

"I give up." A sigh escaped Regina's pursed lips. "But keep it out of my way. If I detect any untoward aromas or parasites associated with its presence, it's gone. Do I make myself clear?"

Grinning, Tillie slid her arm under Annabelle's and turned them in the direction the nice young vet had gone. "What'll you name her?"

"Ms. Pickles."

Regina started laughing. "Why, for God's sake? That's an absurd name."

Placing her hands on her ample hips, Annabelle straightened her bowing back. "Her eyes are the color of sweet gherkins, that's why!"

"It's cute," Tillie said with a quick head bob.

Emitting another undignified snort, Regina said, "It's a ridiculous moniker. I'm going to get the car."

Feeling like she'd burst her buttons, Annabelle clapped her hands and grinned. "Thank God. I was really afraid there for a moment."

Grasping Annabelle's clasped hands, Tillie hopped up and down, smiling. "She likes the cat. She just doesn't know it yet."

"I certainly hope she finds out soon, or both of us will be

searching for a new roof over our heads."

"Nonsense. I don't think Regina ever had a pet. She can't help but be excited, even at her age."

Shaking her head, Annabelle said, "She didn't look excited. I'd say it was more like pained with a smidgen of disgust thrown in."

The horn blared. Annabelle and Tillie headed for the exit.

"This should prove to be an interesting experiment," Tillie said.

"Or a recipe for disaster."

"Ah, but it shouldn't be dull."

Annabelle whispered, "Lord help us."

CHAPTER 4

Frowning at her friend, Regina said, "Tillie, what's wrong? For several weeks now you've been more lethargic and surly than that silly cat."

Ms. Pickles gave a defiant lift of her head and step-hopped over to rub against Tillie's shin.

"Damnable feline," Regina said. "I still can't believe I let you talk me into keeping that filthy flea bag."

"She's a sweet kitty." Tillie gave the cat an affectionate scratch. "The only one with sand in her knickers around here is you."

"Quit avoiding the question. Since Annabelle's been here you've been sleeping more and more, and your skin is the color of oatmeal. And if you get sick, I'll be stuck with my useless cousin and that idiotic fur ball for companionship."

Tillie sighed and sat down, watching the cat resume her post in the center of the rag rug.

"It has nothing to do with Belle," Tillie said. "I've got the energy of a turnip, which pisses me off. Other than an ache here and there, I don't really feel bad."

"You've lost weight. You should call the doctor."

"I'm not sick."

"All right, then I'll call the doctor." Regina stood up and grabbed the phone directory and held it out to her friend. "But you should be the one to do it."

"Bossy bitch," Tillie said. "Just because you're six feet tall doesn't mean you can bully me."

With a sigh, Regina handed her friend the phone receiver. "Please call, Tillie. Let's make sure it's just the flu or something, okay?"

Tillie dialed the doctor's office and asked for the earliest appointment available. "That's fine. See you tomorrow, then. Thank you."

"What time tomorrow?" Regina asked.

"Nine-thirty. Let me borrow the Caddy, will you?"

"Not on your life. I'll drive you and make sure you get there and back without any casualties, especially to my car."

"Get real." Tillie shoved her chair back and leaned over the table. "I won't hurt your red statusmobile."

Regina stood, glancing down on the switchback part in Tillie's hair. "I need to go by the bookstore. I'll drop you and pick you up . . . it's on the way."

"Time for a new smut-fest? I mean novel?" Tillie asked.

"Yes, as a matter of fact. Go lie down or something."

Placing her coffee cup in the dishwasher, Regina signaled that the conversation was over.

Tillie grumbled, "I'm sick and tired of your bullshit. I'm not a child. I'm going to get dressed and go for a walk."

When Tillie reached the second floor, Annabelle emerged from the bath, tendrils of blue hair sticking to her bright pink cheeks. She grinned at Tillie. "Hi. You're up early."

"Not early enough. According to Regal Regina, I've been quite the slug-a-bed. So much so, she's talked me into seeing the doctor." Her head down, Tillie proceeded into the steaming bathroom but turned in the doorway. "I'm baking for the church sale today—bread, cookies, the works. Want to help?"

Annabelle beamed. "I'd love to. I'm almost done with the pile of mending Regina's been saving for the last ten years. I never knew a body could have so many clothes."

"Meet me in the kitchen in fifteen minutes," Tillie said, closing the door.

Regina reached the top step just as Annabelle emerged from the guest room. She gaped at her cousin's ensemble. Annabelle looked like a wilted flower child in a tangerine-colored dress and apple green apron with pink lace.

The woman hasn't one ounce of taste.

"You look quite extravagant this morning, Cousin."

"Clothing can be adornment or camouflage, it depends on who's wearing it and why."

"Well, uh, thank you, I think," Annabelle said.

"Excuse me." Regina gripped the handrail. "I'll be in my studio for a few hours."

She watched Belle's eyes brighten with curiosity. "What are you painting?"

"That's none of your business. Don't you have something to do?" Regina asked and opened the door to the attic.

"I'm helping Tillie with the baking today."

Regina hollered down the stairs. "Don't burn the house up."

At lunchtime, Regina descended from the attic and followed the bouquet of cinnamon and chocolate.

In the kitchen, every flat surface was covered with cooling racks overflowing with cookies and rolls. She slipped an oatmeal raisin cookie into her mouth, enjoying the spicy crunch.

Annabelle, Tillie, and the cat were conspicuously missing, so she helped herself to a chocolate chip cookie, then went searching.

Following the murmur of voices, Regina found Tillie and Annabelle on the back step teasing Ms. Pickles with a dried iris stalk. The screen door squealed in protest, announcing her presence.

A blur of white and blue hair whirled as Tillie and Belle turned to face Regina. All conversation stopped. The cat took advantage of the interruption to capture the object of its torment and roll, triumphant, into the grass.

"All done baking?" Regina asked.

"Nope, taking a break. I see you helped yourself." Tillie grinned and pointed. "That brown smear on your smiling face tells all."

"Busted." Regina's tongue licked at the smudge.

Chuckling behind her handkerchief, Annabelle cleared her throat.

Regina perched on the wooden rocker, sitting next to the iron bakery rack. She studied the faded cotton gloves with brown stained fingertips. "What else are you two cooking up today?"

The chair creaked as Regina began rocking back and forth, arms across her chest.

Exchanging a look, Belle stepped off the stoop and picked up the cat. The wee motor began to sound a scant second later. She avoided Regina's eyes as she passed her to go into the kitchen. "I'll start cleaning up the mess."

"Thanks, Belle," Tillie said.

"All right," Regina stopped rocking and leaned her elbows on her knees. "What did I interrupt?"

"Nothing, really. It's just that we were discussing possibilities. Brainstorming."

"About what?"

"About our future."

"Whose?"

"Mine and Belle's, actually."

"I recommend you start from the beginning and catch me up." Resuming the rhythmic creaking of the rocker, Regina studied her friend. "And since when has Annabelle been your confidant?"

"Since I needed a sounding board."

"Why not me?" Regina crossed her arms, rocking harder. "We've been friends for years."

"Because you'd fuss."

"How can I fuss if I don't even know what you're talking about?"

"There is a remote possibility that the big 'C' has moved in on me again."

Regina sucked in her breath. "I really didn't want to think about that right now. I'm not in the mood for doom and gloom."

"That's why I couldn't talk to you. If it is back, then I need to know you'll be taken care of. With your history . . . well, you can't go it alone with no one but your dead mother for company."

"How did you know?" Regina's rocking came to an abrupt stop. "Never mind. I don't need looking after, Matilda Jean. And her stay here is temporary."

"She's been here a month. It'll be winter soon. Anyway, you wouldn't toss her out in the snow, would you?" Tillie asked.

"That could prove quite enjoyable, but I doubt I could lift her." Regina pushed against the porch with her feet.

"Get serious, girlfriend. She's your family and you need each other."

"I need her about as badly as I need sand in my underwear."

"I see. Well, if the worst situation occurs and I have to go through treatment again, you'll need a hand with the house and the cooking."

"I can cook."

"Yeah, right." Tillie crossed her thin arms over her chest. "All you do in the kitchen is pour coffee and raid the cookie jar."

Regina cleared her throat. Her heart felt grim. "Perhaps that's true, but I don't need old Mother Hubbard scorching all my good cookware should you need a . . . break."

"Regina Louise, you have to face the fact that I might be in deep shit here. I might not survive this time."

Regina could feel the tears building. "What nonsense. You're probably just anemic or allergic to that repulsive feline." A lone tear slipped down her cheek.

Shaking her head, Tillie stood and started for the door. "We have more baking to finish."

Sitting alone on the porch, Regina felt a chill.

What'll I do without her? She's my best friend. She's my only friend. Lord help me, I can't lose her, too. Why do I have to lose everyone I love? And Lord, while we're having this conversation, please don't leave me stuck with Annabelle and that stupid cat.

At seven o'clock the next morning, Regina made coffee and read the paper, savoring the peaceful quiet of the morning. By five of eight she had showered, dressed, and started checking the clock every five minutes.

With Tillie's appointment only an hour and a half away, Regina needed a cigarette.

When eight bongs struck, Ms. Pickles did a three-legged hop skip into the kitchen, one hop ahead of Tillie.

Regina ignored the cat and smiled at Tillie's sleepy frown. "Good morning."

"Yeah. It's morning, I just haven't decided if it's a good one yet." She flopped down on the chair to stare at the full coffee cup set before her.

"Good Lord, you look like you're wearing a cat hair robe. Do you let that flea bag sleep with you?"

"Yup, she takes turns sleeping on one of your quilts and this robe."

"That's disgusting."

Ms. Pickles mewed and turned her back on Regina.

Tillie pushed herself out of the chair to feed the cat. After an affectionate stroke of silky fur, the petite woman topped off her coffee cup.

The chimes marked the half-hour.

"Your appointment is at nine-thirty, isn't it? You'd better get a move on."

"You're raring to go, I see. Don't worry. You won't be late for the bookstore."

Doesn't she even know how much she means to me?

At 9:15, Regina had donned her cashmere jacket and was pacing, her carpetbag bouncing against her hip. She looked up to see Tillie and Annabelle saunter down the stairs.

"How long have you been standing there?" Tillie asked.

"Good to see you're finally up, Annabelle." Regina opened the door. "Let's go," she said to Tillie.

Annabelle smiled and waved them off. "See you." Ms. Pickles joined her on the landing.

They rode in silence, except for the thumping sound of the windshield wipers.

Regina stopped the car in front of Dr. Goodall's office door. She scrutinized her friend, who appeared to have had all the color wrung from her. "Let me know what the doctor says, okay?"

"Sure," Tillie said, reaching for the door handle.

Regina touched her arm. "No, I mean it. You'll tell me everything, won't you?"

"Every gory detail. Want to give me a blindfold and cigarette now?"

"I'll be back in an hour."

"Okay." The small woman goose-stepped toward the stairs without a backward glance.

CHAPTER 5

Situated in the middle of a strip mall, the small independent bookstore specialized in used and out-of-print books. Regina wandered the aisles, unable to focus on the musty but pleasant fragrance of leather and aged paper.

Tillie just had to be all right.

She stopped before the bargain shelves and the rows of cookbooks with bright colored covers and photographs of food too pretty to be real.

Thumbing through the one whose tag line read, "The Chef's favorite," she pictured her friend standing by the stove stirring some delicious creation. There were many luscious aromas that had come out of her kitchen over the past ten years with Tillie. And everyone one of them was stored in her memory.

She laid the book down and wandered to the children's section. Several tots sat around a wooden table listening to a young woman read from a picture book. The picture she showed them was of a gray kitten with huge green eyes, tangled in a skein of red yarn. It even looked a little like Ms. Pickles.

She shook her head and walked on. A pink sign read "New Chick Lit Releases on Sale Now." She picked up a book with a pixie-faced woman with white hair on the front. The title made her chuckle, "Bodacious Babes Unite." *Sounds like a t-shirt slogan Tillie would like.* Her heart hitched in her chest.

I'm losing it. Getting soft in the head.

After forty-five minutes into forever, Regina surrendered to her impatience and headed back to the doctor's office. As the car pulled up, her friend rose from where she'd been waiting on the shadowed bench.

"I'm sorry. Have you been waiting long?"

"Nope." The whitewashed profile of the woman now occupying the passenger seat concerned Regina.

"What the hell happened in there?" Regina parallel-parked close to the curb, hands suddenly sweating. Switching off the engine, she faced her normally exuberant buddy, who stared out the window at the busy street. "How did it go?"

"Oh, fine." Tillie sighed. "I'm tired. Just take me home."

"I don't think so. Tell me what the doctor said." A knot forming in her stomach, Regina reached out and touched Tillie's cold arm.

Tillie's blank eyes gazed through Regina. "They don't know anything."

"What did the doctor say?"

"First, the vamps drained the vein in my left arm, filling vial after vial. Then, they scheduled me for a mammogram at noon tomorrow at St. Mary's. I know for a fact that it normally takes three months to get a boob squashing appointment. We women line up for the privilege."

"Honey, I'm sure it'll be okay. Don't worry." Damn. Regina keyed the ignition, and they drove home, each involved in her own thoughts.

When they arrived, Regina followed Tillie to her room. Ms. Pickles curled up on the robe tossed across the bed. With the cat on guard, Regina wondered if Tillie would sleep.

Heading down the stairs for a cup of tea, Regina encountered Annabelle.

"How is she?" Annabelle held her handkerchief in a death grip.

"Tired. Discouraged. Probably a bit frightened," Regina said.

She poured the hot water from the kettle into her cup and dunked a tea bag.

Mesmerized by the up and down motion, Annabelle's head bobbed in time. "What did they say?"

Pausing with the bag suspended over the steaming water, Regina looked at her cousin's worried face. "They don't know, but something's not right. She goes in for more tests tomorrow."

Sitting in silence, Regina sipped her tea.

Annabelle excused herself from the room but returned a scant five minutes later.

"Was she asleep?" Regina asked.

"No. She's staring at the ceiling. She's so still, lying there in the dark. I'm really worried."

After setting her cup into the sink, Regina and Annabelle walked up the stairs to stand before Tillie's door. Regina held her breath so she could listen for Tillie's breathing. It was too quiet, so she stepped into the room and stood beside the bed. A subtle rise and fall of the covers reassured her.

Regina headed back to the kitchen, placed the pot of water back on the stove, and lit a cigarette.

"I thought you quit," Annabelle said from the doorway. "What would your mother say?"

In response, Regina sat at the table, blew an impressive smoke ring and narrowed her eyes. "She'd be more concerned with your presence in her house."

Annabelle gasped, then stomped across the kitchen to the refrigerator and retrieved the bowl of leftover chocolate chip cookie dough. Pulling out a chair she sat facing her cousin.

"I doubt we'll find consolation or relief in our vices," Regina said.

Or in the relentless chiming of the clock. A grim reminder that time continued, pausing for neither sickness nor health.

★ ★ ★ ★ ★

Late the next morning, the white haired lady gripped the stair rail like a lifeline. Tillie resembled a friendly ghost in khakis and white t-shirt that read: "Aging is inevitable. Maturing is optional."

Her bleached cheeks were stretched by a thin-lipped smile. "Hey Reggie, will you drive me to the hospital for the boob squashing procedure?"

Her friend looked worse than that stupid cat did when they found it. "I'd be glad to take you. Nice shirt."

"Annabelle, would you mind finishing the cookies for the church bazaar? I made the dough yesterday morning but never got them baked."

Annabelle blushed. "Sure. By the way, where's your recipe? I couldn't resist eating a little bit of the dough, so I'll need to mix up another batch."

"A little bit, my foot," Regina snorted. "While I charred my lungs, Annabelle added a pound of dough to her rump."

Tillie laughed and flipped the vanilla stained card to Annabelle, before heading out the door.

Hours later, Annabelle met the quiet pair at the door, wringing her hands. "My goodness, what took so long?"

Regina rolled her eyes at her cousin. "Great, the Drama Queen is here to rally the troops."

"Shut up, Regina." Tillie explained, "The doctor didn't like the films. I'm having a needle biopsy this afternoon."

"Oh, dear," Annabelle said.

Regina strode up the stairs. "Profound, Annabelle, really profound."

At teatime, Regina was conspicuously missing from her perch at the kitchen table.

Tillie joined Annabelle, scooping the cat into her lap for a cuddle.

"Where's my driver?"

"The spoiled brat's locked herself in the attic," said Annabelle. "I heard her creaking up the stairs earlier, and she's not come down since."

"She's afraid for me," Tillie said.

"Piffle. Regina can't handle anything she can't control."

With a firm stride, Tillie headed up to the attic studio. No light shone from under the locked door. She rapped it with her knuckles.

"Regina, are you in there?"

A rustle filtered into the hallway, penetrating the still air.

Pressing her ear to the cool wood, Tillie listened.

"Are you taking me to the hospital?"

"No, I can't."

Tillie shook the doorknob, "What do you mean you can't? Are you okay?"

"I'm busy. Have Annabelle take you. The keys are in my purse."

"Fine." Tillie marched down the steps to inform her newly appointed driver.

The outpatient waiting room was packed. Tillie and Annabelle grabbed the last two chairs and waited.

"Matilda Dawson?" the nurse asked.

Tillie nodded her head and followed her through the swinging doors. She turned back and glanced at Annabelle, whose attention was now on the television hanging from the ceiling.

Annabelle was pacing the floor when Tillie burst into the waiting room, mumbling curses. "Let's go home."

Scuttling to catch up with Tillie's determined stride, Annabelle puffed, "What . . . happened . . . in . . . there? Are . . .

you . . . okay?"

"I'm sore as hell from that heavy-handed brute."

Annabelle huffed and tried to untwist her knotted hankie and still keep up with Tillie. "You mean a man did the test, not a nurse?"

"Men can be nurses, Annabelle. But this woman was built like a cement mixer. I thought she was trying to skewer my boob, not biopsy it."

"Oh, my." Annabelle's cheeks pinked to the roots of her blue hairdo.

"I wanted to punch her, but she outweighed me by ninety pounds, and I was afraid she'd sit on me."

Annabelle tucked her hankie into her sleeve and slipped her vinyl bag back over her shoulder. "It's a good thing that didn't happen, or *I'd* have kicked her butt."

Tillie's mouth dropped open, bringing her up short. Then laughter burst forth, and she slipped her hand over Annabelle's other arm. "I'm surprised to hear that from you, old girl. You can be my bodyguard any time."

"All right," Annabelle said and raised her thumb in the air.

They chuckled and walked out, arm-in-arm.

CHAPTER 6

For the next four days, Regina watched Tillie limp along on autopilot, waiting for the dreaded phone call. The usual delicious fragrances of Tillie's creations were replaced with the smell of charcoal and the sound of the smoke alarm.

Finding escape in the attic, Regina slashed her brush across the canvas, using the colors of her emotions, cadmium red, yellow ochre, and ebony. In between brush strokes, she paced, baptizing herself in a wreath of smoke.

Whenever Regina did venture downstairs, she spied Ms. Pickles under the sofa instead of her usual post on the rag rug by the kitchen sink.

Early on the morning of the fifth day, the shrill ringing of the phone shattered Regina's taut nerves as she tried to mop up the coffee she'd spilled. She looked at Annabelle over the table and held her breath as Tillie stumbled to answer the phone.

"Hello . . . yes . . . this is Matilda Dawson. Uh-huh. Very well . . . Okay . . . Bye."

Thinking they looked like mismatched bookends, Regina breathlessly strained to hear.

Tillie slammed down the receiver and leaned her forehead against the wall. "Shit."

With a cleansing breath, she turned and looked into the stricken faces of her friends.

"Dr. Goodall wants me to come in at five to discuss the test results. I'm supposed to bring a family member. We're also supposed to meet with a specialist, Dr. Camelpotty, or something."

"I'm going with you," Regina said.

Tillie turned to face Regina, her cheeks a flaming pink.

"Thank you for gracing me with your presence *this* time."

"Why not all of us?" Annabelle asked. A tear coursed down her round cheek.

Damned crybaby, Regina thought.

"Annabelle, I'd appreciate it if you'd stay here."

Tillie patted Belle's arm. "Don't worry. We'll deal with whatever comes. Right now, I need to walk." Tillie slammed out the back door.

They'd arrived at the doctor's office in strained silence. The nurse had led Tillie past the examining rooms to the inner sanctum, Regina only a step behind. Dr. Goodall sat behind a massive wooden desk covered with mounds of papers and books. A half-smile creased his doughy face, reminding Regina of a cracked snicker doodle.

Across the room sat a smaller man with rimless glasses and skin the color of toast that contrasted with his gray suit. He flashed a gleaming white smile and stood.

Tiny hairs rose on the back of Regina's neck. "So, this is Dr. Whatshisname."

"Hello, Miss Matilda," Dr. Goodall said and reached out a freckled hand. "Who's this with you?"

"I'm Regina Morgan-Smith. And you look like a quack to me."

"Nice to meet you, Ms. Smith. I'd like you both to meet my colleague, Dr. Nitya Kumbatpati."

After tentative handshakes Tillie sat on the edge of her chair. Regina thought she resembled a bird gripping overhead wires in the Kansas wind.

The GP removed his horn-rimmed glasses and leaned over

his cluttered desk to address his patient. "Matilda, the mammogram showed a suspicious mass. There are also some anomalies on your blood test results. The biopsy confirms that you have a small malignant tumor. I think we've caught it early."

"Well, shit." Tillie shot out of her chair, circling behind it. She gripped the back, knuckles white as her hair, and then slapped the fabric. "Shit, shit, shit. I suspected as much."

Regina watched, hoping for an excuse to take her friend anywhere else but here.

"What are her options?" she asked.

Tillie collapsed into her seat.

Clearing his throat, Dr. Goodall linked his fingers over his burgeoning belly. "I've consulted with Dr. Kumbatpati, and we think a six week series of chemotherapy would shrink the tumor. Then he can perform a lumpectomy. Or, you can forgo chemo, and he'll perform a radical mastectomy, removing the breast and lymph nodes to prevent spread of the disease."

"What kind of options are those?" Regina said. "Tillie, you need another opinion. I don't care what it costs. I'll get you the best care available."

The specialist stood and bowed his head briefly before speaking. "You are welcome to seek another opinion, of course, but do not wait long."

With a snort, Regina dismissed the chubby physician behind the desk and confronted the cocoa-skinned figure before them. "What are your credentials, doctor?"

His soulful, almond shaped eyes held Tillie's gaze as his melodic voice floated through the tension-filled air. "I am a graduate of Johns Hopkins and studied at the Mayo Clinic for two years, following my residency at Boston General."

Regina rose from the chair, towering above him. "So?" Her mind was spinning, trying to catch its tail.

Who does this foreign witch doctor think he is? Screw political correctness.

"I'm the one asking the questions. Leave her alone!"

Dr. Goodall's jowls quivered as he cleared his fleshy throat. "I assure you, Miss, uh, Missus Smith, we have reviewed every possibility."

Tillie grabbed her arm. "Regina, it's okay." She turned to address the new medicine man. "There is another option, isn't there?"

He nodded, continuing in a singsong cadence. "Yes. Given the history of cancer in your family we did consider it, but it's not necessary at this time. Your tumor is about the size of a pea."

Regina stood, hands on hips, feet shoulder width apart. "What option? Tell me."

Tillie took a deep breath and faced her friend. "They can remove both breasts and the lymph nodes all at once."

"What are you saying?" Regina's eyes filled with tears as she sank back in the chair, shredding the ends of her hair. *She'll be scarred, disfigured, demoralized.*

"My mother died of breast cancer. Those freaky mutant cells move from mother to daughter and from one breast to the other. Why not raze the building before the little monsters move to invade my entire body?"

Regina gulped, forcing her throat to open. "You've got to be kidding. I don't believe this. Wake me, somebody, please. I'm having a nightmare."

Dr. Goodall spoke from behind the monstrous desk. "You don't have to make that decision now, Matilda. Sleep on it. Talk it over with your family."

The specialist remained standing. "I concur, Ms. Dawson. A radical mastectomy is not usual for tumors as small as yours."

"Why let this take me apart one piece at a time?" Tears filled

Tillie's eyes. "Let's just get it over with. I'd rather be symmetrical, anyway." She gave a halfhearted smile.

Regina couldn't hold back the tears, so she lifted her chin and adjusted her shoulders against the chair back to steady her shaking. "Tillie, there has to be another way." She'd have to keep it together until she got home.

Dr. Kumbatpati excused himself and picked up the phone. "Miss Carol, please find time on my surgical schedule for Matilda Dawson in the next two weeks. Radical mastectomy."

He hung up and faced her. "Ms. Dawson, you'll have every opportunity to change your mind, right up until we administer the anesthesia. I assure you, it isn't necessary to remove both breasts at this time."

"Thank you for that."

Doughy Dr. Goodall finally emerged from behind the desk and reached out for Tillie's inert hand. He held it in his ham-sized paw for just a moment.

"Think about it and let us know what you decide."

He turned to Regina. "Thank you for coming. She's lucky to have such a devoted friend."

"She's my *best* friend, you arrogant sons of Caduceus," Regina said.

With an apologetic shrug, Tillie wiped her tears and headed for the door. "I hope you realize you'll be the last man to feel me up."

Regina lifted her nose in dismissal and marched beyond the threshold.

CHAPTER 7

Her eyes never leaving the draped canvas, Regina slumped on the barstool in her attic studio. She'd started this painting the week of Tillie's diagnosis, showing it to no one. The swirls of bright color reminded her of Tillie. The somber colors emphasized her mood.

Although Tillie's strength continued to ebb, her friend had always used humor to fight the dreaded "C". She and Annabelle were at the grocer's stocking up on Tuesday sale items.

With the exception of the cat, Regina was alone. *Life sucks, and if I ever doubted it before, I sure as the devil don't now.*

Ms. Pickles step-hopped around the canvases lining the floor. The cat halted before each one, staring and sniffing, giving nods of approval to some, sneezes of disfavor to others.

"If I didn't know better, I'd think you were a connoisseur of art." An amused smile crossed Regina's face as she regarded her feline critic.

The cat mewed in response and resumed her perusal of the canvases lounging against the walls. After completing her circuit, she sat down in front of the easel.

"Curious?" Regina rose and lifted the purple shroud to reveal her work. "You stupid cat. I can't go through this again. I feel like I'm shriveling from the inside out."

Sitting back down on the stool, Regina rested her elbows on her knees, chin in her palms. Tears slid past the corners of her frown, leaving dark spots on the gauze skirt she wore.

For the first time, the cat snuggled against her shin and together they studied the painting.

"I guess this one isn't quite the same style as the others. Not a very pretty picture, eh, Missy?"

Emitting a muted meow, the cat gazed at Regina. They returned their attention to the composition.

Regina imitated the cat with a tilt of her head. "It's rather dark, and a bit frightening, don't you think?"

Her strained chuckle hung in the dusty air.

"If I had it all to do again, would I do it differently?" She straightened her back and sniffled. "Probably not."

It's how I feel—desolate.

Tillie tossed and turned. Though the down filled mattress held her form like a shroud, she couldn't settle into the arms of sleep. When the clock chimed two, she decided her mother's cure for insomnia was in order, hot milk and honey. As she passed down the hall, she heard a moan, then a muffled scream from behind Regina's door.

She tapped on the solid wood before opening the door a crack. "Regina?" Moonlight glowed through the window onto the bed, creating ethereal illuminations that menaced. "Honey, are you okay?"

Regina thrashed in the bed, arms outstretched, clawing the air, groping in the dark. She cried out.

Tillie's cool hands smoothed Regina's heated ones and then stroked her drenched brow. She hoped a familiar voice would penetrate and rescue Regina from the nightmare.

With a snap, Regina awoke. "*Grandmere?*" she said, blinking slow and hard.

"No, honey, it's Tillie."

"Oh. I'm sorry if I woke you."

She strained to rise from the bed. Her hair hung like a damp cloud to her waist. Soaked with sweat, her gown and sheets were tangled around her.

"It must've been a terrible dream." Tillie held her hand. "Want to talk about it?"

Regina hesitated, and then shuddered.

"I was immersed in inky pigment, a quagmire. The stickiness sucked me down into the bowels of the earth. I couldn't escape, no matter how hard I tried."

Grabbing the silk robe from the foot of the bed, Tillie wrapped it around her friend's quaking shoulders.

"Sounds gross and kind of . . . sticky."

"What's going on, a pajama party?" Annabelle asked from the doorway.

"Hardly," Regina said.

Drawing the dressing gown close around her, Regina stared into the gloom. "You two must think that because I have money, good looks, and a big house I have it all."

"Don't you?" Tillie said. Her words held more than a hint of bitterness.

Regina peered at her friend's shadowed face. "No."

"All that money didn't save your parents from dying young," Annabelle said.

"I lost two for the price of one, and I was only twenty years old."

"Honey, *my* parents are gone, too, one right after the other. None of us has cornered the market on loss."

Regina seemed to not hear Tillie's comment. "Neither my position nor my money could keep my husband from sampling the other females who were sucked into his orbit. Devlin died on his way to a tryst."

"At least you had a husband." Tillie sighed. "I didn't realize you knew about the other women. You never said anything."

"Poor Reg, still living the same old nightmare. Wake up and

smell the garbage. You're lucky. Some nightmares go on forever," Annabelle said.

"I've lost anyone who ever mattered, and I may lose my best friend, as well. It just isn't fair," Regina said.

"Give me a break." Tillie massaged her chest. "Life's never been fair. If you want to know the truth, you've had it pretty damned good. Your folks gave you financial security. Something neither Belle nor I have ever known. Not to mention the fact that you're a successful artist. Be grateful for what you've been given and accept the rest."

Shoving her hands in her robe pocket Annabelle said, "I have."

Regina wiped the sweat from her forehead. "Paint and canvas are cold companions. My father was never around when I was a child. And while my dear mother instilled the virtues of class and decorum, she never offered affection. Never love."

Tears filled Tillie's eyes. "Midnight confessions are damned tiring. You need to get a grip, Regina Louise."

"Grandma loved you best, you know. You were her little porcelain princess," Annabelle said.

Closing her eyes, Regina whispered, "You have a child . . ."

"Who worshiped her father," Annabelle said.

With a snort, Regina opened her arms in supplication. "I'd trade my money, my house, even my own life to spare you this disease, Tillie."

Giving her a quick hug, Tillie smiled in the dark. "I know you would."

"I'd even put up with Belle and that stupid cat if the Lord would allow you to stay with me a few more years."

Tillie patted her on the knee, her soft chuckle filling the darkness.

Annabelle sighed. "Careful what you pray for. You might get it."

"You know I'm risking my sanity and a good haunting by allowing you to live here."

"Yes, I know," Annabelle said.

Tillie stood and held out her hand. "Come on."

Regina grasped Tillie's fingertips and held on. She slipped from the bed, a bleak smile upon her face.

They padded to the kitchen where Tillie prepared warm milk and honey with a sprinkle of nutmeg. They sipped in companionable quiet.

As the tension eased from her body, Regina spoke, "There's something I want to show you."

"Both of us?"

Motioning them to follow, Regina ascended the stairs.

She glimpsed over her shoulder Tillie clutching the banister and Annabelle's face full of anticipation. Beads of sweat appeared on Tillie's pale brow. Regina slowed then stopped just outside the door, waiting for them to catch up.

Regina opened the door and crossed to the center of the studio amidst the sound of rustling fabric, and pulled the chain for the light.

It took a few seconds for their eyes to adjust. Regina stood in front of the easel. A purple cloth lay crumpled on the floor. As she stepped away from the canvas, the muscles in her jaw flexed.

Tillie fanned her face.

"What have you painted that is so important you have to show it in the middle of the night?"

"I want to see it," Annabelle said.

In the center of the painting was an old woman; her face twisted, her silver and black braided hair tied around her neck, eyes bulging. Translucent skin covered skeletal hands that clawed at the noose. Bare and knotted feet peeked from beneath a long filmy skirt, bony knees poking through the fabric. The nails of her hands and feet were black, lips blue, and her eyes were the color of blood.

"Oh, Regina." Tillie shook her head. "That's hideous."

"Yuck," Annabelle said, "I've seen better paintings made by the elephants at the zoo."

"Annabelle!" Tillie said.

"Sorry, Regina."

"Why didn't you talk to me about your fears before now? You're not alone anymore. You've got me and Annabelle."

The tiny woman crossed the room and hugged her friend with all her strength.

Regina's cold figure stood stiff like a museum guard devoid of emotion, then she laid her chin on Tillie's head.

"I'm afraid."

"So am I."

"If something that scary hung in my room, I'd have nightmares, too. Cover it back up, please," Annabelle said.

Retrieving the cloth from the floor Regina did as she was bidden. "As my dearest friend would say: Annabelle, bite me."

CHAPTER 8

Annabelle pulled a stockpot from the cabinet and set it on the stove. She'd assembled all of the ingredients they would need to make jelly. As she poured the juice into the pot she began to hum.

"Shush, Annabelle, I'm trying to read the recipe," Regina said.

"Pardon me, Madame. I didn't mean to intrude."

"That's funny, considering you already have. I'm only in here helping because Tillie wants Sand Plum jelly, and you can't do it by yourself."

"How would you know? And I already have what?" Annabelle turned on the burner and stirred the red juice. "Did you measure the sugar?"

Tearing open the new bag of sugar, Regina measured it into the large measuring bowl. "Yes. You intruded. On my life, my house, and my best friend."

"I've got as much right to live here as you do." Annabelle created a slow rhythm of swirls. "As soon as this starts to boil, pour in the pectin, slowly. Wait a second; it's got to be ready."

The juice began an intermittent boil around the slow rotations of the spoon. "Have you forgotten that our mothers were sisters? And as different as any two creatures on this earth."

"As are we. I have class, and you're just crass," Regina said.

Annabelle smiled. "I thought Devlin was the poet."

Regina held the envelope above the pot while Annabelle

continued to stir. "The last time I made jelly was with *Grand-mere*. I must've been fourteen."

"Wait. Okay, now, pour it slow and steady," Annabelle said.

Regina did as she was instructed.

"I was already married," said Annabelle. "The same blood runs through our veins. Morgan blood. We've lived to be older than both our mothers. It's sad really."

"Don't screw it up, Annabelle. What's sad? That you aren't more like your mother? She was elegant and earthy at the same time. I loved listening to her tell stories, and her voice . . ." Regina picked up the sugar and held it above the pot.

"She had a lovely voice. I'd say you're a mirror of your mother, Regina, only taller. The rods up your backs match perfectly. I can't think of anyone who can compete in the snob department." Annabelle stirred. "Okay, now add the sugar. Dump it in all at once."

Regina dumped the sugar, then slammed the bowl on the countertop. "If you hate me so much, why don't you move out?"

"And go where? There's no room for me at Liddy's. I don't hate you, not really. I'm mad. You had your mother six years longer than I did. You have money and the family residence. Everything I own fits in my Pullman. I don't have anything besides Liddy, the grandkids, Tillie and you."

Wiping her hands on a dishtowel Regina folded her arms across her chest. "And a fat lot of good Liddy and the grand-kids are to you. We won you by default, or maybe you're the booby prize. That'd be just my luck. I've got things to do."

Without stopping the rhythmic motion, Annabelle reached out to grab Regina's sleeve. "You're not going anywhere until we're done. This is for Tillie. So, is that the real problem? I've butted in on your exclusive friendship. You poor dear, can't have her all to yourself anymore."

Regina pulled away from Annabelle's grasp and picked up the jelly jars, moving them closer to the stove. "For someone with limited options, you certainly know how to narrow them even further. You disrupted my life, Annabelle. Not a word in eight years, not since your husband died. Why?"

Staring at the red liquid, Annabelle continued the mechanical motion. "What was there to say? Hi Regina, how's your bank account? Mine's empty, and the creditors are auctioning the farm to pay our debts. How have you been? Up to your elbows in silk and china? Selling your paintings in England and New York while I take in sewing from the local dry cleaners and scrub floors at the church? You could've called and asked if I needed help."

"You're right. I could have. If you needed help, you should've asked."

Annabelle turned to gaze into the depths of Regina's blue eyes. "I should have asked the one person I knew who hated me as much as or more than my daughter. She blamed me for David's death, for my lack of funds. It was about that time that her husband left her a single mother, raising three kids, and one of them a baby." She reached over and turned off the stove. "I took care of Megan until she went to kindergarten. When the baby cried, she wanted me and not her mommy, and Liddy hated me more. What could I possibly say to you that would've mattered?"

"Mother always said that poor relations would bleed us dry, but I didn't know how much trouble you were in. No one told me."

Annabelle poured the boiling red liquid into one jar and then another. "You never asked. No one cared."

Holding the hot jar with a potholder, Regina screwed the lid on and reached for another. "What do you want me to say? I'm sorry? I am. I'm sorry I didn't make the obligatory call to inquire about your health and welfare. I'm sorry I didn't send you a box of money when you lost your home, but I didn't know. I'm sorry you lost your lovely mother so young. I'm not sorry your father and husband died because they were both bullies and didn't deserve either you or your mother. But all the things that happened to you are no fault of mine."

They went through the process of filling and sealing each jar without word or thought.

"It seems odd that you'd ignore your remaining family," Annabelle said.

"You never called, either. Never hinted that things were so dire for you and Liddy."

"How would you have responded to a call? 'Oh, Hello Annabelle, what do you want? Money? I might've known you'd come begging.' I had some pride left that David hadn't beaten out of me."

"You chose him," Regina said.

Dumping the pot in the sink, Annabelle turned the tap on and watched the water flow down the drain like her dreams.

"Daddy chose him. I had no say in the matter. Momma had been gone three years, and he wanted shed of me and the farm. David was willing to take the farm, and I was the price. After a few years of drought and debt, he decided neither one of us was worth the cost, and that's when I started paying dearly."

"You could've left him."

"Run away? Like you? And do what? I'd never done anything but garden, can, and sew. I'd never worked in an office or store. And I had a little girl." She turned the spout so it would fill the sticky pot.

"Did he hit her, too?"

"No, thank God," Annabelle said and pulled her hankie from her sleeve. She waved it like a flag. "But he taught her well enough. I was to blame for all of our misfortune, not the weather, or bad luck, or booze. Me. It was all my fault, and after a while I began to believe it myself." She added soap and ran the scrubber around the edges of the pot.

"I always knew you were no rocket scientist, but you had to know you couldn't predict the weather, let alone dissuade your husband from the bottle. He was a brute and evil to say so. What do you want from me, Annabelle?" Regina screwed on the last lid and faced her cousin.

"A family. A home."

"You don't want much."

Annabelle started to clean up in earnest. "Some support and friendship would be nice."

"I'm trying," Regina said and wiped her hands.

"Isn't that what everyone wants?"

"I suppose."

Regina began drying the dishes while Annabelle filled the coffee pot with water and grounds. "And let's not forget Tillie's cooking," she said and flipped the switch.

"That, my dear cousin, is, without a doubt, the smartest thing you've ever said. Life without Tillie's cooking would be hell on earth, especially with you in the kitchen. You really do need to work on your culinary skills, Annabelle. Frozen fish sticks? Bottled applesauce? Powdered cheese and macaroni? Those things are barely food."

"It's what we could afford. Fresh fruit was a luxury, and a pound of meat had to stretch for three people for two days. I got commodities from the church, dried beans, rice, and powdered milk. Once in a great while we even got cheese."

Drying the last dish Regina sat down at the table. "Processed, no doubt."

Taking two cups from the cupboard Annabelle poured. "We were thankful for it, too. We did what we had to do to survive, while you drank wine with the main course and sherry with dessert."

Regina stepped over to the counter and sipped the hot coffee. "I'm sorry. I didn't realize, and I'm still having some difficulty visualizing anything edible coming from powdered milk."

"Don't knock it until you have nothing else. It beats starving." Annabelle eased into the chair and sighed, her weariness evident.

"You don't look like you've missed many meals."

"I had to eat to work, and not all of us can afford to visit the gym or hire a personal trainer. Did you ever have one of those?"

"Don't be ridiculous." Regina finished her cup and placed it in the sink.

"Try walking around in someone else's slippers before you turn up your nose."

"Only if they are washed first," Regina said. She picked up a jar of jelly and looked through it. "It's clear. I really am sorry, Belle."

"I know."

CHAPTER 9

The silence in the house was comfortable for a change as Regina and Annabelle shared the parlor. Regina ignored the knock at the door and continued to read.

Setting aside her crocheting, Annabelle went to answer the door. "Oh, my goodness, what a wonderful surprise. Come in," she said and ushered in her three grandchildren.

Megan had wrapped her arms around her grandmother's waist while Peggy hugged her shoulder. "Hi, Gram. How are you?"

Standing back a step, Tad's face was split with a grin. "Hey, Gram. I'll bet you're surprised to see us."

Reaching over to pull him into the group hug, Annabelle began to cry. "It's so wonderful to see you all. You've grown so much. Regina, look who's here."

Regina stood and extended her hand. "These must be the grandchildren you go on about. It's nice to see you again."

Taking her hand, Tad shook it.

Removing her backpack, Peggy took off her jacket and flopped down on the sofa. "Cool house. It's *so* old."

"Almost a hundred years old," Annabelle said.

"I missed you, Gram," Megan said, taking her grandmother's hand.

Tad dumped his backpack on the floor and walked around inspecting the furnishings. "Geez, that's even older than you, ain't it, Gram?"

"Considerably older," Regina said.

Stopping before a photograph of an older woman, Tad asked, "Who's that? She looks like she could eat nails."

"That's my Aunt Victoria. Regina's mother. She was rather stern."

Peggy crossed to have a look. "She'd be pretty if she smiled."

"She really looks pissed," Tad said.

"Come and sit down and tell me how you kids got here," Annabelle said.

"We took the bus," Peggy said, sitting beside her sister. "We wanted to see for ourselves where you were living and to make sure . . ."

"Everything okay, Gram?" Tad asked, looking at Regina.

"I'm fine, sweets, but does your mom know you're here?"

Squirming, Peggy stood. "No. We can't stay long. We ought to be able to get home before mom does if we leave in a few minutes."

His nose rising in the air Tad sniffed and stumbled toward the kitchen. "Is that cookies I smell?"

"No, actually, it's jelly, but I'll bet there are some cookies in the cookie jar. Tillie makes sure of that. Regina has a sweet tooth . . ."

"Excuse me," Regina said, "I have work to do."

"She looks like her mother. Lead the way to the cookies, Gram, I'm starving," Tad said, rubbing his thin stomach.

The kids gathered around the table while Annabelle set the cookie jar in the middle and went back for the glasses and milk.

"Tad eats all the time now, which really gets to Mom. Did you see the size of his feet? Gram, do you think he'll be tall like . . . like . . . Daddy?"

"I suppose it's possible," Annabelle said.

"How tall was he?" Tad asked.

"I don't even remember what he looked like," Megan said.

Peggy put her hand on her little sister's. "He was a lot taller than Mom."

"Yes, I think he was about six feet or so . . ." Annabelle began pouring when the doorbell chimed, immediately followed by a pounding on the door. "Oh, my. Excuse me, children."

Annabelle opened the door to find a scowling Liddy.

"Where are my kids?" She stepped in and looked around.

"They're in the kitchen having milk and cookies. Do you want some?"

"Not hardly. What are they doing here, Mother?" Liddy's hands were on her hips.

"They just stopped by on their way home from school to say hello. They weren't planning to stay long."

"This is *not* on their way home from school. Get 'em."

Regina glided into the room, and Liddy's face became a mask.

"Hello, Lydia. How are you?" Regina asked.

"Fine. I . . . I was worried about my kids. Are they here?"

"I believe I heard something about cookies and milk in the kitchen. Why don't you join us?" Without waiting for a reply, Regina walked away.

"Yes, please," Annabelle said. "Stay for a bit. I haven't seen you all in quite some time. Tad has really grown."

Dragging her feet, Liddy followed them. "Okay, but we can't stay long, the kids have . . . homework . . . and . . ."

Regina's entrance into the kitchen caught the kids' attention, but the presence of their mother stopped them mid-bite.

"I was worried when you didn't answer the phone. This was the only place I could think of to try, besides the mall." Liddy stared at Tad. "How did you find it?"

"We're not mall rats," he said, lifting his chin. "We looked Cousin Regina up in the phone book and took the bus. No big deal."

"Next time . . . tell me before you go off on your own

somewhere. You know how I worry," Liddy said.

"Since when?" Tad said.

Peggy jumped up. "Mom, I've got a ton of homework. We'd better go."

Crossing to the cupboard Annabelle reached for a cup. "Not yet. Liddy, wouldn't you like some milk? Coffee? A cookie?"

"You know I hate milk. I could use a cup of coffee, though," she said.

"Sure thing. How about you, Regina?"

"Actually, no. I think I've had enough stimulation for one day." Regina moved the cookie jar closer to Tad. "Tad, you look like you could use another couple of cookies."

"Sure," he said, reaching into the jar. "I won't turn down cookies. Did you make 'em, Gram?"

"Tillie and I made them. She's a chef, so we always use her recipes," Annabelle said.

One corner of Liddy's lip rose. "A chef. How convenient."

With his mouth still full of cookie crumbs, Tad asked, "Does she cook a lot of weird stuff with grass sticking out of the top like on TV?"

"She leaves the grass out for us," Regina said. "We have much simpler tastes than the Bistro customers she serves."

"I'll just bet," Liddy said. "Lucky, seeing as how you're such a crummy cook, Mother."

"She's taught me a lot. I'm much better in the kitchen these days."

"Yeah, right. You always were a lousy liar," Liddy said.

Pulling on her sleeve, Peggy said, "Mom, we really need to go. Tad and I have homework. Can you give us a ride?"

Liddy stood and dragged Tad into the doorway. "Thanks for the coffee and for showing me how the other side of the family lives. I'd forgotten."

"Please let the kids come again," Annabelle asked. "I've

missed them so much."

All three kids hugged their grandmother.

"You kids are always welcome to raid the cookie jar. Tillie keeps it well stocked," Regina said.

"Would you tell her we're sorry we missed her?" Peggy asked.

"And tell her she makes awesome cookies," Tad said. "Love you, Gram."

Liddy stood in the open doorway, her face nearly white.

"I love you, too," Annabelle said as Liddy slammed the door.

"To say that woman was pissed would be an understatement. They should've let her know where they were going," Regina said.

"If they had, she wouldn't have let them come. I hope she doesn't . . ."

"They'll be fine, Annabelle. It won't be long before they'll be driving and dating, which is far worse than them visiting their grandmother. The two older ones are nearly grown."

"I know."

Regina resumed her seat by the window and picked up her book. "Lydia was almost pleasant. Maybe she's grown up some, too."

"It's what I pray for," Annabelle said, closing her eyes.

CHAPTER 10

Regina peered through the hospital room door, her nose wrinkling from the antiseptic smell. Her friend sat propped up with pillows; wisps of wavy white hair touched the collar of her peach gown. Blue tracks showed on the backs of her tiny hands. A magazine rested on her stomach.

Gazing up with a smile, Tillie called out, "Hey there, Regina."

"Hey, yourself." Regina strolled to the bedside. "I hope you're finding something good to cook. If you don't get home soon, Annabelle's going to kill me with boxed macaroni and frozen fish sticks."

"Hum, how about something with a little kick?" Tillie said with a wink.

"You know I've got a cranky colon. You and Annabelle are the only ones left who can handle spicy food." Regina sighed.

"This won't hurt anybody's innards, I guarantee." Tillie's eyes twinkled. She turned the magazine over, flashing a page of shiny, bronzed men, without clothing.

Regina flipped her hair behind her shoulder with mock disapproval. "Matilda Jean Dawson, you old pervert."

Tillie laughed.

"I'm just admiring one of God's better creations. A real life version is on the night shift. His name's Todd, and his biceps are the size of cantaloupes. It's a shame he's gay. I bet I could straighten him out."

She leaned back against the pillow and closed her eyes, a dreamy look spreading across her wrinkled face. "I may be in my fifties, but I'm not dead yet."

"How do you know he's gay?"

"I asked him. He is just too damned yummy." Tillie shook her head. "Don't worry, he wasn't offended. Was quite proud in fact. Told me all about his partner. Now, don't you say anything to anybody. We don't want to get that boy into trouble."

"I wouldn't dream of it."

Regina shifted the carpetbag on her shoulder and leaned close. Silver crescent moons and stars tinkled at her ears. "How are you, really?"

Tillie's black eyes emptied for a moment, then she grinned. "Shoot, I don't need breasts. They just get in the way, you know, a shelf for me to spill stuff on." Her voice softened as she continued, "I'm okay. They cut it all out, and I'll be fine in a few weeks. The drains will probably come out before I come home. My arms hurt like hell, but Doc says I can start cooking any time I feel like it."

Tears filled Regina's eyes.

"Now don't you start blubbering! I lost ten pounds from surgery, five per boob. If I'd known they weighed so much I would've whacked them off long ago."

"You're full of shit, you know that?"

Regina reached out and squeezed Tillie's slender arm, careful to avoid the tubes and wires. She sniffed and wiped her eyes with the back of her ringed hand.

"Yeah, I know, and so does everyone else."

With a vase of freshly cut flowers, Annabelle entered and handed a paperback to Tillie.

"Hey, Belle. What beautiful flowers, and thanks for the bodice ripper."

"Those are from my garden, and that's *my* book," Regina said.

"One of your favorites, if the dog-eared pages mean anything. I thought you'd like something from home," Annabelle said and kissed Tillie's cheek.

"Thanks, Belle. That's very thoughtful of you. Did she underline the good parts?"

Regina crossed her arms, "Not likely. How'd you get here?"

"I took the bus. There's one that picks up less than a block away from the house. If the kids can do it, so can I."

"If I'd known you were coming, I'd have given you a ride," Regina said.

"Thanks. I'll take you up on that going home."

"Speaking of home," Regina said to Tillie. "When do they release you?"

"Not until the end of the week. The drains may even be out by then. The insurance company won't allow any more time than that."

"Heartless creeps," Annabelle said.

"We're all just numbers and a bottom line," Regina said.

Tillie looked at her friend. "Funny."

"What?"

"Funny that someone with unlimited resources even knows about what the rest of us go through," Annabelle said.

Tillie patted her arm. "Sorry, Reg. Nothing personal."

"Yes it is, and Annabelle's right."

"You're learning, Cousin."

Not bothering to stifle a yawn, Tillie pulled the sheet up to her chin. "If you two don't mind, I'm feeling dopey and tired. The pain meds are finally kicking in."

"Call when you know for sure they're discharging you," said Regina. "And if you need more time, we can manage until you're on your feet again, eh, Annabelle?"

"Yes. I think we can, but we miss you," Annabelle said.

"Thanks, gals, I appreciate—everything."

"Come on, Annabelle, let's go before the flood gates open."

"Who's crying? Scram. I don't need any sob sisters around here. Besides, I want to get started on this throbbing manhood book."

With a grin and a shake of her head, Regina escorted Annabelle out the door as Tillie opened the book.

Two days later, Regina drove to the hospital to pick up her friend.

Tillie leaned on a wheelchair full of flowers, a scowl on her petal soft face. A nurse in turquoise scrubs stood beside her, hands on hips, forehead creased.

"What seems to be the problem?" Regina asked.

"This." Tillie pointed down at the wheelchair. "They worked on my chest, not my legs."

Regina grabbed two of the potted plants. "It's hospital policy, and the last bit of pampering you're likely to get."

"Oh, all right." Tillie scooted onto the gray vinyl seat, slipped her feet onto the footrests, and scrutinized the nurse. "Pop a wheelie, will you, dear?"

"Not a chance. I only do wheelies every other Tuesday." The corner of the nurse's mouth rose slightly as she gave the chair a little extra push.

"Go, girl." Tillie grabbed for the wheels.

"No, you don't." The nurse was quicker, maneuvering her away from the automatic doors.

Annabelle stood in the portal of the front door. Her blue hair haloed her beaming face as she greeted Regina and Tillie at the door.

"Welcome home."

She took Tillie's hand and led her into the dining room. In the center of the oak pedestal table sat a picture perfect cherry pie.

"I know everyone hates my cooking, but I can bake. Come in and sit."

Tillie sat down at the head of the table.

"How sweet. And this tablecloth. Why it's beautiful. You embroidered it, didn't you, Belle?"

Annabelle smiled at the compliment and cut them each a slice of pie. Dark red cherries oozed from the golden crust.

"Smells good," Tillie said, taking a huge bite.

Annabelle started eating with gusto.

Regina saw Tillie's eyes water, but she had already taken a mouthful. She coughed and spewed cherries all over the lovely white linen. She gasped for air, gulped her water and growled, "You old fool."

"Belle," Tillie wheezed. "You used salt instead of sugar."

Annabelle was too busy shoveling in every crumb to notice the others' reactions. She licked her fork clean and patted her tummy. "What did you say? Aren't you girls going to eat your pie?"

Regina and Tillie burst out laughing, tears sliding down their cheeks.

Annabelle's brows met over her nose in a scowl. "What's so funny?"

"Oh, it hurts to laugh." Tillie crossed her arms over her sensitive chest. "Stop!" She gasped.

Rolling her eyes heavenward, Regina sighed. "Now I know why you still eat spicy food, Annabelle. Your taste buds have already crossed over to the other side."

Under graying eyelashes, Annabelle smiled at Tillie. "It's good you're back. I'm better at growing things than cooking them."

Regina gathered up the plates.

"Let's feed this masterpiece to Bone Crusher. The disposal has eaten pretty damned well while you've been gone, Tillie. Welcome home."

CHAPTER 11

It had been a couple of weeks since her stitches were removed. As Tillie walked up the street, a black BMW Z3 slowed to keep pace. She glanced over her shoulder and noticed the stunning silver-haired driver. His smile enhanced the classically molded features of his face.

With a lift of her chin, she turned her stroll into a power-walk, marched up the steps of the porch, and plopped down beside Annabelle on the swing.

Tillie pointed to the kitchen towel her friend embroidered. "Who's that for?"

"I make these every year for the church bazaar. Do you like it?" Annabelle's eyes disappeared behind her round-cheeked smile.

"Pretty." Tillie pushed at the deck with her feet to start the swing.

Annabelle continued to stitch, despite the swaying.

Across the street, the sports car pulled into the drive, and the man unfolded his long legs from behind the wheel. He waved and smiled. The ladies gawked.

"Do you know who that is?" Tillie asked, craning her neck to see over the porch railing.

"No, but I saw him at the Riverside Tea Room last Saturday. He's quite handsome."

Tillie hopped up and headed for the front door. "Not bad, at least from a distance."

"Oh, he's even better close up." Annabelle blushed and returned to her stitching.

Come evening time, the three ladies sipped decaf and lounged around the kitchen table. They'd filled their stomachs with Tillie's sumptuous mushroom Swiss meatloaf, broccoli, garlic-mashed potatoes, and peach cobbler.

Ms. Pickles lay curled in the middle of the rag rug, sending kisses with her eyes to each of her mothers. Hayden's "Minuet in D" drifted from the CD player down the hall.

The doorbell disturbed their individual musing.

"I'll get it." Regina glided across the polished oak floor to the entry.

Tillie glanced after her. "Wonder who's here."

The answer came in the towering form of the hunk from across the street. He filled the doorway and dwarfed Regina's five-foot-nine-inch frame.

"Mr. Joseph Linden, please meet Matilda Dawson and Annabelle Hubbard. Would you like some coffee?"

Regina motioned toward her empty chair and headed for the counter, not waiting for a response.

"Evening, ladies. Black's fine, thanks."

Tillie couldn't help but notice that he was at least six-foot-six. His green eyes were the color of Astroturf, crinkled at the corners, and his presence warmed the room.

"Welcome to the neighborhood, Mr. Linden," Regina said, then set a steaming cup before him. She pulled up a chair from the pantry for herself and sat beside him.

"Please, call me Joe." As he tasted the steaming brew, his green orbs met Tillie's black ones over the rim of the china cup. "I've noticed you walking the neighborhood the past couple of days."

Tillie held his gaze, choosing to ignore his comment.

"Where do you hail from, tall man?" she asked.

"Here. I used to live in mid-town, but decided to buy a place by the river. I love these old homes."

"Oh, so do we," Annabelle said. "Why, your eyes are the same color as Ms. Pickles'." Her hand fisted in her mouth, and her cheeks bloomed.

"And who is Ms. Pickles?"

Regina nodded at the sleeping cat apparently unperturbed by the intrusion.

"I see." He reached across the table and patted Annabelle's hand. "What a nice compliment."

Annabelle stared at the tabletop and whispered, "Thank you."

Tillie's brow was furrowed as she continued her cross-examination. "What do you do?"

"Retired air force. Thirty years. My last assignment, McConnell." He scrutinized Tillie's petite stature. "You're a scrappy little bit, aren't you?"

Rising up to her full five-foot-one inches, Tillie thrust her hands in her pants pockets, peering down her nose. "Damned right, and don't you forget it."

She wondered if he was as good as he looked, feeling more alive than she had since the big C took hold again.

His teeth gleamed like a lighthouse beacon as his face broke into a grin.

"I doubt you'll let me," he said.

Annabelle choked back a laugh and covered her mouth with her handkerchief.

Regina cleared her throat.

"More coffee, Joe? You're a nice addition to the neighborhood."

He gulped down the hot liquid and slowly rose from the chair. His eyes never left Tillie's as he rose above her by more than a foot. "Thanks. I need to be going. Maybe I'll catch up with you some morning while you're steaming down the sidewalk." He nodded to Annabelle and Regina and gave Tillie a lopsided lift of the lips. "Nice meeting all of you. I'll see you later."

Tillie's warm cheeks belied the tough stance she had yet to abandon. He stirred a hunger in her that had nothing to do with food. The slam of the screen door made her jump. "Well, I'll be damned. You were right, Belle. He's even better close up."

Regina put the dirty cups in the dishwasher. "Let's go into the parlor and enjoy the music."

Annabelle rose to follow. "I need to work on my stitching."

Tillie hesitated, turned to the cabinet and retrieved her recipe box. "I need to do some baking." *Momma always said the way to a man's heart was through his stomach. Might as well start there and see what develops.*

Enticing aromas of yeast and cinnamon floated down the hall to the noses in the parlor, which lifted in unison.

"Shall we see what's cooking?" Regina said. She marked the page in her book and headed to the kitchen.

Hanging back, Annabelle watched Regina stroll into Tillie's domain.

Flour up to her elbows, Tillie rhythmically flipped, kneaded, and pounded the dough on the countertop, oblivious of her audience.

Ms. Pickles sat lopsided at her feet, head moving at the same tempo as Tillie's busy hands.

"Who are you trying to impress?" Regina smiled.

"No one in particular. The Bistro needed some additional baked goods," Tillie said, never breaking the rhythm.

Annabelle peeked around Regina's shoulder. "What is that wonderful smell?"

After a final smack, Tillie began to roll out the dough. "Caramel Pecan Rolls."

Regina's brows shot up. "What's the occasion? Or should I ask, who?"

Joe and I would've made a nice couple. Oh well. There's no competing with Tillie's Caramel Rolls, so why suffer the humiliation.

Tillie's head snapped around to meet Regina's eyes. Her spine stiffened, and then relaxed before she replied. "I made some extra as a nice welcome for our new neighbor. And don't worry, I've make enough for us, too."

Letting out an enormous sneeze, the cat lolled over and closed her eyes.

Regina snagged Belle's arm. "We'll leave you to it, then." She put a finger to her lips, and then crooked it at her cousin.

Annabelle whispered, "What's the big secret?"

"Come up to my studio, and we'll talk." Regina led the way to the attic.

Pulling the stool up, Regina motioned for Annabelle to take the rocker, oblivious to the odor of oil and turpentine mixed with dust.

Annabelle lowered herself into the chair. "You've got me nervous. What's going on?"

"I know how keen Tillie's hearing is, and I don't want to upset her."

"Go on."

"Well, if I'm reading the signs correctly, Mr. Linden and Matilda are interested in each other."

"Oh? I think that's wonderful, don't you?"

"I'm not sure. Tillie puts on a tough façade, but she's very vulnerable right now. It hasn't been all that long since her surgery."

"I see." Annabelle frowned, staring at the gold band on her left hand. "Are you worried about a physical relationship?"

"Yes. We don't know Mr. Linden, or how sensitive he'll be to a woman's image of herself." Regina crossed her arms over her chest.

"Aren't you worrying a little too soon? They only just met."

"I don't think so. I've known Tillie for a long time. She's . . . how shall I put it? A very sexually aware woman."

Annabelle blushed. "But she's never been married."

"Annabelle, don't be naïve. That doesn't mean she's been celibate. Tillie's had several very serious relationships over the years."

"What can we do?"

"Not much. I just didn't want you meddling." Regina sighed. "Let's see how it progresses. I might be reading the signs all wrong. We'll be there if she needs us."

"Sounds to me like you're the one who is meddling." Annabelle's eyes were drawn to the covered canvas. "What's that?"

"It's something I've been working on. I don't share works-in-progress until I feel they're ready for viewing."

"Oh, really?"

Regina cleared her throat. "We'd better go back downstairs."

Annabelle went first.

Regina hesitated before turning out the light.

Perhaps it was time to start something new.

CHAPTER 12

For the days prior to Thanksgiving, Regina noticed that Tillie spent her time away from work with Joe Linden. When he'd taken her for a ride in his convertible, she'd donned a red scarf and black Audrey Hepburn sunglasses. Something was definitely going on.

On a particularly balmy day Annabelle sat at the window seat with her stitching. Regina watched as Joe and Tillie left on his Harley Davidson motorcycle. He'd presented Tillie with a shiny black helmet to go with the leather bomber jacket she'd found at a thrift shop.

Annabelle paced and fretted the entire time they were gone.

When the phone rang, both ladies jumped up to answer it.

Regina reached it first.

"Hello . . . hold on."

She covered the receiver and whispered. "It's your daughter."

"I'll take it. Hello . . . No . . . I'm having Thanksgiving with Regina and Matilda this year. Tell the children happy holidays from me. And thank you . . . for asking."

Annabelle hung up and leaned her back against the door jam. "Liddy protested, but I know she was relieved I won't be there for the holiday. The kids probably begged her to call."

"You miss the children, don't you?"

"Very much."

Regina waited behind the door as Joe escorted Tillie into the house. "Hello, Joseph." She dismissed him with a nod and

87

turned to her petite friend. "It's Sunday, and you missed dinner. Again."

Tillie smiled. "We went for a ride at the lake. It's beautiful in the morning."

"You look flushed. Maybe you should lie down."

"I am a little tired." Stretching up on tiptoe Tillie kissed Joe's cheek. "Thanks."

He touched her lips with his. "You're most welcome."

Regina and Joe stood at the bottom of the stairs watching Tillie float up to her room.

When the door clicked shut, Regina turned to Joe. "Do you have a moment, Joseph? I have some questions."

"About?"

"You. Your family."

"Please, call me Joe, and, no, I've never had a family of my own. My parents are deceased and three of my four sisters have passed away. Is that what you wanted to know?"

Discomfort choked her voice. "I'm sorry about your sisters." She led him into the parlor. "Please tell me about yourself."

"My youngest sister, Tabitha, is traveling overseas. She and her husband are doing an extended tour of Europe, but should be home at Christmastime."

"Oh." She cleared her throat again. "What are your plans for the holidays?"

Tillie spoke from the doorway. "I forgot to tell you. Joe's having Thanksgiving dinner with us."

"If that's all right with Regina and Annabelle," Joe said.

"They won't care," Tillie said. "*I'm* the one who's cooking."

Good manners overruled her heart as Regina responded. "We'd be happy to have you join us, Mr. Linden."

"Thank you." He gave Regina a tentative smile, then turned the high beams on Tillie.

"Back to bed, Little Bit. I'll see you tomorrow."

"Yes. You're taking me shopping. I've got some new recipes to try for Thursday." She slipped her hand in his.

"Whatever you say. You're the boss." He wrapped her in a warm embrace, and they walked out of the room.

Regina watched in silence.

A smile of satisfaction spread across Regina's weary face. All three of them had spent Wednesday afternoon polishing and wiping every surface on the first floor. Only a slight aroma of lemon oil remained.

She admired the embroidered falling leaves of orange, red, yellow, and brown embellishing the scalloped edged tablecloth. Annabelle's handiwork.

Her own holiday contribution graced the center of the table. Pumpkin colored tapers in shining silver candlesticks. Nice touch.

But the appropriate response for Tillie's domain was awe. The kitchen sparkled from Tillie's efforts with soap and water. Despite her diminutive size, she could muster a massive amount of elbow grease. She announced to Regina, "No ammonia today. Let's enjoy the fragrance of pumpkin, turkey, and all the fixings."

The fact that Tillie was up before the sun that morning, had coffee on, and pies in the oven when Regina came down to break her fast belied her delicate health. Regina found Tillie mixing up corn bread for the stuffing she'd prepare Thursday morning. A half dozen stained and scribbled index cards lay on the table.

Perusing the menu Regina said, "Pavlov's dogs couldn't possibly be salivating as badly as I am right now."

There would be oyster bisque soup bubbling in the pot the next morning. A huge turkey, stuffed and roasting in bourbon with mustard glaze. The senses would be filled to bursting.

"Can I help?" Regina had asked, knowing full well the answer would be no.

"Nope. All I have left today is the wilted winter greens with black eyed peas and curried sweet potatoes. I'll be done by noon."

True to her word, Tillie had finished her cooking and started cleaning when the clock struck twelve.

Regina waltzed across the kitchen floor and put a hand on her friend's shoulder. "It looks and smells glorious. I for one am exhausted. Let's take a nap, then call in a pizza for dinner."

"We do good work, don't we?" Tillie said. Pale splotches mixed with the flush on her cheeks.

"The silver's all polished," Annabelle said, entering the kitchen with a smile.

"Good. We were just discussing a break from our labors. Tillie and I feel a nap is in order."

"I imagine so, what with all the work you two did. I could've done more, you know." Annabelle went to the refrigerator for a glass of iced tea.

"I appreciate your doing the tedious job, Belle. It wouldn't have gotten done otherwise." And nothing was broken. Regina patted Annabelle's hand and motioned Tillie toward the door. "Time to rest, dear."

"No arguments here." The last of Tillie's energy had been spent. She dragged her feet across the floor and up the stairs to her room and flopped, face down on the bed.

Regina closed the door on her already sleeping friend.

The doorbell announced Joe's arrival Thanksgiving morning.

"I came early to help," he said, handing Regina a festive arrangement of autumn colored mums and roses.

"How lovely. Thank you."

He followed her into the formal dining area between the

parlor and kitchen where Annabelle was setting the table with gleaming china and silver. Pumpkin orange linen napkins were rolled inside maple rings carved with thistles.

"Tillie's in the kitchen. I recommend we stay out of her way. She'll call if she needs any assistance," Regina said. "Would you like some coffee?"

"That would be great," Joe said.

A gleaming silver coffee service held center stage on the carved walnut sideboard. A matching cabinet with bowed glass held china and crystal.

"Black, right?" Regina poured.

"Yep."

"My, what a wonderful meal. You certainly know the way to a man's heart, Tillie-me-darlin'."

Tillie flushed with pleasure.

Annabelle rested her pudgy fingers on her rounded tummy. "I don't think I've ever eaten so much in my life."

Looking at their satisfied faces, Regina dabbed at a tear that escaped, but not before being noticed. "We truly have been blessed."

"Indeed," Joe said and began helping Annabelle gather dirty dishes.

Tillie and Regina took their coffee into the parlor and sank onto the sofa with a duet of sighs.

"You outdid yourself today, Matilda Jean."

"Thanks, Regina Louise. I was inspired, you know."

Tillie's black eyes darted to the kitchen door where clattering and voices drifted down the hall.

"Damned if I'm not falling in love, again."

"I suspected as much."

"I haven't told him about the surgery yet. I guess that's next, but I wanted to wait until after today. He makes me horny as hell." Tillie sobered. "Do you think it'll matter?"

"I don't know. If he's worth his salt, it won't." Regina patted her hand.

"Guess I'll find out soon enough."

The china sparkled as they finished stacking the last piece in the cabinet.

"Thanks for your help, Annabelle," Joe said, squeezing her wrinkled knuckles.

She blushed. "You're welcome."

He held the door open for her as they headed to the parlor to join the others. Bowing before Tillie, he took her hand and kissed it.

"Will you join me at my house for a nightcap?"

Regina cleared her throat. "You've been up before dawn for two days, Matilda Jean. Don't you think you should retire for the day?"

Without hesitation, Tillie rose from her seat and took Joe's hand in hers. "I've got an ounce or two of energy left, and I think I'll spend it with Joe."

"Thank you all for sharing your holiday with me," he said. He tucked Tillie's hand in the crook of his arm and headed out the door.

"He's such a charmer," Annabelle said.

"Yes, he is." Regina opened her book, but the words blurred. "Damn," she whispered. "He's going to break her heart."

Gathering up her sewing, Annabelle sighed. "I think I'll take a hot bubble bath before bed. I feel like an overstuffed sack of potatoes. Do you think Tillie will be home late?"

"Probably," Regina said. She stared out the window facing the street and Joe Linden's house. "Good night, Annabelle."

Tillie and Joe sat on the deck, sipping wine under the stars.

"Tillie, sweetheart. Do you think you could find it in your

heart to make love with a wrinkled old fart like me?"

"I guess so, but I want to tell you something first."

"Sweetie, I'm falling for you. I don't think I can wait." His big warm fingers closed on her small ones and tugged her up from the glider seat. "Let's talk upstairs, in private."

She followed, torn between excitement and terror.

What if he was put off by missing parts? Maybe it wouldn't matter.

The parts still remaining were warm and moist in anticipation.

Her hand slid along the banister. A dim light shined from the doorway at the top of the stairs. She hesitated on the threshold, examining the interior of his bedroom with curiosity, hoping to find the courage to speak.

He gently tugged her to the queen-sized bed, sat, and pulled her between his legs.

"Wait." She grabbed his hands and stepped back. "I'm not whole."

"What do you mean? You're the sweetest package I've seen in a long time."

"I've had a radical mastectomy."

"That doesn't matter, sweetheart, we're all missing a few pieces here and there by age fifty." A sensual grin spread across his stubble cheeks.

She laid her hand against his beating heart. "Joe, I had cancer."

"Oh."

Reality must've dawned.

He looked at the floor and dropped his hands from her hips. "I wasn't really paying attention, I guess. I don't think I'm ready for this after all."

"Shit. I was afraid of that. Nice knowing you, shallow man." She turned to exit the room.

"No, you don't understand. You're the sexiest little bit I've ever seen. I get worked up just watching you walk down the street. It's not the absence of breasts that I can't handle, it's the *cancer.*" His eyes were glistening with unshed tears.

Her brows twisted in confusion. "The surgeons got it all. I'm not even taking chemo or radiation treatments."

"I've lost three of my sisters to cancer. I'd go out of my mind if you died on me, too."

Tillie sat down beside him and held his hand. "We all go sometime."

The tears still refused to fall. "I guess this just hits me too close to home right now."

"It's all right, Joe. I understand."

They lay down beside each other in silence for a half-hour. Tillie kissed his forehead and slipped off of the bed.

"I'm sorry." His voice sounded hollow.

"Me, too." She touched his shoulder and slipped out of the room.

CHAPTER 13

Tillie and Annabelle decided that only a six-foot Scotch pine would do the century-old house justice. They trooped off to the Christmas tree farm north of town to cut one fresh. After a ride on the hay wagon and a cup of hot cider, they wrapped the tree they'd chosen in a tattered quilt and tied it to the trunk of the Cadillac.

A mile from the farm, Tillie snorted. "Christmas will be over by the time you get this heap home. I don't know how you talked me into letting you drive. Regina will have a fit. Step on it, Belle. We have an appointment with spiced eggnog, Bing Crosby, and tinsel."

"What about Regina?"

"She'll come around. Christmas can be great fun. She'll quit being such a dotard and enjoy my famous sugar cookies."

"Grandma Morgan used to make us iced sugar cookies with sprinkles. The house smelled heavenly," Annabelle said. She stared in the rearview mirror, as if searching for the past.

They pulled up beside the house and dragged the tree up the porch steps, leaving a trail of needles in their wake.

"Lord, what a mess," Regina said, wrinkling her nose.

"Hi, there." Tillie grinned. "Did this glorious pine scent reach all the way upstairs?"

"That's not exactly the trail I was following." Regina pointed to the path of green needles littering the carpet.

"Oops," Tillie said. "It could've been worse. They shook the

95

dead ones off before we brought it home."

"That's hard to believe."

Annabelle made a quick exit.

Tillie frowned, gazing after her deserting friend. "Did you find the Christmas decorations?"

"No, I was busy," Regina said.

"Fine, but the tree will look naked without some ornamentation. What will the neighbors say?"

"Joe won't mind," Annabelle said. She returned with the sweeper. "He's got a little silver tree with twinkle lights. Nothin' fancy." Nabbing a cookie she started the vacuum.

"Well, I mind," Regina said, then proceeded back up the stairs

When the vacuum's roar stopped, Regina joined Annabelle and Tillie in the parlor, carrying two cardboard boxes with XMAS marked on the sides. Even Ms. Pickles gathered around to examine the treasures the boxes contained, while Bing crooned about Christmas in the background.

Regina wondered if the shining ornaments, strings of lights, fuzzy stockings or the tree skirt would be too much temptation for the three legged cat. The next time she turned from the tree she saw Ms. Pickles balanced on her back foot, leaning as far into the box as possible before promptly falling on her head. She emerged with a wad of tinsel stuck to her fur and made her disgust apparent with a massive sneeze.

The laughter started deep in their bellies and grew as they watched Ms. Pickles fight off the glittering demons and scamper underneath the sofa. A lone piece of silver clung to her tail.

"Stupid cat." Regina's smile softened as she lifted a snarled garland from the box and began hanging it from the top of the tree.

"Tillie, do you remember the first time we met?"

Tillie beamed from dimple to dimple.

"How could I forget? It was the university's English department Christmas party. I knew who you were the minute you floated into the room." Tillie handed Annabelle a string of lights. "She was wearing a black silk sheath, single string of pearls, with her black hair hanging to her butt. Elegant yet understated. Hated by every dowdy wife in the room."

"I always wondered how you became friends," Annabelle said.

Regina's brow wrinkled. "At first I thought Tillie was just another one of Devlin's groupies. Petite and sassy in that backless flaming red dress she was almost wearing."

"Not hardly." Tillie barked a laugh. "Most men can't satisfy one woman, let alone two. Plus, I don't share. Devlin was a brilliant scholar, but totally governed by his gonads. I never could figure out why he was so attracted to brass and glass when he had platinum and diamonds at home."

Regina let the coldness of that comparison slide.

"Some folks always want what they don't have," Annabelle said.

"Devlin always talked about Tillie this and Tillie that."

"He did not," Tillie said.

"I beg to differ. I couldn't believe some of his outrageous tales," Regina said.

"Like what?" Annabelle asked

"Like Ms. Matilda Jean's trip to the tattoo parlor with the janitor and the head of the basketball team."

Tillie draped tinsel on Regina's shoulder. "Can't prove it by me."

"I'd begun to suspect they were having an affair. It wasn't until later that I realized it was the ones he didn't talk about that were the real threat."

Regina turned back to the tree and adjusted the beaded garland. The silence hung like bats from the ceiling.

"Is that when you two became close?"

Regina and Tillie exchanged a knowing look.

"Much later. Tillie was refreshing and a far cry from the stuffed academics. Quite the grown up in diminutive form."

"Thanks, Reggie," Tillie said.

Putting her hands on her hips, Regina mimicked her friend's voice. "The first words out of her mouth that night were, 'So, you're the artist, entrepreneur, scholar, and Queen Regina I've heard so much about.' "

Tillie plopped down on the floor beside the box and rolled with laughter, tears streaming from her eyes.

With a frown, Annabelle listened. "So, you were friends when Devlin died?"

"Not really. More like friendly acquaintances."

Regina resumed wrapping the garland around the base of the tree, then put her hands to the small of her back.

"I need fortification and drugs. How about some eggnog and a cookie?" Tillie said.

With tiny bits of cookie, Annabelle coaxed Ms. Pickles out from under the couch and into her welcoming lap.

"Devlin died this time about twelve years ago," Tillie said, popping a pill from her pocket and chasing it with a sip of eggnog.

Stroking the cat's soft fur, Annabelle nodded. "That's what I thought."

"She was a mess after Devlin died. If it weren't for me, she'd have wasted away in grief," Tillie said.

"Really?" Annabelle asked.

"Absolutely not. After the funeral I found several notebooks of Dev's poetry. For days I drank coffee, smoked cigarettes, and read," Regina said. "When I finished the last page, I slept for twenty-four hours, then I called Tillie."

"When I got here the house smelled and so did she. Anyone else would've locked her up in the psych ward, but that wasn't what she needed."

Regina looked into her friend's sparkling black orbs before continuing. "I needed a friend. She came over, cooked a wonderful meal, and read with me. Then we cried. She allowed me to grieve. Mother never approved of weakness."

"Aunt Victoria was rather stiff." Annabelle sniffed.

"We decided to have his best work published. The university agreed, and within a year his poetry was in print," Tillie said.

"But he cheated on you," Annabelle said.

Regina set her cup on the table. "Yes, he did, but Tillie helped me celebrate his work and remember the happy years."

Although some of her questions were answered, the real puzzle was not. Annabelle paused, then said, "But how did you come to live here together?"

Regina stood and resumed her decorating.

"I'll try to fill in the gaps," Tillie said. "Let's see, about a year after Dev passed away, my dad died of a heart attack. He'd been in the gas and oil business, but the economic recession ate up the reserves."

"How awful for you and your mother," Annabelle said.

"Mom went a year later from breast cancer, but I think she really died of a broken heart."

"They were really close, then?" Annabelle asked.

"They went together like peanut butter and jelly," Tillie replied.

"That's when things got really rough for you, didn't it?" Regina said.

"The medical bills were enormous. I had to sell everything, including the house. At age forty-eight I found myself homeless."

Annabelle patted Tillie's hand. "I know how you feel. But it's still sad to lose so much in such a short time."

"That's when Regina decided I could live here with her. She

can't cook worth a damn," Tillie said.

Regina faced them, composure restored. "This big old house needed new life, she needed a home, and . . ."

"As simple as that?" Annabelle asked.

"Simple? Not hardly," Regina said. "This was *my* house, and I'd lived alone for years. No matter how much I appreciate Tillie's energy and honesty, she's still irritating."

"Yes, but I'm one hellova chef," Tillie said.

"That's the Lord's truth," Regina said.

Tillie smiled.

"You like it quiet and orderly, and I'm neither. Are you sorry?"

"Only on occasion," Regina said and turned her attention back to the tree.

Annabelle glanced out the window. "There goes handsome."

"Too bad he's such a wuss," Tillie said.

CHAPTER 14

It'd been nearly a month since they'd seen Joe, and Christmas was almost upon them. Tillie moped around in the kitchen most days after her walks.

Regina found Annabelle gazing out the front window several times, her brow furrowed, a hankie wadded in her fist. On Wednesday morning she moved to the front door and watched Tillie round the corner, arms pumping, panting white puffs into the icy air and saw her discover Joe waiting on the porch steps. Tillie came to a military halt in front of him and waited with the patience of a drill sergeant.

"Mornin', Little Bit. Did you have a nice walk?"

"Yes." She crossed her arms over her chest and tapped her booted foot.

"I've been thinking about you ladies and thought I'd come by."

"You're a little late." She marched past him and into the house, slamming the screen.

He hung his head and then glanced over his shoulder. All three ladies stood in the doorway, scowling.

Regina opened the screen door. "Don't just sit there. Come in and have some coffee. Tillie's made sticky buns."

Annabelle beamed. "Oh yes, do come in, Joe."

He dragged his tall frame from the step.

Tillie hung back while Regina and Annabelle headed for the kitchen.

"Quit acting like a kid who's lost his marbles." She opened the screen further.

"I missed you," he whispered. "All three of you."

"Well, of course you did, you big oaf," Tillie said. "Now crawl in here where it's warm."

"Yes, ma'am."

The lack of conversation blanketed the kitchen like thick fog settling on the Arkansas River. An occasional chink of a china cup and the ticking of the clock were punctuated by sipping sounds.

Having had enough, Regina spoke. "Tell us what you've been doing since Thanksgiving, Joe."

"I've been doing a lot of thinking. Remembering, really."

"Good memories, I hope," Annabelle said.

"Some. I'd like to share them with you. When I was growing up I had three older sisters to torment."

Tillie laughed. "I'll bet you did a bang up job, too."

"Yep. But they'd take turns mothering and then picking on me. I think they drew broom straws to see whose day it was to do what to Little Joe."

"Little Joe?" Annabelle said.

"I've grown a bit since then. Abigail was the oldest. She once fed me a white paper sack full of chocolate Ex-lax and told me it was candy. I had the runs for two days."

Regina chuckled.

"She was the worst, but she'd also beat the bejesus out of anybody outside of the family who messed with her 'Joey'." He sighed and took a drink of the cooling brew.

Tillie refilled his cup and gave him a tentative smile.

"Mary Jane came next in the pecking order. Quiet, studious, and devious. Her favorite prank was letting the seam out of the rear end of my trousers. I'd have to sit on the bench instead of playing ball at recess, so she'd join me, silently grinning from ear to ear."

"I think that's a terrible trick," Annabelle said.

"I thought so, too, at the time. I think she just did it to get my undivided attention.

"Janice was the sweet one. She loved to bake and experiment with recipes. I was her favorite guinea pig. I would eat anything that didn't eat me first."

"No doubt that's how you got to be so big," Tillie said.

"One time she did some creative cooking, caramel chocolate something. It was so bad you couldn't chew it for fear your jaw would lock tight, cemented by the gooey stuff. I made the mistake of telling her 'this isn't fit for pigs,' so when my birthday rolled around she made me a special pie. It had a luscious meringue and flaky crust, but the inside was mud, baked hard as a brick. Momma said I had to eat 'just one bite,' and I did, washing it down with a half gallon of milk. I learned a valuable lesson that day. Women are mean and stick together."

"We know about special pies, don't we, Belle?" Regina said.

The twinkle sneaked back into Tillie's black eyes.

"I may have to try *that* mud pie recipe."

When the chuckling died down, Joe's eyes filled with tears. "I lost them all to cancer in less than five years. I didn't think I'd survive. A huge hunk of my heart just withered away with each one's passing."

Patting his hand, Tillie said, "We don't get out of this life alive. We've just got to make the best of the time we're here."

"True enough," Joe said.

"We've all lost loved ones," Tillie said, clasping his large brown fingers in hers.

"In other words, grow up, Joseph." Regina rose from her chair with a flourish.

He wiped his eyes and sat up straighter in the chair. "Spoken like a true military commander."

"No kidding," Annabelle said.

CHAPTER 15

As the year wound down, so did the temperatures, and Regina's bones creaked louder than usual. Christmas had quietly come and gone, and Annabelle gave Tillie a break from kitchen duties.

Annabelle experimented with the copy of *Gourmet Cooking* she'd found in her Christmas stocking. Only one major mishap occurred that week, when she tried to caramelize sugar and scorched the ceiling instead.

Regina phoned the fire department, and then Tillie made a quick call to the local pizza parlor. A Mondo Veggie Supreme and several handsome firemen showed up on their doorstep, which seemed to go a long way toward improving the situation and Regina's mood.

The afternoon of the thirtieth, the winter wind slashed exposed skin and brought tears to Regina's eyes. She sat curled up on the window seat, reading, the Christmas quilt she'd received from Annabelle wrapped snuggly around her legs.

A thunderous crash followed by a loud curse came from the back of the house.

Regina marked her place, slipped out from under the wrap, folded it, and pointed a long finger at the cat. "Keep your furry fanny off my new quilt."

Following the muffled growling to the pantry, she found her cousin, sitting in the middle of the floor, covered from head to foot with flour. The stool lay overturned behind her.

Surrounded by cans of vegetables, there was no good place for Annabelle to leverage herself up and out of the mess. Tears cleared a path down her whitened cheeks, as she wrung her apron and kicked her feet.

"What a fine mess you've gotten yourself into, Annabelle."

With a snarl and a raised hand Annabelle shouted, "Oh, shut up and help me."

Regina clasped her cousin's hand, then gave a yank. "Lord, it's a good thing I'm strong."

"You can afford to be."

"What's that supposed to mean? I've got a good mind to push you back down and leave you there."

"Face it, dearie, some of us worked while others went to the gym." Annabelle shook the flour from her blue locks. White dust formed a circle around her feet.

With hands on her hips Regina glared down on her shorter cousin.

"Maybe if you'd worked a little harder, you wouldn't have gotten so round."

Stretched to her full height Annabelle barely reached Regina's chin.

"I wasn't blessed with lithe genes or money to fritter away on the latest diet craze."

"Hey!" Tillie hollered and startled them both.

"Girlfriends, I'll go get the socker boppers and a whistle. Marquis of Queensbury rules?"

"No, I think not. I've been shut up in this house too long." With a flip of her braid, Regina left them to clean up.

In the parking lot north of the Ulrich Museum, Regina saw Joe's sports car, with the "GI JOE" ego tag. Unable to locate his impressive form in the vicinity, she walked up the concrete staircase leading to the double doors of the entrance.

The glass doors slid closed behind her, enveloping her in quiet warmth. Enormous brass Greek gods flanked the entry.

"May I help you?" The squeaky voice matched the person sporting a black bob, a pierced eyebrow, and a name badge that read "Amee" on the lapel of her jacket.

Looking down her nose at the young woman, Regina said, "Did you say something, child?"

"Excuse me? Could I be of service?"

Tempted to scare the willies out of the imp, Regina paused. She opened her mouth, but her neighbor's soothing baritone cut off any reply.

"Hello, Regina." He bowed slightly at the waist and tipped his Scottish driving cap. "I was just admiring your work."

"Joseph," she said and turned on her smile.

The pixie began hopping on her black platform shoes and wringing her hands. "Oh, oh, are you Regina Morgan-Smith?"

"Careful dear, you'll break an ankle. Yes, I am she. Please stop your bouncing and show me to my exhibit."

Joe watched the exchange with his arms crossed and expressed his amusement with a grin.

"My pleasure." Amee led them down the hall, chattering. "I love your work. Especially the nightmares."

Regina raised an eyebrow. "Nightmares?"

"I mean, the landscapes are nice, but the dark scenes are so passionate."

"I don't believe you've lived long enough to know real passion, young lady," Regina said.

Giving the rebuffed Amee a wink, Joe followed Regina across the carpet to the largest painting, dominating the room. "So, Regina, you're passionate about your painting?"

"Yes, I suppose I am."

The spotlight centered on a woman's face. Surrounded by black, burnt umber and ultramarine, with only a hint of her torso, she seemed to float out of the pitch. The sunken cheeks, blue on white, were strangely luminescent against the background of night.

Joe whispered over her shoulder, "She looks like she's dying or dead."

"She's both."

"She reminds me of you."

Regina stepped to the right where a much smaller painting hung.

He joined her. "Now this one is much more fun. I especially like the glint in the bright green eyes. Was Ms. Pickles a cooperative subject?"

"Not especially."

Regina moved to the next display. "This one was a joy to create," Regina said, with a self-satisfied grin.

"You've captured the peculiar shade of blue in her hair quite nicely. The posterior angle, however, is not very complimentary. Her dress reminds me of an old bedspread my grandmother had. You'd better hope Annabelle never sees it."

"I've no doubt she will, someday."

They continued their path around the room and exited together. Amee was nowhere to be seen.

"I'll walk you to your car," Joe said, taking her arm.

Enjoying the attention, she wondered why he preferred petite women. She might consider redirecting some of her passion, given the appropriate encouragement.

"Joseph, why don't you help us ring in the new year tomorrow night? We're having champagne and hors d'oeuvres at ten."

She unlocked the car and slid into the seat.

He hesitated, but finally answered. "Okay, but I'll bring the champagne."

"Very well, as long as it's not domestic."

Regina started the car and backed out. She saw him in the

rearview mirror as he stood at the vacated spot, watching her drive away.

After they had finished an early supper, Regina cleared her throat. "I ran into Joseph at the museum today."

The heads of the other two snapped up.

"Ah, I see I have everyone's attention," Regina said.

"What was he up to?" Tillie asked and began clearing the table.

"He came by to see my exhibit."

Annabelle frowned and picked up her plate. "How long will your work be there?"

"It's a special show, so only a week or two."

Strangely silent, Tillie continued to scrape the crumbs into the disposal while Annabelle began filling the dishwasher.

"I've invited him to join us for new year's tomorrow. He's bringing the champagne."

In mid-movement the plate slipped from Tillie's hand, shattering on the unforgiving porcelain. She slowly pivoted, black eyes flashing, piercing Regina's cool blue gaze.

"Nice of you to include us in your plans."

Annabelle shrank back.

With a slow smile, Regina accepted the challenge. "You don't mind, do you?"

"Not really. Should be interesting. Will you finish up here, Belle? It's time for my walk." Tillie slammed out the back door, rattling the glass.

"What are you up to?" Annabelle said, as she tore off her apron and threw it on the counter. "You know she's still sensitive to that man."

"Oh? And you're not?"

"What? I've had enough of men to last a lifetime. Are you panting after him now?"

"Not any more than you are."

"You selfish bitch. She *was* your best friend. Probably your only friend."

Knowing full well what she had done, Regina took her time dressing. She smiled at her reflection in the cheval mirror. The creamy silk skirt floated beneath the matching cashmere sweater. An amber brooch and earrings hung to her shoulders. She added a hint of coral lipstick and stepped back to take a look at the whole package.

Not bad and ready for any number of possibilities.

Regina descended the stairs as the clock struck nine-thirty. The Christmas tree shimmered with lights and tinsel, and Ms. Pickles, having made peace with the silver demons, was curled asleep on the velvet tree skirt underneath.

In the hearth, fire crackled and pine cones popped, scenting the room and adding cozy warmth. A shimmering champagne bucket stood in a stand to the right of the sofa.

Regina picked up her novel while Tillie rearranged tiny morsels a fraction one way, then the other on the serving platter. She noticed that once again, Tillie had used her culinary prowess to tantalize and seduce. However, the most elegant presentation was the cook herself, with her black lamé pantsuit and cowl neck blouse. Her white hair glimmered in the firelight.

"Matilda Jean, you're clearly loaded for bear and ready to conquer," Regina said.

Ignoring the bait, Tillie rearranged the trays.

Although the fire blazed, the climate in the room sported icicles.

Wearing a long navy dress, Annabelle joined them. Her sensible shoes were replaced with shiny black slippers. A string of pearls disappeared between her ample breasts. Wisps of blue hair curled around her flushed cheeks and ruby red lipstick.

When the doorbell rang, they all froze like mannequins in a holiday display. Regina paused to pinch her cheeks, then opened the door with a flourish. "Welcome, Joseph."

"Thank you, Regina. You're looking stunning this evening."

Her eyes popped at the sight of a lovely woman accompanying him. She stood a good three inches taller than Regina and carried herself with the grace of a dancer. Her shiny blond hair was streaked with gray and did a saucy flip at her shoulders.

Lord, is there no end to his arrogance?

"I'd like you to meet my little sister. She flew in early, and I knew you wouldn't mind me bringing her. Tabitha this is Regina Morgan-Smith."

He guided Tabitha in by the arm and handed Regina the promised magnum of champagne.

Regina pursed her lips and hung their coats on the brass butler. "It's French, thank the Lord."

"The Lord had nothing to do with it," Joe said.

With her nose in the air, Regina led them into the parlor and jabbed the bottle into the ice bucket.

"What a wonderful room," Tabitha said. "I love a comfy fire."

"As do I." Regina flipped her slender fingers toward her waiting roommates and slid onto the sofa.

Why waste any more of my time? He's obviously ignorant with no quality of breeding. Right, Mother?

Joe's green eyes found Tillie, who stood next to the loaded refreshment table.

He led his sister across the room and took Tillie's delicate hand in his.

"This is the little spitfire I was telling you about."

Caressing her palm with his warm lips, Joe smiled. "You look wonderful. I'd like you to meet my sister. Tillie, this is Tabitha."

Tillie extracted her hand from his and offered it to his companion. "I'm very pleased to meet you."

With a smile, his sister took Tillie's proffered hand and gave it a sound shake. "My brother's description didn't do you justice."

"Figures. Would you like something to eat?"

"Absolutely. Joe tells me you are a gourmet cook, as well as the love of his life."

Joe slid his index finger under his collar, which didn't appear the least bit tight. "Guilty of the former, but I'm not so sure about the latter." With military stiffness, Joe eyed his sister, then turned his attention to Annabelle.

"You look very nice tonight, Annabelle. This uppity female is my baby sister. Her husband had to return to Seattle on business, so she decided to invade my domain for the new year."

"How do you do?" Annabelle's cheeks were aflame.

"Fine, thank you," Tabitha said, with a slight nod.

Joe's eyes lifted to be captured once again by the black-eyed temptress.

Regina shoved her book off the sofa. The thump jolted Annabelle, Tabitha, and the cat. However, Joe and Tillie didn't appear to notice.

Maybe the cat will vomit a fur ball and get their attention. Regina sulked like a teen, and she knew it.

Tillie gave Joe a wink.

"You look good enough to eat. Thank God you brought a chaperone."

"You look wonderful." Joe bent at the waist and kissed her hand a second time.

With a chuckle, Tabitha pushed her brother out of the way and smiled at Tillie. "Quit hogging the chef, Joseph."

Her eyes were brilliant green like her big brother's and didn't appear to have missed anything, including the complicated dynamics emanating between those assembled in the room.

While Annabelle hovered at the doorway, twirling a lace

handkerchief between her hands, Regina worked out her frustration on the champagne cork.

Joe excused himself and crossed the room.

"Regina, let me do that."

With a twist, he had the wire off and wrapped a dishtowel over the cork before giving it a nudge with his thumbs. It expelled with a muffled but audible poof, sending the cat scurrying under the sofa again.

"I'll get another glass," Annabelle said.

The jovial conversation made the evening progress quickly for everyone, except Regina. For her, ringing in the new year had become an interminable process.

CHAPTER 16

Tillie and Tabitha became inseparable during the last days of her visit. They had lots in common, not the least of which was Joe. There was a honk outside at ten each morning, and off they'd go to take advantage of all the sales.

After four days of this routine, Regina had had enough.

"Annabelle, why don't we go shopping?"

"Excuse me?"

"Those two can't be allowed to buy up all the bargains," Regina said.

"Well, I do need some yarn and some embroidery floss."

"That's it? Where's your sense of adventure?"

"Regina, are you feeling all right? I'm on social security, remember, I can't afford to be adventurous."

"Fine, then we'll go to the fabric shop and get you some string. Then I'll take you to lunch. My treat." Regina retrieved her pocket book from the sofa.

Annabelle took off her apron and shook her head. "You've obviously been cooped up too long."

Tabitha's departure came much too soon for Tillie, who squinted at her watch. "What possessed you to take a plane in the middle of the night?"

"It's six A.M. The sun is up!" Tabitha said and hugged her new friend.

"Not yet. That's a mirage," Tillie grumbled and returned the squeeze.

Joe wrapped his long arms around them both. "Tabby, Little Bit believes in getting her beauty sleep. She doesn't usually see daylight until nine."

"I didn't think there was daylight before nine." Tillie poked him in the ribs before turning to Tabitha. "I've had such a good time this week. Hell, girl, you wore me out, and I'm broke. But, it was worth it."

Tabitha's dark lashes filled with tears that spilled down her smooth cheeks. "Thanks for everything, Tillie. Watch out for my big brother, would you please?"

"Somebody needs to."

Standing side-by-side in front of the terminal entrance, Tillie and Joe watched Tabitha approach the security checkpoint. She threw them a kiss, which they returned in kind.

"I'm going to miss her," Joe said. He swiped his eyes with his hand.

"Me, too."

They headed to the parking lot.

"Want to get a bite to eat?"

"No. I'm really tired. Could you just take me home?"

"Sure." He unlocked her door before heading to the driver's side.

Tillie scooted in and laid her head back against the rest. Her eyes remained closed until they pulled into the drive.

His brows knit. "You okay?"

"Just tired. See you later." She threw him a kiss and went straight up to bed.

The grandfather clock struck twelve. Tillie stretched, pulling herself from slumber.

Unintelligible, angry voices reverberated up the stairwell.

115

Tillie stared at the ceiling, taking inventory of her tired bones. *Dammit. I feel like shit. They said they got it all. Liars. I gave up both breasts, and for what? Now I suppose I'll have to go through chemo. Poisonous crap. Probably lose my hair and turn green like a freaking alien.*

She dragged herself from under the covers, opened the wardrobe, and pulled on a hot pink t-shirt printed with, "Growing Old Ain't For Sissies" on the front. She slipped her cold toes into fuzzy green slippers and peeked into the hall. The coast was clear, so she headed to the bathroom.

Frowning at the haggard woman in the mirror, Tillie said, "Momma, I didn't need the big C genes. Why couldn't I have the double-jointed ones instead? Then I could've joined the circus."

Voices and slamming doors penetrated her thoughts.

She closed her eyes, splashed cold water on her face, and pulled in a calming breath.

"Lord, thanks for four months free of disease. Give me strength and help Regina and Annabelle stop biting each other's heels. I may not be around to referee much longer."

She patted her cheeks, tried on a smile and headed for the coffeepot.

Nose-to-nose across the table, one cousin breathed fire, and the other ice.

"Lord, here we go," Tillie said, entering the ring.

Regina straightened and smiled at Tillie. "What did you say, dear?"

"Never mind." Tillie's slippers flopping on the linoleum floor brought the cat sliding between her ankles. Tillie poured the last of the thickened, warp-factor-ten brew and took a sip. "When are you two going to realize you need each other?"

Lines creased Regina's brow. "Drink up, dear, you're delirious—and looking a peculiar shade of gray this morning, I must say."

With a snort, Annabelle slammed her coffee cup on the counter.

"Nice. Tillie, in case you've forgotten, Regal Regina doesn't *need* anyone!" The stout woman stormed from the room.

"Certainly not *you,* Bossy Belle."

Regina opened the back door and turned to Tillie. "Perhaps I'll see you later."

The cat's back arched as she rubbed against Tillie's bare shin. Tillie bent down to scratch the purring feline behind her ear. "What am I going to do, Ms. Pickles?"

The gray kitten curled up on her slippers and went to sleep.

Tillie contemplated her future in the molten java she'd yet to finish.

My relapse will probably send Joe running for the hills. Too bad. Maybe I can change his mind. An erotic last wish, perhaps?

The black, soggy dregs formed an ominous pattern in the bottom of her cup. If these were tea leaves, she was doomed.

"If I've got to do this thing. I may as well get on with it."

She raised her mug in salute. "Lord, how about I let you drive and I'll ride shotgun?"

With a heavy sigh, Tillie put her feet under the warm fur of the kitten and wiggled into her slippers. It was time to make a phone call.

CHAPTER 17

It'd been two weeks since Tillie agreed to Dr. Kumbatpati's recommended eight-week regimen of chemotherapy.

"I don't have much choice, do I?"

"You always have a choice," he said in his singsong voice.

"Not really. I didn't choose to get this damned disease. It's a royal rip."

For the past two Thursdays, she'd sat in a green vinyl recliner, surrounded by gray walls decorated with pink and red construction paper hearts, tethered to an intravenous line. A plastic trashcan sat within easy reach.

The soap opera on television appeared to be even less promising than the worn two-year-old magazines on the table. A new "bodice ripper" sat unopened on Tillie's lap while she counted the ceiling tiles and sang. "I gotta get out of this place, if it's the last thing I ever do . . ."

The soft tap of loafers on tile made her lose the rhythm.

"I'm still here," she said to the doctor as he approached from behind.

"How are you doing today?"

"Dr. K., I see you're as starched as ever. Did you know that you're totally screwing up my love life? I've been sick every Friday and Saturday night."

He wiped his glasses on the corner of his lab coat, a tinge of red highlighting the tops of his ears. "I'm most sorry, Miss Matilda, but it is only for six more weeks."

"Easy for you to say. I'm not getting any younger and don't have many weekends left to party."

He smiled. "You are doing quite well and will no doubt live to party much longer."

"I bet you say that to all the good looking women."

"Yes, but do not tell my wife. She would not understand."

Tillie chuckled. "Your secret's safe with me. By the way, when I took my shower this morning I found *Cousin It* clogging the drain."

"Cousin It?"

"Sorry. I forgot you didn't grow up around here. My hair's falling out. Isn't there anything you can do?"

"No. The medication you are taking has to be quite strong to kill the cancer. Unfortunately, hair cells are as fast growing as the malignant ones and react to the chemotherapy as well."

"I'm not into wigs. They're too itchy. I'll freeze my noggin at this rate. I guess I'll have to accessorize. Ever been to Hat Man Jacks?"

"No. But, I will investigate it if it would please you."

He bowed his brown head to show her the few black strands that covered it. "I, too, have thinning hair, but mine will not grow back like yours will."

"Good point. You could try hair plugs."

He slowly shook his head.

"You're probably right. Better to go natural than look like a newly sprouted field," she said.

By Sunday night, Tillie was able to withstand the smell of food, but Regina and Annabelle were conspicuously absent.

"No doubt they're going ten rounds somewhere out of earshot, while I fend for myself."

She shuffled into the kitchen, banged a few pots and pans, and then nuked a can of soup.

"Always be prepared," Tillie said. She pulled out a new trash bag and slipped it over the sash of her robe. "Not exactly *tres chic*, but it'll be a handy barf bag."

She mumbled while the electric can-opener whirred. "Selfish bitches. Am I friend or chief cook and china washer?"

By the time the soup was hot, Regina had slipped in to join Tillie at the kitchen table. She scrunched up her nose.

"How can you tolerate that plastic spoon? It's totally uncivilized."

With a slight tip of the corner of her lips, Tillie said, "I'm lucky to eat at all. Silver flatware makes everything taste like metal, and it makes my teeth feel like I'm chewing aluminum foil."

"Everything Annabelle knows how to cook tastes like cardboard. She wouldn't know an herb if it bit her ample behind. It's unbelievable. I need you."

"You could cook, Regina Louise."

"Yes, but I can't find a thing in the kitchen since you took over. You've spoiled me. Besides, cooking makes Annabelle feel useful."

"Right. And you don't enjoy giving her hell for making a mess."

"Perhaps." Regina grinned.

Pushing away from her half eaten bowl of broth Tillie sighed. "I'm tired. Annabelle and I are going to watch *It Happened One Night*. Care to join us?"

"You've seen it at least ten times. Surely you must have the dialog memorized by now."

"Yes, but it's so sweet."

Flipping her braid over her shoulder, Regina said, "I think I'd rather be in a coma."

"Suit yourself."

Annabelle passed them in the dining room. "I'll make us

some popcorn," she said.

"None for me thanks," Tillie said. "I'm full of soup."

"That's not all you're full of," Regina said and crossed to the bay window, picking up her book.

"I love the smell of buttered popcorn," Tillie said.

"That's not what I smell . . . Annabelle!" Regina screamed.

With a weak, "I'm sorry," Annabelle waved as the smoke billowed down the hallway. Tillie leapt from the sofa and dashed for the bathroom.

The cat waited patiently outside the door.

"Well that was a waste of good soup," Tillie said. She resumed her place on the couch.

"I'm so sorry, Tillie, would you like some juice?" Annabelle waved her hankie in the air to dissipate the smoke.

"A soft drink might be better."

Annabelle fixed glasses of soda for them both before settling down to watch the movie.

Snuggled into a ball, Ms. Pickles fell fast asleep in the crook of Tillie's knees.

"Annabelle," Tillie whispered. "Would you crochet something for me?"

"Sure. Would you like a new afghan?" Annabelle asked.

"No. Do you remember the little skull caps that women wore in the forties?"

Annabelle laughed. "My mother used to wear those. I have a picture somewhere. You thinking about bringing them back in style?"

"It's better than looking like a shrunken Kojak."

From across the room, Regina looked through her lashes, obviously straining to hear their conversation.

"Any particular colors?" Annabelle asked.

"Well, as a matter of fact. Several would be nice. If they're not too hard to do."

"Not at all," Annabelle said.

Regina slammed her book shut. "What's this about caps? You don't wear caps, Matilda Jean."

"I will be wearing them."

Regina's brow creased. "Why?"

"Because I'm losing my hair."

Her hand went to her breast and Annabelle choked. "Oh, no, your beautiful white hair," Annabelle said.

"What did you guys expect?" Tillie looked from one to the other. "Dr. K. says it'll grow back. In the meantime, I'd like a little camouflage. Geez, it's only hair."

With a sniffle, Annabelle pulled her handkerchief from her pocket and dabbed the tears that threatened to roll.

Tillie reached over and patted her friend.

"Quit sniveling, Annabelle," Regina said and tucked her nose back into her book.

The cat hopped over Tillie's legs and rubbed against her stomach. With a conspirator's smile, Tillie nudged Annabelle and casually lifted her finger in Regina's direction.

Annabelle shrugged her shoulders and mouthed the word, "What?"

Tillie's black eyes gleamed as she cleared her throat. "Hey, Reg, when did you start reading upside down?"

Regina's head snapped up, and the book slapped shut. Her eyes glistened. She slowly stood. "If you'll excuse me, I have work to do." Regina headed for the stairs.

"See you later." Tillie spoke to her retreating back.

"Take a look at my yarn. Pick the colors you like best," Annabelle said.

"Well, Ms. Pickles," Tillie said, as she stroked the furry head. "Old Regina's not as tough as she lets on. But we already knew that, didn't we?"

Annabelle followed Regina out, but not quickly enough to

overtake her, so she veered to her room for her crochet bag.

The attic floor creaked in protest as Regina crossed to the light bulb string. She held it for a moment, scanning the room in the dim glow of the setting sun coming through the dormer window. A lifetime of work crowded the floor along the walls in stacks two or more deep.

She pulled the cord, and the harsh incandescence made her squint and turn away. She wiped the tears that had appeared again and pulled out a new canvas to replace the jet black and crimson woman hanging by her braid that occupied the easel.

"Oh, mirror to my tortured soul, you give me the shivers. I feel like spiders are crawling up my arms."

Regina began the methodical task of sorting through her oil paints, stopping only to glob pale colors on her wooden pallet.

With no conscious effort, she added layers of color to the canvas. First titanium white, blending to a blush of peach, then a wisp of sky blue; the sable brush guided by feel alone. Once again, she allowed herself to be controlled by the driving emotions hidden beneath her surface calm.

When the night was spent, she stared at the finished product. The gold of the morning sun penetrated her consciousness and brought a glow to the painting.

Staring at the winged woman with wavy white hair and black eyes that hovered on the canvas, Regina asked, "Is that you, Tillie? Are there wings behind that devilish smile?"

As she descended the stairs, Regina saw Annabelle in the parlor making a cap to adorn Tillie's soon to be bald head. "This is much too plain for you, my spunky little friend," Annabelle said aloud. She set the barely started row aside. "Have you been up there all night?" Annabelle asked.

"Yes, and I'm tired. I can't face losing my friend."

"I imagine so. Were you painting all this time?"

"Yes." *And crying. And remembering.*

"Oh. Well, I have a favor to ask."

Leave me alone.

"What?" Regina asked.

"Do you have any of *Grandmere's* old beads? I'd like to put them on Tillie's caps."

Regina frowned. "Why?"

"I'm making these for Tillie, and I thought the beads would be a nice touch," Annabelle said.

Staring through her portly cousin, Regina saw *Grandmere* handing a gangling twelve-year-old a balsa wood box, with a cameo and roses burned on the lid.

No, they're mine.

"I suppose," Regina said.

"Now, please, I can slide them on as I stitch," Annabelle said.

"Fine." Her face a blank mask, Regina escorted Annabelle to her bedroom.

Annabelle stood just outside the doorway while Regina rummaged in the closet.

She came out with a Flemish jewelry box and handed it to her cousin.

"There are several loose pieces in the bottom drawer." Regina shut the door in Annabelle's face.

"Thank you." Annabelle spoke to the wooden panel. Cradling the old box to her chest Annabelle hurried to her own bedroom to examine the treasures inside.

Lifting the delicately burned lid, Annabelle found several compartments with disintegrating satin lining. There were brooches of malachite, jet, and sapphire. A lovely black cameo she recalled her Grandma wore to funerals.

With reverent care, she laid the pieces back in their compartments like hollow eggs before she opened the bottom drawer of the chest.

"Jackpot," Annabelle said.

Using her finger, she sorted dozens of tiny glass beads by shape and color into piles on the stained satin.

"Grandma, I remember, you always wore the black beads with a red satin blouse and the garnets on white lawn. Sometimes Regina reminds me of you."

Annabelle added ebony beads to the jet black cap, creating a delicate wave design. And while the rest of the house slept, she crocheted.

By midafternoon, Annabelle had finished the black and created a red cap sprinkled with tiny garnets and clear glass pearls that twinkled like captured stars.

When her stomach threatened to eat her from the inside out, Annabelle stopped and headed for the kitchen. But when she passed Tillie's closed door, she heard a muffled sound. She pressed her ear to the wood, then pulled her clean handkerchief from her sleeve and tapped.

"Tillie?"

Without waiting for a response, Annabelle slipped into the dim room and crossed to Tillie's bed. She handed her the hankie and sat on the edge.

Tillie blew her nose with a honk. "Want to join my pity party? Look." She placed a wad of fine white hairs, the size of a ping pong ball, into her friend's warm palm.

"I feel like one of those hairless Chihuahua's. Pitiful looking things."

"But, dear, didn't the doctor say it would grow back?"

"Yes, but until then I'll look dreadful, and Joe will be back soon."

Annabelle gently touched the remaining gossamer strands.

"Wait here a minute."

"I think I'd rather be bald." Wiping her leaky nose Tillie sniffled.

125

When Annabelle re-entered the room, she held a mirror in one hand and something black and red in the other.

Tillie turned on the bedside lamp. "What have you got there?"

"Close your eyes."

"How can I see with my eyes closed?"

Tillie flinched when Annabelle slid the soft cap onto her head.

"Okay, you can open them now."

Her eyes widened as she looked into the mirror Annabelle held for her. The glimmering red cap sat at a jaunty angle, with wisps of white poking out around the bottom.

"Well, I'll be. You made this scarecrow look pretty spiffy."

Annabelle's heart swelled. "Do you like it?"

"Of course. It makes me feel kinda foxy. Thank you, Belle."

"You're lovely, even without hair. No doubt my head is all lumpy. And I'll bet Regina's is pointed."

A giggle started low in Tillie's chest, like thunder, then erupted into sidesplitting laughter. Tears spilled from the corners of their eyes as the ladies fell upon each other in a comforting hug.

Annabelle's stomach grumbled, which started the giggling all over again.

Tillie patted Annabelle's protesting tummy. "I think we'd better feed that before it gets loose."

"It's already as loose as Jell-O. How about some peanut butter?"

"Actually, that sounds pretty good. Is there any Sand Plum jelly left?"

"I believe there's some in the pantry."

"How'd you learn to be such a good jelly maker, Belle?"

"Momma taught me. We had such fun. We'd put on long sleeved shirts and jeans, because of the thorns, you know. We'd wear hats and spray each other with bug repellent. Nasty smelling stuff, but it kept the stingers away. The bees and wasps love plum thickets."

Tillie managed a smile.

"The plums were usually ripe about the fourth of July, so we'd get up early, before it was hot, and fill our buckets. We'd come home and sit in the shade of the porch and cut out the worms and talk about happy things. Momma would tell me about when she and Aunt Victoria were little girls. It took almost all day, but the results were worth it."

"I can't argue with that." Tillie headed to the kitchen, admiring herself in every reflective surface.

CHAPTER 18

Annabelle picked up the ringing phone. "Hello."

"Hi, Belle. This is Joe. Is Tillie around?"

"Why, hello. Where have you been? We haven't heard from you for quite a while. Almost a month, I'd say."

"Yes, I know. I've been in Seattle visiting with Tabitha and her husband. Is Tillie there?"

"No. How is Tabby?"

"As sassy as ever. When will Tillie be back?"

"Why do you want to know?" She wound the cord around her finger.

"Excuse me?"

"I said, why do you want to know? You've been gone for weeks and haven't called. You should've been with her, especially now."

"What do you mean?" he asked.

"Oh, come now, Joe. I'm not blind. You two are head over heels for each other."

"You've been reading too many of those heaving bosom books you women like so much."

"Is that so?" Annabelle said.

"When will she be home?"

"It's Thursday, and she's gone all day."

"Don't tell me she has a new beau? Where's she hanging out on Thursdays?"

"She's getting chemotherapy," she said.

He sucked in his breath, nearly gagging. "What? What's happened?"

"Right after you left, she wasn't feeling up to par, so Regina took her back to see Dr. Kamelpotty, or whatever his name is, and he said *it* was back."

"Shit. Oh, sorry, Annabelle."

"That's okay. This is her third week of treatments."

"Is she doing all right?" he asked.

"It makes her tummy queasy and wears her out. She sleeps most of the weekend." Annabelle couldn't disguise the tears in her voice.

"Does the doctor think she'll get better?"

"They don't know. They pat her fuzzy head and tell her what a good girl she is. It's degrading. If she wasn't so pooped, she'd probably punch them."

"Has she asked about me?" he asked.

"No, she just looks out the front window for hours. I think she's disappointed. She misses the fun you two had together. When are you coming home?"

"I don't know."

"What are you afraid of?"

Joe cleared his throat. "Do you remember when I told you about my oldest sister, Abigail? I was so mad at her for dying and leaving me. When Mary Jane went so quickly, I thought I'd never get over the shock. After Janice got sick, I became this avenging angel, determined to conquer her cancer with my strength of will. In the end we were both defeated."

"That was a long time ago, and you were just a young man."

"True. Tabby said I took on this devil-take-it-all attitude that scared the life out of her. She figured my military career was an obsession with danger and death."

"That was then, and this is now, Joseph Linden. You're a grownup."

"Sometimes I'm not so sure," he said.

"Joe, are you in love with Tillie?"

"I think so."

"Okay, then what's the problem?"

"Love is unnerving, but cancer is terrifying."

"You may not have forever to be with her. Why are you wasting time?"

"Don't you understand?"

"I guess not," Annabelle said.

"I can't watch another loved one die."

"So don't." Annabelle straightened her spine. "Stay away from that lovely woman, be lonely and afraid, and know that she may not be here when you finally get up the nerve to come back."

"Now you're being nasty," he said.

"Wake up. She's might live for years. Wouldn't you rather she share those years with you?"

"Yes, but I'm a coward."

"Good. Now we're getting somewhere." Annabelle grinned into the receiver.

"Dammit. I'm coming home."

"You've hurt her, Joe. Don't do it again."

"I know. I'm sorry," he whispered.

"Don't say you're sorry to me. What I feel doesn't matter. It's Tillie who needs to know you won't run out on her again."

"Okay. I'll take the first plane home, probably tomorrow."

"Call before you come. She may not feel up to company."

She heard the tears choking his voice. "Thanks, Annabelle."

When Regina picked Tillie up from the clinic, she was limp as soggy spaghetti, her skin the color of paste. Her thinning body was a glaring testament to the harshness of the fight against disease.

"Would you mind acting the chauffeur today, Reg? I'd like to lie down."

Regina nodded, extracting the newest additions to the vehicle: a small plastic trashcan, lap robe and embroidered pillow, then opened the rear door.

Tillie shuffled to the car and leaned on the hood prior to lowering herself into the backseat. Sweat beaded on her upper lip. She collapsed on the cool white leather and slept fitfully all the way home.

When they pulled into the drive, Annabelle was waiting on the porch, handkerchief in hand.

Regina helped Tillie out of the car, then followed a step behind her as she dragged herself up the stairs.

Lord, she's just got to make it through this.

Grinning from ear-to-ear, Annabelle said, "Joe called."

With only a slight hesitation, Tillie continued the climb, determination in every step.

Flailing her hankie, Annabelle opened the screen for the sick woman to pass through.

"He's been out of town and said he'll call as soon as he gets home tomorrow."

Regina shot her a glare, her lips a stark line across her face.

Like a clumsy puppy, Annabelle hopped out of Tillie's way. "He's concerned about you."

Tillie stopped with obvious effort and smiled at her friend. "That's nice, but right now I don't want to talk about Joseph Linden. I want to go to bed."

"Oh, of course. I'll tell you all about it when you wake up."

"Fine," Tillie said over her shoulder and continued up the stairs.

Regina hissed at her cousin. "Shut up, you old fool."

Annabelle looked startled. "What did I say?"

131

In quiet whispers they spat back and forth at the bottom of the stairs.

Tillie shook her head and proceeded. When she reached the top she spoke. "After my nap I think I want one of you to shave my head. I'm tired of the straggly hairs poking out every which way."

Regina and Annabelle stood in stunned silence.

Tillie turned and went to her room.

Chapter 19

Seated at the breakfast table, Regina sneaked a peek at the other ladies over the edge of the newspaper.

"Liddy called," Annabelle said.

Regina sniffed. "So, what's the evil darling want now?"

"She needs me to babysit over spring break. She has to work, and the kids fight too much to be left alone."

Tillie's head snapped up, black eyes blazing. "You aren't going, are you?"

Annabelle lifted her nose. "Well, yes. I miss my grandkids."

"Are you nuts?" Tillie asked. "Don't you remember what happened the last time you stayed with her?"

"I don't know what you're talking about. Nothing happened to me then, and it won't now," Annabelle said.

"Besides, *I* need you right now . . ."

Regina folded the paper then scooted her chair on the linoleum, the sound shifting attention to her. "Belle, I think we all know Liddy hit you."

Tillie chimed in. "No shit."

"No, no, no. She was going through a bad time, and I just made it worse. She never hurt me."

Regina snorted. "What makes you think things have changed? What about her worthless ex-husband? Was he the one?" She watched as Annabelle fidgeted and failed to meet her gaze.

"I'll be fine. It's just a week. She's my daughter, and she needs me."

Tillie's voice tightened. "Will you be home every night?"

"No." Annabelle wrung the cloth napkin in her lap. "Liddy's too tired after work to bring me home, and I can't afford to pay a week's worth of taxi fares."

Although her body was poisoned with chemicals, Tillie summoned up the spirit to command the regal mistress of the house. "Regina can take you and pick you up."

Eyebrows lifted, Regina's cool blue stare met the snapping black orbs of her friend. "Hold on, Tillie. I'm not her chauffeur. She's a grown up. And who'll take you to treatments if I'm taking Annabelle hither and yon?"

"Joe can chauffeur me to the torture chamber. It'll do him good. Just because I can barely lift my arms doesn't mean I can't make a phone call."

"Joseph may not be available. The wimp would stand in front of a firing squad before partnering you to chemo."

Regina turned to Annabelle. "What time do you have to be there each morning?"

"Probably six forty-five. Liddy has to be at the aircraft plant at seven-thirty, and it's clear on the south end of town. Come on, Tillie, don't worry, it's only a week. It'll be easier for everybody if I just stay with Liddy and the kids."

Tillie reached across the table and clasped Regina's rigid hand. "Can't you take her and pick her up? It's only for five days or so."

Frost formed on Regina's straight shoulders. She gently dislodged her hand.

"I don't think so. Although it's difficult for me to admit, for once, Belle is right. It's a week. She's a grown woman and can take care of herself. It's her family, not a den of serial killers."

With a sigh and slump, Tillie said, "You will call us if anything happens?"

Giving her friend's arm a pat, Annabelle smiled. "I'll be fine.

Save your strength. If I've learned anything the last few months with you two, it's how to stand up for myself."

"Humph," Regina said with a throaty chuckle and left the room.

On Sunday evening, Regina drove Annabelle to her daughter's house on the northeast end of town. She lived in a once prosperous neighborhood now fighting decay and neglect, and losing. Broken toys, tricycles, and bikes lay helter skelter on patchy lawns of crab grass and dirt.

Regina wrinkled her nose and slowed over the potholes in the street. "Looks like things need a bit of attention around here. Not to mention an exterminator."

She stopped in front of a sagging tri-level house. Baby poop yellow paint peeled off the siding, and a half-dead elm leaned precariously close to the postage–stamp porch.

Annabelle's voice began to rise with her dander. "Liddy does the best she can. Since Tom left, she's managed to keep the house without any money from him. He can't hold a job long enough to pay child support, and what little he does make mysteriously disappears."

Changing the subject seemed prudent at this point. "Then it's probably a good thing he's not around. How old are the kids now?"

Her cousin's voice softened. "Peggy's thirteen, Tad's twelve, and Megan's almost ten."

"Good Lord, I'd say the brats are old enough to stay by themselves and help out around the house. Why, you and I babysat when we were twelve."

"Oh, I'm sure they help when they aren't doing school work. Things are different now. There's just too many ways for them to get into trouble," Annabelle said.

The blue haired woman didn't wait for the next scathing

remark. She exited the car, dragging her bag, and bent down to say good-bye through the window. "See you Friday."

"I'll pick you up at five-thirty, unless I hear otherwise." Regina hesitated before pulling away from the curb. "Take care, Cousin."

If I'm lucky, she'll stay. If she's lucky, she'll survive the week.

Annabelle stood with her mouth agape, then shouted as the car pulled away, "Watch after Tillie!"

Doing her best royal wave Regina didn't look back.

Annabelle thought aloud, "I wonder which is worse. Living with someone who hates you, but takes good care of you; or living with those you love who hurt you?"

As she approached the house, she saw her daughter standing in the doorway. Liddy had her father's sharp chin, angular body, stringy dishwater-blond hair, and perpetual frown. Arms akimbo and facial features obscured by the screen, there'd be no wave or warm greeting between them.

Annabelle mumbled, "One week, no more. Surely I can manage for seven days."

With a scowl, Liddy held open the torn screen door. "I see you brought a bag, so you're planning to stay after all?"

"Yes, you said it would be easier. Cousin Regina was nice enough to give me a ride."

A strangled laugh escaped the wrinkled lips that marked Liddy's smoking habit. "Nice? Since when?"

"Now, Liddy. We're her only family. She has no children to comfort her aging years."

"She has all that money to keep her company, Mother."

Annabelle stood in the shabby entry and faced her daughter. "That's uncalled for."

"Maybe not. From the look of that Cadillac and her mansion, there won't be anything left for us poor relations, anyway," Liddy said.

"That's enough." Annabelle detected the smell of stale cigarettes and dirty socks. The living room was cluttered with toys, magazines, shoes, and dirty dishes. Clothes were strewn across the sofa back and chairs.

Two screaming girls peeled down the hall. Peggy was the image of her mother, tall and thin. The youngest, Megan, was small and round, very like her grandmother.

"Navel lint!" Megan shouted.

She stood on the third step, bringing her nose-to-nose with her older sister. "Toe jam."

Her cheeks purple with anger, Peggy made a grab for her little sister, screeching, "You little douche bag!"

"Girls!" Their mother's bark caused a momentary lull in the squabble. "Your grandmother's here."

"Oh, shit," spilled from Peggy's red painted lips. She dashed up the stairs and slammed the door.

Megan's face blossomed with her smile of triumph and welcome. With one long leap, she launched herself from the steps and dove for her grandmother. Her chubby arms wrapped around Annabelle's soft middle.

"Hey, Gram! I haven't seen you in so long. You look great. Have you lost weight?"

Annabelle drank in the joy sparkling in Megan's coffee colored eyes. She kissed her favorite grandchild's shining mahogany locks and hugged her back.

Tad didn't attempt to disguise the sarcasm in his voice. "Nice hair, Gram. It reminds me of the old Ford on blocks down the street."

"Hello to you, too." Annabelle smiled. "And your sister?"

With a flick of his thumb, Tad pointed upstairs. "She's peeling off her mask."

Megan giggled, still latched onto her grandmother's thick waist.

"She's wearing make-up now. All the girls do."

Tad grunted. "Yeah. Mom says it's okay, as long as she doesn't wear it outside in the daylight. Wouldn't want the freak to scare the little kids next door."

"Well, I'm sure I'll see her soon. Megan, honey, show me where I'll be sleeping."

"I'm so glad you're staying with us again, Gram."

The little girl heaved and tugged her grandmother's Pullman down the hall. "Mom said to put you in that old room off the kitchen. It's more private."

Annabelle turned a questioning look at Liddy, but all she saw was the back of her daughter retreating up the stairs. Wiping away her frown, she turned to her escort and patted her shoulder.

"I'm sure it'll be fine."

Dragging the bag behind her, Megan held the handle with both hands, chattering like a squirrel.

"Peggy and I fight so much that Mom had to separate us. She's got our old bedroom, now that she's a princess—that's what Mom calls her. Tad the Toad has a room because he's the only boy. I'm in the dressing closet between Mom's room and the bathroom. It's little and stuffy, but I like it. I pretend I live in a cave. So, I guess you're stuck in the old pantry."

"It's only for a week," Annabelle said.

Thank you, Lord.

"I brought you my fluffiest pillow and that blue quilt you made, so you'd be cozy."

"Thank you, dear." Belle kissed Megan's pudgy pink cheek.

Peggy didn't make an appearance all evening, so Annabelle decided it was time to visit her eldest grandchild. She left Tad and Megan in the living room watching a scary movie. They assured her it was "no big deal" and they'd seen it lots of times before. The violence on the screen gave Annabelle the shivers.

She paused on the stairs. Both Liddy and Peggy's doors were closed. She saw a light under both, but the rumbles of rock 'n roll reverberated from behind door number two.

She rapped, hoping the sound would be heard, and waited. A person she almost didn't recognize flung open the door. Electric blue shadow masked soft brown eyes, while purple lips pulled back from a gum-smacking sneer.

Peggy appeared to be a smaller version of her mother. Thankfully, her granddaughter did not mirror her mother's flat, muddy brown eyes filled with nothing but bitterness. *I failed Liddy, but somehow, I've got to make it up to these kids.*

"Hey, Gram. What's up?"

Annabelle tried not to stare at the extraordinary paint job. "Hello, dear. I missed seeing you all evening." She searched in vain for a glimpse of her young Peggy.

The florescent yellow crop-top showed a hand span's worth of skinny stomach, only a hint of a burgeoning bosom, and the short shorts rivaled anything Daisy Mae had ever worn in the comic books. Hot pink hoops hung from Peggy's ears, and assorted rainbow colored bangles clanked on her wrists.

"Cool shade of blue, Gram."

Annabelle patted her hair, cleared her throat and forced a smile. "I got it done last week. May I come in?"

The girl slowly opened the door and stepped aside. "I guess."

Annabelle nearly staggered under the force of the music. "Would you please turn that down?"

"What?"

"Please, turn down the music."

"Oh." Peggy stomped across the floor and slapped the toggle switch to her stereo. "There, happy?"

"Thank you, dear."

She sat on the edge of the only chair; mounds of clothes

draped the slatted back.

With a flop, Peggy bounced on the bed and crossed her legs Indian style. The sheets and bedspread were in a turquoise snarl, knotted with multicolored clothing, jewelry, and shoes.

"You don't need to babysit me, Gram, I'm thirteen. You're just here to keep an eye on the brats."

"Really?"

"Yup. Mom said so."

"Won't you be bored up here all alone? We could bake cookies and watch movies. And you kids can all play ball."

"Jeez, Gram. That's little kid stuff. I'm not into cookies and ball games anymore. Major boring."

"Yes, I see you're into the make-up stage of your life. What does interest you, honey?"

Peggy shifted, leaned on her elbows, her knees up and a good amount of fanny displayed.

"Nothing around this dump."

"Your mother works very hard to provide for you kids."

"Yeah, I know."

"You still have time before you're grown up. Why not enjoy being a kid a little bit longer."

With a frown Peggy said, "Kids don't have any choices."

"What would you choose to do?"

"I'd marry a rich man, live in a mansion bigger than Cousin Regina's, drive a white Mercedes Benz with leather seats, have a maid and a cook, and eat escargots and caviar every day."

"You're a little young to be thinking about marriage. Do you even know what escargot and caviar are?"

Peggy shrugged and rolled her eyes.

"They're snails and raw fish eggs, honey."

"No way!" The young woman wrinkled her nose and stared at the ceiling. A tinge of pink bloomed on her pale cheeks.

Silence fell between them. Annabelle took advantage of the

opportunity to examine the room more closely.

Posters decorated the walls. A beautiful blond model clad in a black evening gown lay draped over the hood of a red sports car. A young actress Annabelle vaguely recognized posed in a tight white suit and hefting a laser gun over the caption, "May the force be with you." Another showed a huge white castle on a hilltop, mist and fog obscuring the base.

"Don't lose your dreams, my dear Peggy, but remember, dreams come with a price. And things don't always turn out quite like we plan. There's more to growing up than money."

Peggy flung herself back on her bed. "At least I won't have to listen to Mom anymore."

"Then you'll have a boss, or a husband or a minister."

"Minister? You know we don't go to church. That's for rich folks with fancy clothes."

Annabelle let that one pass. "Just because we're adults doesn't mean we always get our way. Play while you can, Peg. Enjoy your youth."

Her granddaughter sat straight up, crossed her arms over her chest and snorted. "Are you going to lecture me all week?"

Annabelle heaved herself from the chair. "I'll try not to. How would you like to be roommates this week?"

"No thanks, Gram, I need my space."

Peggy turned the music back up, the bass punctuating the end of their conversation and bouncing her grandmother from the room.

CHAPTER 20

Ensconced in the pantry on a two-dollar, garage-sale rollaway, according to its scribbled tag, Annabelle listened to the noises of the house. The cot fit around her like a coffin, the width of her shoulders and just long enough that her feet didn't hang over the end. She'd tried sleeping on her side but kept falling onto the floor. Lying on her back was the only safe option, so she snuggled into the cocoon of covers, catching snatches of comfortless slumber.

Her thoughts traveled the night, a tormenting mixture of worry and fear.

What would happen to Tillie? Both Regina and Joe need her so much. Would Regina give away her room? She might have to, for Tillie's sake. To a nurse, perhaps. Dear God, she hoped not. Would she be incarcerated in this tiny room, tangled in her daughter's anger forever?

"No, I won't let that happen."

She would help the children find a way to avoid despair, unlike their mother or herself. She could see changes in them after only a few months.

Sometime near dawn she dozed. Hundreds of birds greeting the morning woke her. Squinting at her wristwatch in the dim light, she saw that it was already a quarter past six. Liddy would have to leave for work soon.

Stiffness occupied every joint in her body, but she managed to groan her way into a cotton dress, printed with huge pink cabbage roses. She shuffled to the kitchen for coffee and an aspirin.

"My back is killing me," she mumbled.

No wake-up elixir had been brewed, so she hummed while filling the pot from the tap, her back to the living room door.

"Good, God, Mother. You look like you're wearing a bed-spread."

Annabelle's shoulders tightened. She turned off the spigot before greeting her daughter.

"Good morning. Ready for work?"

Wearing faded chinos and a black t-shirt, Liddy's stringy hair was scraped into a ponytail. Her bony hands gripped her narrow hips, and her permanent scowl was firmly affixed. "Not quite. I expected coffee by now."

"Really? Well, I don't have a clock in my room, so I had no idea of the time. Don't you normally make your own?"

"Not always. Sometimes I pick it up at Mickey D's. I keep hoping some stupid server will spill it on me so I can sue and quit work."

"There's nothing wrong with working for a living," Annabelle said.

"How would you know, Mother? Everything you ever got was a result of someone else's hard work."

Fighting unwanted tears, Annabelle blinked.

"It takes more than one person to work a farm. Your dad worked the fields while I kept up the house and garden. And when he died, I cleaned houses until I got down in my back."

"Oh, I forgot. But you weren't much of a cook or a maid, were you, Mother?"

Turning her back to her daughter's spite-filled stare, Annabelle opened the cupboard door. "We do the best we can with the hand we're given."

In the cabinet she found a moldy loaf of white bread, an

empty box of toaster pastries, and half of a box of sugared cereal. "Could you stop by the store on your way home tonight, honey?"

She stuck her head in the fridge to inventory its stores. Only enough milk and juice for a couple of days.

With a dramatic sigh Liddy stared at her mother. "What do you want, Mother?"

Annabelle took a quick peek in the freezer and found several packages of hamburger and box of fish sticks. She moved to the lower cabinets, which contained ample canned food choices and several boxes of cheese and macaroni.

Liddy stomped over to the coffeepot. "Well?"

"Some bread, milk, and juice should do it. There are enough staples that the kids will eat fine during the day."

"And what about dinner?"

"I'm not sure there's enough for the whole week. Why don't you pick up a roast? I can make BBQ beef and hash from the leftovers. That should take care of it."

"Anything else?" Liddy's voice dripped acid.

God, help me.

"I don't think so, dear."

"Good. I'm not made of money, you know."

"Yes, I know."

Annabelle poured herself a cup of warm coffee from the decade old pot and sat down at the scarred Formica table. A magazine propped up one leg that had long since lost its cap. The mismatched chairs made an interesting collage of style and decrepitude. She sipped and tried not to let her hackles rise.

Without another word, Liddy and her coffee cup slogged through the house and out the front door. The screen door slammed in her wake.

An hour later, three sleepy children stumbled into the kitchen.

"What's smells so good?" Tad leaned over his grandmother's

shoulder. "Holy cow, Gram. Pancakes?"

Megan came to attention and crowded around the stove.

Sitting down at the table, Peggy said, "But, we don't have any syrup."

"Ah, but you're forgetting that I know how to make all kinds of things from scratch."

The two younger kids inhaled deeply and moaned their pleasure.

"It smells buttery." Megan nearly hummed with contentment. "I'll set the table."

"I'll get the juice if you'll get the glasses." Tad poked Peggy's bony shoulder.

With only a few scuffles, the children had the table ready when Annabelle put a plate full of steaming pancakes before them.

They dug in with enthusiasm.

Syrup dripped down Tad's chin. "These are great!"

The girls' faces were pink with pleasure, and Peg's face was scrubbed clean of the war paint from the night before.

"What did you find to make these with?" Megan asked.

"I'll write it down for you. You could make them. It's easy."

Megan licked her sticky fingers. "Can you show me how to make syrup, too?"

"You bet."

After they had eaten their fill, Megan and Tad made a mad dash for the television remote, while Peggy lingered by the kitchen door.

With a pose just like her mother's, she scolded. "Geez, you're slow, Gram. It'll be dinnertime before you get finished."

Annabelle raised an eyebrow and held out a towel. "Then come and help me."

Peggy took her time drying the dishes while Annabelle hummed with joy.

"Want to walk off those pancakes?"

"It's only March, you know. It's cold out. I'd rather watch TV," Peggy said. She flopped on the sofa, snatching the remote from her little brother.

With a shake of her blue haired head, Annabelle pointed at the trio of couch potatoes. "What a bunch of wimps. I saw a garage sale on the next block. Let's go see what treasures we might find."

"Okay," Peggy and Megan said in unison.

Shaking his head, Tad turned off the television and dug his shoes out from under the chair.

"Girls. Born shoppers."

Leaning close to her grandmother, Megan whispered, "We don't have any money."

"I have a little bit," Annabelle said.

The foursome walked down the dreary street with a spring in their steps. Megan skipped along beside her grandmother while Tad sprinted to the stop sign and pointed.

"There's the sign. Let's go, slow pokes."

Megan chased him around the corner.

"Walk with me, Peg."

Her eldest granddaughter slowed her pace, concentrating on her feet. "Gram, are you rich now that you live with Cousin Regina?"

"No, honey. I live with Regina and Tillie, but the only money I have is from social security."

"Is it very much?"

"Not very. Enough to help out with food and buy a new pair of shoes now and again."

"Oh. Mom buys our clothes at the thrift store. It's so embarrassing."

"She does her best. Besides, you can get some pretty nice stuff at the secondhand store. Tillie and I get all our clothes there. She finds things with designer labels and mixes them with very stylish accessories."

"She's sick now, isn't she?"

"Yes, dear, very sick."

"Will she die?"

"I don't know."

For less than five dollars, they all found something worthy at the sale.

Tad, the artistic one in the family, picked a box of watercolor paints. A pink angora scarf, with very few holes, was Peggy's choice. There were two "Ramona" books that Megan hadn't read yet, and Annabelle found a black vinyl pocketbook with hardly any wear.

They talked and laughed all the way home, bragging to each other about their loot.

By midafternoon, the refrigerator door boasted two original works of art by Tad. Megan lay on the sofa halfway through her first book.

Peggy wrote down the pancake and syrup recipes, then helped Megan and Annabelle get things ready for dinner.

"You're too little to help in the kitchen," Peggy said to her little sister.

"Am not!"

The consummate peacemaker, Annabelle stepped between the growling sisters. "It's much more fun to cook together."

Although Annabelle had forgotten to take the hamburger out of the fridge in time to thaw, she showed the girls how to do it slowly in the skillet.

"This is the way they did it in the olden days, right, Gram?" Megan giggled.

"In the days before microwaves, anyway."

They whipped up goulash and canned green beans and had

just turned the stove down to low when Liddy came home from work.

Tad shouted above the television. "Hi, Mom."

A grocery bag in each hand, Liddy stomped towards the kitchen. "Tad, get off your lazy butt and close the door."

"Yes, Mom."

Peggy and Annabelle were standing shoulder-to-shoulder at the stove, chatting and laughing, oblivious to Liddy's presence. Megan stood in the pantry doorway.

Slamming the bags on the table, Liddy broke the plate set in front of her chair.

"Oh, my," Annabelle said, covering her heart with her hand. "You startled me."

"You were too busy yukking it up to help me with these bags, and now I've broken another dish. Thanks a lot, Mother."

Her eyes wide, Peggy stepped back.

Megan escaped into her grandmother's makeshift bedroom.

Annabelle watched Liddy lift the milk and juice from the brown paper bag and toss them onto the shelf in the refrigerator. She pitched the beef roast in next, then threw the bread on the cabinet.

"There, that took the last of my cash. Luckily, I get paid day after tomorrow."

"Thank you, dear." Annabelle reached across the table, her hand shaking. She picked up the broken plate pieces, trying to avoid her daughter's angry gaze.

"Dinner's ready. Kids, wash up."

Tad slipped into the kitchen, his new paint box held out for inspection. "Look what we bought today. I got these, Megan got books, and Peggy got a scarf."

Liddy glared at her son. "Oh? And where did the money come from?"

"I gave it to them," Annabelle said.

"You can't buy them, Mother. Is that what you've learned living with the rich part of the family?"

"Stop it. They're garage sale items and hardly cost a thing. Besides, Regina's never done anything to hurt you."

The kids stood back and watched their mother and grandmother verbally spar, feet cemented to the floor with tension.

"What did she ever do for us? Daddy always said she acts like her shit don't stink and we do."

"That was a long time ago. She's been very good to me."
Sort of.

An unbecoming snort precluded Liddy's next comments. "It looks good to society to take in your poor relations. Bet Aunt Victoria is having a fit in her gilded heaven, thinking about you soiling her satin sheets."

"Aunt Victoria is dead, and Regina is nothing like her."
Not quite as bad, anyway.

"You're a fool, Mother. Do you think she cares a hoot about you? About us? I'll bet she was real tickled to see you and your suitcase on her doorstep."

Annabelle wrung her hankie. "She was surprised, I'll grant you that. But no matter what, we're the only family she has left."

"This is a stupid conversation, Mother. I suppose dinner's cold now. Way to go."

Peggy lifted the lid on the goulash and grinned.

"Smells good, Gram."

With a jerk, Liddy pulled out her chair.

"Tad, Megan, shut your gaping mouths and sit down."

Megan slid into her seat, then leaned over to her grandmother and whispered, "Thank you for the books."

Annabelle whispered back, "You're most welcome, sweetie."

The children were subdued as Annabelle served the meal.

"Liddy, did you see the lovely artwork we have to brighten

up our meal?"

"Huh?" Liddy lit a cigarette and blew smoke above the table.

"Tad is quite an artist," Annabelle said and patted his hand.

"Yeah, right."

Tad's eyes welled with tears, but he didn't let them fall.

"Liddy, you need to eat. Put out that cigarette."

"Don't tell me what to do in my own house. Daddy always had a cigarette before he ate. He said it made your cooking taste better."

"Your father was a jerk, and the smoke isn't good for the children."

Surely I can survive a few more days.

Putting out her stub in the goulash, Liddy grabbed her mother's arm and began to squeeze. "How dare you bad mouth my father. If you'd been a decent wife he wouldn't have died."

"Not now. Let go."

As Liddy removed her fingers, her mouth curled in a sneer. "And why not? The kids should know their grandmother is a whining leech. My father worked himself to death. What did you ever do?"

Annabelle looked at the red welts forming on her arm. "I raised you. And quite poorly, too."

The rest of the meal was eaten in silence. Peggy picked at her food, casting secret glimpses at her mother and grandmother in turn.

Having cleaned her plate Megan cast hopeful glances at her brother's untouched portions. She whispered, "It's good, Tad, eat."

He gave a barely perceptible shake of his head, his eyes glued to his lap.

Liddy lit another cigarette, signaling the end of the meal. Tad bolted from the kitchen to his room, slamming the door.

Taking Megan by the hand, Peggy led her away from the table.

"But I want to stay with Gram," Megan whispered.

"Come on. I'll braid your hair." Peggy put her hand on the small of her sister's back and guided her to the stairs.

With a final puff, Liddy crushed her cigarette butt in the remaining food on Tad's plate, leaving Annabelle to clean up.

Annabelle cleared the table and began washing the dishes, contemplating her daughter.

Liddy had absorbed every hateful word spoken in their family, some of them her own.

Maybe now was her opportunity to help the kids, if she could just stay out of Liddy's way.

CHAPTER 21

A huge thunderclap jolted Annabelle from her fitful sleep. A spring storm was brewing, severity guaranteed in the middle of converging fronts. Her experience with the antics of Mother Nature on the farm instilled in her a sense of awe and respect, sprinkled with a hint of fear.

She could barely bend at the waist, so she rolled from the cot onto her hands and knees on the floor. Using the close proximity of the wall, she pulled herself up. Her knees and back screamed in protest.

"I don't think my old body can take any more nights on this blasted cot. Maybe, I'll try the couch."

As it presented the lesser challenge, Annabelle chose to wear a button-up house dress, afraid she couldn't lift her arms above her head.

This faded green and purple plaid should blend quite nicely with my blue-do.

She fumbled for her toothbrush and dragged her feet toward the kitchen.

The smell of coffee brewing was a pleasant surprise.

Liddy was spreading peanut butter on bread, ignoring her mother's struggles. "Make the roast for dinner. The kids can eat peanut butter for lunch."

"I don't mind fixing them something hot."

"Don't spoil them." Liddy shook the limp sandwich. "This is their reality."

"I'm only here for the week. Why can't I spoil them? That's what grandmothers are supposed to do."

"Oh, really? And what about when you're gone? I don't have time to make them pancakes for breakfast. You can't bake or buy your way into their hearts, Mother."

Annabelle filled her coffee cup and faced her daughter.

"That's the silliest thing I've ever heard. Honey, you should make more time for your children."

With a snarl, Liddy swung her right hand, connecting with Annabelle's cheek. A streak of lightning sliced the sky as the soft skin below Annabelle's eye split, and the coffee cup shattered on the linoleum.

"You old bitch," Liddy said. She shoved her mother against the counter. "What the hell do you know about anything? Especially raising kids!"

Annabelle lifted her arms in defense but not before Liddy's fist hit her in the stomach, then connected with her nose. Blood cascaded down the front of her dress. She held her broken nose with both hands and watched a red drop splash between her feet. She slowly lifted her head.

"I shouldn't have said that."

"That'll teach you, just like Daddy used to do. You know it's your own fault. He always said so."

Her lips back in a feral smile, Liddy handed her mother a dishtowel. "Clean up this mess. I have to go to work."

While Liddy grabbed her sandwich and stuffed it in a paper bag, three terrified witnesses disappeared from the doorway. Their grandmother watched them scramble behind the couch as their mother strode to the door without a second glance.

Annabelle sagged into a chair, a red stain spreading across her lap.

The slam of the door brought the children from their hiding place. They halted in the doorway, stunned.

Megan burst into tears. "Oh, Gram! I didn't think she'd hit you, too."

Tad dashed upstairs and returned with a shoebox, a clumsy red cross and the words "First Aid" marked on the lid in crayon. With a vengeance, he threw its contents onto the table, looking for who knows what magical cure.

Her eyes filled as Peggy gently pulled the reddened towel from Annabelle's hands and replaced it with a clean one.

"I'm sorry, Gram. Does it hurt?"

A wave of nausea caused Annabelle to weave in the chair. "You saw?"

Tad grabbed her shoulders and hugged her to his skinny chest.

"The storm woke us."

"I'll call 9-1-1," Peggy said.

Annabelle reached for her and gurgled. "No-call-Regina. 838-2551. Ask her and Tillie to come."

"Okay, Gram." Peggy dialed the phone.

Annabelle could hear Regina's austere voice as she answered.

"Hello. Uh, this is Peggy, Liddy's daughter? Uh-huh." Peggy voice quivered. "It's Gram. She's hurt. Can you come? No, ma'am. She told me to call you instead. Please, she's bleeding all over the place. I think her nose is broke. Hurry."

When the bleeding seemed to slow, Peggy helped her grandmother change into a clean dress.

Megan and Tad sopped the blood from the floor and table. The discarded towels, dress, and slippers were put to soak in the kitchen sink full of cold water.

Joe, Regina, and Tillie arrived with a screech of tires a short time later.

They burst through the door, Tillie shouting. "Annabelle, where are you?"

"In here," Peggy said.

Joe's long legs ate up the length of the living room. He stopped in the doorway. Regina and Tillie bumped into his back.

Megan sat at Annabelle's feet, her head resting against her knee. Tad had his arm around his grandmother's shoulders and a look of challenge on his frightened face. Peggy helped her grandmother hold a towel to her swollen and purple face.

"She's really done it this time, hasn't she, Annabelle?" Regina said.

Tillie pushed her way through them. "Bloody hell. How did it happen? As if I didn't know. If you say you fell I'll pull the rest of my hair out."

The cloth she held in front of her face muffled Annabelle's reply, "The bleeding won't stop."

Peggy frowned at her grandmother. "Mom hit her."

The half-cleaned swirls of blood were visible on the floor at Belle's feet.

"First your husband beats you, then your daughter. Where will it end?" Regina asked.

Annabelle closed her eyes, tears falling over the puffy skin, soaking the towel. "She didn't mean to . . ."

Megan sniffled. "She hurt our Gram."

"Who's the tall guy?" Tad asked.

"I'm a friend of your grandmother's."

Tad lifted his chin. "Oh. Can you help her?"

Regina straightened her shoulders and gestured to Joe.

"Joseph, please take the children into the other room. Annabelle, it's time we got you out of this place."

Tillie and Regina turned on all the lights and peeked under the blood soaked towel that covered most of Belle's face.

Tears filled Tillie's eyes. "Oh, honey, she did a number on you."

Regina looked her cousin in the eye and announced, "This

has got to stop. We're taking you to the hospital, and you won't be coming back here."

"What about the kids?" Annabelle asked.

"One thing at a time, Cousin, let's get you fixed up first."

Tillie gasped at the sight of the sink filled with crimson water. "You've lost a lot of blood. Are you dizzy?"

"A little."

The tiny woman darted around the kitchen, cleaning, tears mingling with the reddened water. "I told you not to come. Oh shit, where's the bathroom?"

Pointing toward the living room, Peggy responded, "It's at the top of the stairs."

Tillie made a dash in the direction Peggy pointed.

The sound of retching drifted down the stairs.

"She's really sick, isn't she?" Peggy said.

Annabelle nodded.

"Where are your things?" Regina asked.

Annabelle pointed.

Regina gathered Annabelle's meager things from the pantry.

Joe stood in the doorway, looking first at Annabelle, then towards the horrid sounds Tillie was making upstairs.

Looking miserable, they all waited for the little woman to return. At the sound of the toilet flushing, conversation resumed and Regina took control.

"Joseph," Regina said. "Pick Belle up and get her to the car. We're going to the hospital."

Tillie joined them, pale but controlled.

Removing the towel from her face, Annabelle said, "You okay, Tillie?"

"I am now." Determination was written in her furrowed brow.

Megan clung to Tad and said, "Can we come, too?"

Peggy grabbed both their shoulders. "We'd better not. Mom might not understand. Will you call us, Cousin Regina?"

"Of course. I'll let you know when we get her home." Regina placed her hand on Peggy's pale cheek. "She'll be fine. Will you be okay?"

"Yes, ma'am. I'll watch the brats." Peggy gave her siblings' shoulders a squeeze.

Tad pushed out his bony chest. "We can take care of ourselves."

Joe put his arm around Annabelle and reached behind her knees to lift her.

"No, Joe, I'm too heavy. I can walk."

"Nonsense, woman." He picked her up and cradled her in his arms, then carried her to the car and helped her into the back seat.

Tillie slid in beside Annabelle and wrapped her friend in her skinny arms.

Annabelle whispered, "What set you off back there?"

"I dunno. The smell of blood, I guess."

Regina turned in the passenger seat catching Tillie's eyes. She held their gaze, pain and understanding passing between them.

CHAPTER 22

Annabelle's labored breathing punctuated the quiet inside the car. They soon pulled into the emergency room parking lot.

Regina went inside to get things moving while Tillie and Annabelle argued.

"I don't need a wheelchair."

Slinging his arm around Annabelle's torso, Joe bent to pick her up.

Annabelle raised her right hand like a traffic cop, the left still holding the sodden towel. "Joe, I can walk."

He halted, leaning over to look her in the eye. "It's either me or the wheelchair, your choice."

Her cheeks flamed. "Well, in that case, give me the chair."

Joe straightened and winked. "You've broken my heart."

Annabelle giggled behind the towel.

Tillie started towards the row of wheelchairs parked near the door, but he stopped her in midstride.

"I'll get it, darlin'." His long legs covered the area in seconds.

Black eyes twinkling like the beads in her skullcap, Tillie gave him a warm smile. "Thanks."

The sliding doors whirred open to reveal a pensive Regina, hands on her hips. "What's the hold up? Belle, they're waiting for you."

"I'm coming," she eased back in the chair just as Joe slipped it behind her knees. She mumbled her thanks.

With an exaggerated eye roll, Tillie stepped back for them to precede her. "Don't get your knickers in a twist, Regina Louise."

Regina muttered something unintelligible and stormed back inside, her silver braid flapping against her rigid shoulder blades.

"No doubt her majesty has whipped them all up into a fine frenzy." Joe's voice was filled with laughter as he spoke over the top of Annabelle's head. "She should've been in the military. The way she barks is just like a general."

Placing her small hand on her friend's shoulder, Tillie whispered, "Tell the truth about what's happened, Annabelle, or I'll kick the parts of you that aren't already purple. Liddy has to be stopped."

"I know. Tillie, I'm worried about the kids."

Tillie and Joe were strangely silent.

"Does she hit the children?" Joe asked.

Tillie emitted a seal-like snort. "Who's to stop her from hurting her babies? The woman is twisted. She beats her mother, for pity's sake."

Tears filled Annabelle's eyes, but before she could comment, a lovely middle-aged nurse in chartreuse scrubs intercepted them.

Her white smile gleamed against her dark chocolate skin. "Mrs. Hubbard? I love your hair. It matches your face. Now, if you was my color, them bruises would hardly show at all."

Annabelle gave her a watery smile. "Thank you, dear."

"Why, honey, you call me Lou. What happened? Did you get hit with the steering wheel?"

Tillie grumbled under her breath. "No, she got hit by her damned daughter."

Lou took over the pilot position and proceeded through the double doors as they buzzed open. She wheeled Belle straight to the back of an empty row of cubicles.

"Excuse me for a moment, Mrs. Hubbard. I'll be right back," Lou said.

She closed the curtains and stopped Tillie and Joe before they could enter.

"Are you all immediate family? If not, you'll have to wait outside."

"We're better than family. We're her best friends," Tillie said at the top of her voice.

"Please, return to the waiting area."

Joe spoke gently to Tillie, "She's just doing her job, Little Bit."

"I know, dammit."

Five minutes later, a male nurse escorted a beet-faced Regina into the waiting room.

"Listen, you Neanderthal. I will not be treated this way. As her family, I have the right to know what the doctor proposes to do."

Though biceps the size of melons strained his uniform shirt, his voice was quiet. "Due to the nature of her injuries, the doctor would like to visit with your cousin in private."

Stretched up to her full five feet, one inch, Tillie put a finger in the man's muscular middle. "Listen here, you moose. Don't you try to frighten her. She's had a rough day."

"We'll take good care of Mrs. Hubbard, ma'am. Don't worry."

Regina glared through the doorway at the nurse's back, surprised at the extent of the anger she felt. The unbidden feelings of protectiveness, however, confused her more. About halfway to Annabelle's draped enclosure, Lou fell into step beside the male nurse. They looked to Regina like a dynamic duo.

Annabelle felt tiny and vulnerable in the sterile, cold room. The starched white curtains that separated each area blended with the gray walls and floor. The place felt frigid and forbidding.

She huddled under the paper-thin sheet, shaking to her marrow with shock. Only her curly blue hair and bruised eyes peaked out as she considered her options.

A thin man with a shiny bald head and horn-rimmed glasses cleared his throat as he entered. He wore a white coat, a black-tube stethoscope around his neck, and he carried a clipboard in his smooth white hand. His tie was covered in tree frogs.

"Mrs. Hubbard, I'm Doctor Campbell. I'd like to examine your injuries."

"Okay."

Lou came in behind him and flashed Annabelle a reassuring smile.

He handed his clipboard to the nurse and probed Annabelle's battered face. "Do you have any other contusions?"

"What?"

"Are you hurt any place else?"

"My stomach's a little sore."

After softly plying her doughy middle, he spoke to the nurse. "Order an X-ray. Head and abdomen."

He jotted notes in the file folder, then turned back to Annabelle. He removed his glasses, and his steel gray eyes held her wary gaze.

"It would appear you have a broken nose. I'll know more when I see the films. Can you tell me what happened?"

She squirmed under his directness but knew she would have to admit her failure with Liddy. "I got punched in the stomach and face."

Although the doctor blinked, he didn't turn his gaze away. An invisible thread linked patient to healer, while time seemed to grind to a stop.

"Who assaulted you? Don't be afraid to tell me."

Tears filled Annabelle's eyes as she searched the room for an ally, stopping on the nurse's comforting face. "Do I have to?"

"No, but you should," Lou said.

Dr. Campbell touched Annabelle's shoulder. "Mrs. Hubbard, you should file charges."

"I can't. She's my daughter."

The doctor's lips thinned as he patted her clutched hands. "All right, just relax while we arrange for the X-rays."

While the nurse wheeled Annabelle to radiology, Dr. Campbell joined the anxious group in the waiting area.

"We're taking Mrs. Hubbard to X-ray. Her nose appears to be broken, and she has some abdominal tenderness. We'll know the extent of her injuries in about thirty minutes."

He paused, then asked, "Does she have a safe place to go? If not, then we can give her some information about a safe-house recommended by Adult Protective Services."

Regina straightened her spine. "She'll be staying with me from now on, Doctor. Her daughter is not welcome in my home."

"Good. I may want her to stay here tonight. Depending on the test results."

"Fine, then we'll take turns being with her," Regina said.

Joe and Tillie's eyes widened before they nodded in agreement.

"Very well." Dr. Campbell slid across the vinyl chair cushion. "We'll know for sure in about half an hour."

Regina stood and held out her hand. "Thank you, Doctor."

He returned her firm handshake.

Neither of them smiled.

Slumped on the sofa, Tillie addressed her roommate. "What kind of a monster is Liddy?"

"She's a twisted, bitter soul, just like her father," Regina said. "David used to smack Belle around in front of the girl, and he convinced them both his brutality was Belle's fault. He married

Belle for the farm, then blamed her when it failed."

Joe put his arm around Tillie's drawn shoulders.

Tillie's voice cracked. "Why did she put up with it?"

"Probably thought it was normal. She grew up watching her father beat her mother."

"Oh, my God. Poor, Belle." Tillie turned her face into Joe's chest.

Regina's voice was quiet, but firm. "That's part of the reason for the rift in the family. Mother couldn't stand to watch her little sister being abused, so she pretended the abuse didn't exist. Father believed in using brains, not physical brawn, to control a situation. He dismissed my aunt's family as ignorant trash, and my mother followed suit, as did I."

"My God." Tillie turned a face of fury to her best friend. "How could you? Belle and her mother were victims. They didn't deserve any of this. Your family had the resources to help, and you walked away?"

Her face paled, but Regina's chin did not lower.

"I'm not proud of what we did. We didn't interfere in others' personal lives back then. And I believed my father when he told me there was nothing I could do. Then my parents died, and I was too caught up in surviving on my own to give much thought to my cousin."

Tillie sniffled and wiped her nose on Joe's proffered handkerchief.

"It's so unfair." After a dainty honk, Tillie handed it back. "What about those children? What are we going to do?"

"We? Wait a minute. I'm only just getting used to the idea that Annabelle is now a resident of my home. You can't expect me to take on three kids, too. Mother will haunt me for certain."

"They're your family!" Tillie said.

Joe reached for Tillie's hand. "They aren't Regina's responsibility. They have a mother and a father. Belle's in no condition

163

to take on three children right now."

Looking from Joe to Regina, Tillie's face was ablaze. "Then we'll take them."

Regina's eyebrows rose. "Matilda Jean, that's kidnapping."

"Maybe, but I doubt Liddy gives a hoot. We've got to help those kids."

"And how do you propose we do that, my friend?" Regina gave her braid a flip.

"Joe and I can go visit Liddy. We'll let her know that if she hurts them again, we'll sue for custody and charge her with assault and battery. Then we'll wait and see what happens."

"I'll tell you what will happen." Joe's eyes looked grim. "She'll probably punch you in that lovely face of yours, and then I'll be arrested for smacking her back."

Regina held up both manicured hands for silence. "Let me talk with Sam Duncan, my lawyer, and see about our options."

CHAPTER 23

The hospital staff broke a medical community record that day. Forty-five minutes after they'd wheeled Annabelle to X-ray, Dr. Campbell greeted Regina, Tillie and Joe with a slight smile. "There are no internal injuries, but Mrs. Hubbard's nose is definitely broken. You can take her home if you'll promise to keep her in bed for at least three days and take her for a follow-up visit with her physician in one week."

"Very well, Doctor." Regina stood and shook his hand before turning to her friends. "I'll take care of the discharge papers if you two will gather up Belle."

"No problem." Tillie beamed. "Joe, let's get our girl."

Tillie and Joe found Annabelle lying down with a puzzled frown on her colorful face.

"The doctor said I can go home, but where?"

"Riverside, of course," Tillie said. "Want me to help you dress?"

"Oh. Uh-huh."

With a wink, Tillie gave her beau an affectionate nudge. "Okay, bud, hit the road, but don't go too far."

He bowed at the waist and headed for the curtained entrance. "I'll be in the hall, if you need me."

The ladies giggled.

Easing her legs over the side of the bed Annabelle whispered, "He's such a charmer."

"Yes, and a thief, too." Tillie's eyes twinkled.

"What do you mean?"

"He's taken my heart, Belle, but don't tell him. It'll just scare him off again."

"Okay," Annabelle said.

Annabelle consented to have Joe push the wheelchair while Tillie opened doors. Regina joined them at the exit, and they loaded up the Cadillac. The four were quiet, shrouded in the mist of their own thoughts, and arrived at the house in minutes.

A yowling Ms. Pickles greeted them at the door.

"What's with the mad-on, pussycat?" Tillie said. She scratched beneath the furry chin.

The cat responded by scolding them all the way up the stairs to Annabelle's room. After she was tucked in, the vocal feline settled into a nice ball on top of Regina's velvet throw at the foot of the bed.

"Damned cat." Regina shook her head. "I'll make some tea."

Joe pulled the pink brocade chair close to the side of the bed.

Tillie sat on the quilt and took Annabelle's pudgy fingers into her tiny white hand.

"Is there anything we can do?" she asked.

"I'm worried about my grandkids."

The silver haired gent cleared his throat.

"If you want, Regina can check with a lawyer and see what can be done to gain custody," he said.

"Liddy would never agree, just for spite. Megan told me she hits them sometimes."

Tracing the green veins mapping the back of Annabelle's hand Tillie said, "Do you want us to go fetch them?"

"We can't without Liddy's permission. I've seen it on TV. Whenever a non-custodial parent takes the kids without permission, they go to jail for kidnapping. And I don't want my grandchildren to be on the side of a milk carton."

"We'll think of something," Joe said. "You just rest."

As soon as Regina showed up with the tea tray, Joe and Tillie made a speedy exit to his house across the street.

"I need a drink," Tillie said

"All I've got is beer."

"That'll do me just fine, if you don't mind finishing it for me. I'm only good for about half a bottle," she said.

They sat at the kitchen table and downed the first one in fairly short order. Tillie declined the second.

"What's on your mind, Little Bit?"

"Those kids." She started to peel the label from the bottle.

"I know, honey, but what can we do that won't land us in jail?"

"I'm not sure, but I'm not going to sit by and wait to read about them in the papers. Let's let Liddy know she's being watched. Maybe it'll cool her jets."

"Honey, I don't get the impression she gives a rat's ass what anybody thinks."

Tillie shredded the gold and brown paper. "We've got to try."

"All right, but I think it's a bad idea. You let me do the talking. I know how to speak with control freaks. There are quite a few of them in the military."

"Personally, I'd like to rip her hair out."

"You could do it, too. And she wouldn't have anything to grab on your pretty head in retaliation," he said.

She gave him a friendly punch in the arm. "Move it."

It was nearly dinnertime when they pulled into Liddy's drive. The curtains parted, then quickly closed as Tillie walked across the crabgrass to the front door. Joe was at her heels.

Before they could knock, it opened and a stone-faced Liddy greeted them. "What do you want?"

With a slight bow, Joe spoke. "We'd like to speak with you

privately, ma'am."

Liddy took a drag off of her cigarette, blowing the smoke through the screen toward their faces. "Who are you?"

Tillie pushed in front of Joe. "We're friends of your mother's."

"So?" She took another drag and sucked the smoke up her nose.

Joe gave Tillie's hand a warning squeeze. "May we speak outside?"

"Talk."

"All right. We had to take your mother to the hospital after what you did to her. A report was filed. If it happens again, you'll find yourself in someone's crosshairs," he said.

"Fine, I won't miss the old bat. What did she ever do for me?"

Tillie sucked in air and rose to the balls of her feet.

Joe held tight to her hand.

"We're naturally concerned for the safety of your children," he said.

"They're mine, and nobody can tell me what to do with 'em." Liddy blew a smoke ring through the mesh. "Is that it?"

Narrowing her eyes Tillie poked a finger at Liddy. "They're not your property. They're human beings."

Stepping in front of Tillie, Joe's nose nearly touched the screen. "Just know this. We're watching you and so are the police."

"Thanks for the warning, crew cut."

Liddy slammed the door in their faces.

They looked at each other, and Tillie felt all warmth drain from her. "Did we make it worse?" she asked.

He took her hand and led her to the car. "I don't know. I hope not."

As they drove away, he pointed to the glove box. "Get out the cell phone, darlin'."

"And call who?"

"Call Regina and see if she and Belle would enjoy some Chinese food. Tommy Wong makes the best Subgum Chow Mien in town."

"Sounds good to me. As long as it's to go and I don't have to smell it cooking, I should be able to keep it down."

They showed up at Regina's with armloads of white and red cartons with wire handles. Tillie set the teakettle to boil while Joe went up to fetch the cousins.

He carried the protesting patient down the stairs while Annabelle clutched the lapels of her worn robe in both hands. "My nose is broken, not my legs."

Joe set her in a chair, then scooted up to the table between her and Regina. "Mind if I join you ladies?"

"Don't be silly, Joseph," Regina said.

A bareheaded, smiling Tillie poured the green tea before sitting down across from Joe. "Let's eat. I'm starved." She rubbed her head. "See? My hair's fallen out from lack of nourishment."

Like tennis spectators their heads snapped in unison, and their mouths opened. After a moment of stunned silence, laughter exploded from the group.

"You've got quite the attractive fuzz covered noggin, Little Bit." Joe grinned.

"Well, thank you. You aren't too bad yourself. No offense, but sometimes I just need to let my poor head breathe. Helps the hair grow."

Annabelle blushed through her smile. "I think you look cute."

"Tillie, it's about time you regained your appetite."

Egg rolls were handed all around.

"Joseph, there's enough food here for a squadron. We'll never be able to eat all this."

"Just make sure you eat up the fried shrimp. It won't keep, but the rest can be my lunch tomorrow," he said.

B. D. Tharp

Tillie kicked him under the table. "Don't be a pig. We can all have lunch tomorrow."

"We'll see." He chuckled between bites.

Although they did serious damage to the cartons of food, there was still enough left over for at least one meal, if not two.

Tillie and Regina cleaned up the kitchen while their gallant neighbor carried the blushing patient back up to her room.

Later, Tillie walked Joe to the door. "You were great today. Thanks for being there."

He bent his head down and kissed her lips, then rubbed her head. "Do I get a wish?"

"I'm not a round bellied Buddha, but if I were, what is your desire?"

"You, in my bed, with nothing on." He winked.

"Hum, interesting concept. May have to give that some thought."

"Ready when you are, little darlin'," he said.

She searched his green eyes for the truth. "Are you sure?"

"As sure as I've ever been. I love you, Tillie. I want you."

Her cheeks pinked. "Well, damn. You sure know how to sweet talk a girl."

He stepped out on the porch.

"You coming?"

"Not tonight, but can I take a rain check?"

He blew her a kiss. "Yep. Any time."

CHAPTER 24

Relishing the peaceful house, Regina sipped her morning coffee. Tucked in a quilt on the window seat, she gazed through the lace curtains, and listened to the companionable sounds of the birds and the creaking of the old house.

Out front, a beat up, rusty sedan of an undeterminable color bumped into the curb. Three bleary-eyed kids stumbled from the backseat, an assortment of bags and backpacks in hand.

"Oh, Lord, what now?"

She set down her cup and tightened the sash of her robe on the way to the door. Regina stepped onto the porch and witnessed Annabelle's daughter pushing the pale children toward the house. Their clothes were rumpled, shoes untied, hair still snarled from sleep. The boy's left arm was covered with a turquoise cast from the tips of his fingers to his elbow.

They reached the bottom step where Liddy shoved them forward. "You want them so bad, you take them."

"Excuse me? Have you lost what little mind you were born with?"

"That's a good one." Liddy cackled. "Insanity is a luxury saved for the rich. I'm leaving this dump of a town and starting over."

"And what about these children?"

"If you and my mother are so concerned about 'em, you take care of 'em." She made a washing motion with her hands.

Regina stretched up to her full height and stared down her

nose at Liddy. "There's not much experience raising kids in this house, but at least they won't be afraid."

Poor, dirty, scruffy things.

The children stood like miniature lawn statues, tears cascading.

"Mom? Don't go!" Peggy said. She pulled at her lopsided ponytail. "Please! I'll take care of the kids. Don't leave us."

Liddy pointed at Regina. "Reality check, Cousin. Here's a real dose of family."

"What about their father?" Regina said.

"He skipped out on us years ago."

"Ran, more than likely," Regina said. "What happened to the boy?"

"He fell," Liddy said.

With a wave of her hand, Liddy flipped her stringy hair from her face and walked to the car, calling over her bony shoulder. "Have fun. I plan to."

Tad and Megan watched their big sister run across the yard toward their mother's car.

"Don't go!" Peggy shouted.

The engine revved as Liddy screeched to the corner. Peggy stopped in the middle of the empty street and dropped her backpack on the asphalt, her shoulders shaking.

Regina witnessed the young girl age years in the seconds it took her mother to disappear.

Peggy sniffled and wiped her nose on her sleeve before trudging back to her siblings. She approached with teeth firmly planted on her bottom lip.

Regina held open the door.

"Guess you'd better come on in."

The dejected trio dragged their belongings up the steps.

Megan hesitated, peering through the leaded glass front door. "Where's Gram?" Her thumb disappeared into her mouth, up to the second knuckle.

Tad hugged his football to his chest with his injured arm. His eyelashes clumped from tears, now dry, matched the uneven blond spikes on his head.

Leading them up the steps, Regina opened the first door at the top of the stairway. "Why don't you put your things in here, young man."

Tad walked into the center of the room and slowly turned.

The rich blue bedspread and curtains accented the deep azure wallpaper and white painted baseboards and window casings. Watercolor paintings of boats and lighthouses lined the walls. The massive dark wood furniture was designed for a man.

Megan and Peggy peeked around the jamb, their mouths agape.

"This is the blue suite. It used to be Devlin's. He wasn't an athlete like you, but he did enjoy boating and fishing."

"Great, I get to sleep in some dead guy's bed," Tad said.

"It's not like he's still in it. Go on. You're not scared are you?" Regina asked.

"You wish," Tad said.

"Ladies, follow me." She took them next door.

"Where's Gram?" Peggy asked.

Directing their gaze with a manicured index finger, Regina pointed down the hallway.

"Your grandmother is in the rose room at the end of the hall. Tillie is across from her, and my room is in the far corner. You ladies will have to share the sun room."

"I hope we don't get lost." Megan's eyes were the size of dessert plates. "Will Momma be back for us?"

"Sure, she will," Peggy said. She firmed her jaw, grabbed her little sister's elbow, and dragged her into the bright room. The white painted canopy bed was draped with a pale yellow comforter and adorned with lace. The morning sun suffused the room with light.

Megan sat on the edge of the bed, clutching her pink backpack with one hand, sucking the thumb of the other. The head of a nappy haired doll peaked out of the pocket of her knapsack.

Peggy reached out to Regina who stood in the doorway her hand paused in midair. "What are we supposed to do now?"

"It's spring break, right?" Regina said. Her hand remained on the doorknob.

"Yes," Peggy whispered.

"We don't have to go back to school till Monday," Megan said, then stuck the wrinkled digit back in her mouth. She'd dropped the pack and was twirling a lock of hair.

"It's only a quarter past seven. Why don't you children lie down until the rest of the house wakes? We'll figure out what to do then."

"Okay," Peggy said.

Regina saw tears in the child's eyes.

"Why did Mom leave us?" Peggy asked.

"I don't know, honey. Let's not worry about that now. We'll go downstairs after a while and have some of Tillie's famous waffles and see if we can figure out what the best course of action will be." She patted Peggy's cold fingers.

"*Grandmere* Morgan, who was lovely and wise, used to always say, 'Don't look back.' "

"Why?" Peggy asked.

"Because we're not going that way," Regina said, then smiled and eased the door closed.

She glanced in to find Tad lying wide-eyed on the bed; a tattered stuffed animal tucked tight under his chin. His ragged tennis shoes sat on top of his duffel bag with the football on the floor.

"Does your arm hurt?"

He shook his head, then turned on his side to face the wall.

She proceeded down the steps to the kitchen and a much-needed cigarette.

Three kids. Mother will bring the ceiling down.

Regina paced and puffed her way across the kitchen floor for the next half hour, contemplating the disruption of her peaceful home.

"Whatever am I going to do with three children?"

Well, Mother, hang onto your broomstick, the house has been invaded by poor relations.

She envisioned Victoria's disapproving face in the smoke of her third cigarette.

"It's a dirty, nasty habit you've developed, Regina."

So you've said. That's not the real issue, though, is it?

Regina watched as the apparition moved closer.

"Hardly. What do you think you're doing?"

"I'm doing the right thing."

"Ah, the great and glorious Regina Morgan-Smith, now benevolent caretaker, rescuer of the downtrodden. Help someone who'll be grateful. Send money to Bangladesh."

"They're family. And they need me."

"How noble. How droll. They want our money."

"No, my money, Mother."

"They won't appreciate it."

"Stuff it, you royal spook. Didn't you see those children's faces? They're frightened. They've been disappointed and deserted by their father and now their mother. I'm betting she's responsible for the cast on that boy's arm, too."

"What about social services?"

"No. I remember how it felt to be left behind, when *Grand-mere*, then you and Father died. They deserve better than well-meaning strangers."

"They have Annabelle."

"She's weak. They need someone strong to look out for them."

"*You, I suppose.*"

"Yes. They need a stable environment in order to grow and explore their possibilities. You want to know something? It feels good to be needed. Hard to believe, isn't it?"

"*Piffle.*"

With a resigned snubbing-out of her cigarette butt, Regina blew through the smoky form before her. Threads of white dissipated in the air and she whispered, "Why don't you go and haunt someone else? I've got things to do."

Regina tiptoed up the stairs. The door to the blue room stood open, now empty, except for dirty sneakers and a duffel bag. The door to the sun room was ajar. One peek revealed another deserted bed.

If they're not in Annabelle's room, we'll have to call the police.

Regina eased the door open and found Annabelle snoring from beneath the rose comforter, her mottled face serene.

Megan and Tad lay on top of the covers, snuggled one on either side of their grandmother, sound asleep. Their arms were linked over Annabelle's slowly rising chest.

Tear tracks marred Peggy's pale cheeks.

From her position in the doorway, Regina watched the cat, Ms. Pickles, hitch across the carpet and curl at the teenager's feet.

Chapter 25

Skirting the edge of consciousness, Annabelle felt an odd pressure on her chest. Not a bad feeling, somehow comforting. But as the reality of the day penetrated her brain, she became aware of the sounds around her—birds singing, and instead of the purring sound she expected, there was a garble of young snores. Her eyes snapped open in momentary confusion.

Tad's spiky blond hair rested on her right shoulder while Megan snuggled into the crook of her left arm. Peggy's face lay next to hers on the pillow, but she appeared to be sitting on the chair next to the bed. How strange. "If this is a dream, it's a very noisy one."

Peggy was the first one to wake. She raised her head, pushed hair from her eyes, and sat back. "Hi, Gram," she whispered.

Annabelle smiled. "What a wonderful sight to greet the morning. Where did you three come from?"

Megan's head popped up, her doe eyes unfocused. "Mommy left us."

"She probably just went to work," Peggy offered.

Tad's muffled voice responded. "No. She dumped us like trash on the curb."

"What happened to your arm?"

"I fell." Tad snorted. "Mom doesn't care about us. Never did."

Annabelle cleared her throat. "That's not true. She's your mother. She loves you."

Through her tears, Megan hiccoughed. "Not anymore."

"People don't punch the people they love," Tad said.

Annabelle struggled to sit up while Peggy fluffed the pillow behind her. "Now, listen here." Her ample arms pulled the two youngest close to her warm body, but her gaze held Peggy's. "Your mother is going through a bad time right now. That doesn't mean she doesn't love you."

The eldest girl's eyes glistened. "Sure. She'll be back when she feels better."

"That's right," Annabelle said. She gave the little ones a squeeze.

"Bullshit," Tad said.

His grandmother poked his shoulder.

"She's your mother, and you'll show her respect."

"What, like she does you?" He rubbed the spot she'd touched.

"Your mother doesn't mean to hurt me. She's like her father. She hits without thinking."

Megan sat back and looked at Annabelle closely. "Why do they always hurt you?"

Annabelle sighed. "Good question. Because I let them. I used to think I deserved it, but I realize that's not true."

"That's dumb," Tad said. He moved away from Annabelle's embrace, cradling his injured limb.

"Yes it is. But sometimes, when you love someone, you do dumb things. You kids don't have to be dumb."

His back to her, Tad's shoulders slumped. "Yeah, right," he said.

"What happened to your arm since yesterday?"

"I fell."

Belle and Peggy's eyes met. Peggy shook her head.

The cat had hidden under the bed at their waking. She chose that moment to announce her presence by hopping up onto the bed. She emitted a loud "meow."

Megan giggled, snuggling closer to her grandmother.

Reaching out a tentative hand, Peggy stroked one silky, pink-lined ear.

"What happened to its leg?" Tad asked, arms folded across his skinny chest.

Annabelle scratched the cat behind the head. "This is Ms. Pickles. She lost her leg in an accident when she was just a kitten."

"She looks like a pickle face," Tad said.

Ms. Pickles sneezed in response, making the wide-eyed Megan giggle again. "She doesn't like you, Tadpole."

His stomach growled before he could respond.

Annabelle stretched her aching shoulders. "I think it's time to get up. Maybe we can talk Tillie into making us a gourmet breakfast."

"I don't like gourmets," Megan said.

"It's not a food," Peggy said. "It means fancy. Right, Gram?"

"Oh, yes. Tillie's a chef. She makes heavenly food."

Megan frowned. "Does that mean it's good or you wish you were in heaven instead of eating it?"

Tad laughed and poked at his little sister's tummy.

"She probably makes mud pies."

With a shake of her head, Annabelle pushed back the covers. "Why don't we go and see?"

While the children were visiting with their grandmother, Tillie and Regina discussed the situation over coffee.

"What the hell am I going to do with three kids in the house?" Regina asked.

"Feed them?" Tillie gulped down the dregs of her coffee and pulled her recipe box down from the counter. "This calls for a special breakfast. I think best when I'm cooking."

"Are you sure you're up to it?" Regina asked.

"Give me a break, Regina. I feel great. I just won't be doing any pull-ups for a while yet."

"You have been eating better, and you're the color of peaches and cream instead of ashes."

"Oh, that's nice. Did you notice the white fuzz growing on top?" She rubbed her head, black eyes sparkling.

"Actually, yes. It's quite becoming."

"I wasn't crazy about the cue ball thing. Belle's caps helped."

"She did well with them, I must admit."

"I bet that hurt," Tillie said.

Regina coughed. "There's no need to be nasty, Matilda Jean."

"I'm not. I'm proud of you. You're growing up."

"As my dearly departed mother would say in a situation like this—Piffle."

Tillie laughed deep down in her chest. "What's that mean?"

"I haven't the vaguest."

Regina watched her friend gather ingredients onto the countertop. A welcome vitality had returned to Tillie's movements. She'd finish her last chemotherapy treatments soon, and the specter of death no longer loomed large. But something else disturbed Regina, and the realization gave her a start.

Shit, she's in love. Lord, what had happened to her quiet existence? It's departed, along with loneliness, and frankly it scares the hell out of me.

Regina shook her head. One crisis at a time. "What are we going to do with the kids?"

"First, breakfast. Then we see what Annabelle wants to do."

"No doubt she'll want to keep them."

Tillie emitted a very un-ladylike snort. "And what's wrong with that? They are her grandchildren. Hell, woman, they're your family, too."

Regina flipped her braid over her shoulder. "Yes, I suppose they are."

"Really, your royal hiney, why don't you admit it. You're just as worried about them as we are."

"Yes, I suppose I am," Regina said.

"You suppose." Tillie rolled her eyes. "So, let's help them out."

"Okay, you feed them, and I'll . . . what'll I do?"

"Love them?"

"Novel concept. Tillie, I don't know a thing about half-grown children."

Thumping footsteps sounded on the stairs. A chorus of voices tumbling on top of each other grew in volume and intensity.

A smiling Tillie turned her attention to the stove. "Something tells me you're about to learn."

After a scrumptious meal of apple stuffed pastry, scrambled eggs and bacon, the kids chased each other around the table.

Grabbing Megan, the closest, Annabelle wrapped both arms around her and kissed her head. "Whoa, you guys need to take it outside."

Snuggling into her grandmother's embrace, the little girl smiled. "And do what, Gram?"

"Well, there's a garden out there. Tillie can show you where we found Ms. Pickles. You guys can clean up the dead leaves and sticks and put them in the trash barrel."

With a parting squeeze, Megan turned to her siblings.

"Let's go," she said.

Peggy scooped up the cat and followed Tad, who dashed out the door first.

Regina had the dishwasher filled by the time Tillie returned. She sat at the table with Annabelle, waiting in silence for their sidekick.

Tillie slid into the chair, leaning her elbows on the table. "Geez, Regina, don't look so glum. They're nice kids."

Annabelle cleared her throat. "I'll take care of them."

"How? Look at you? You're battered and bruised, supposed to be in bed, living off of your dead husband's social security—in someone else's house," Regina said.

Tillie punched her pompous friend in the arm.

Although Annabelle's eyes were full to the brim, the tears did not fall. "That's true, but I'm their grandmother. I'll find a way to manage it. I'll get a job, if I have to."

"Doing what? The only jobs you've ever had were punching bag and domestic servant. Neither pays very well."

Annabelle lifted her chin and straightened her shoulders. "Witch."

Tillie held up her hands. "Time out. Neutral corners, please. May I make some suggestions?"

Annabelle nodded. "I'd appreciate it."

"Very well," Regina said, worrying the end of her braid. "If you can take what I dish out, you might just be able to handle those three."

With a sniffle, Annabelle crossed her arms and glared at her cousin.

Tillie proceeded to outline her plan. "While Annabelle is healing, the kids can stay here. Joe and I will figure out a way to get them to and from school while Regina looks into the legal ramifications of this situation. We need to know our options and what needs to be done to protect those kids."

Annabelle looked at her cousin. "Well?"

Regina nodded. "It's the right thing to do."

The back door burst open, and the children stumbled in, leaving a trail of dirt. Their sneakers squeaked across the linoleum floor. Peggy cradled the cat in her arms.

Megan squealed. "Miss Pickles ate a bug!"

CHAPTER 26

Thursday morning Regina made an appointment with her attorney, Sam Duncan. She gave his legal assistant the *Reader's Digest* version of the situation, demanding that he be prepared to discuss their options that afternoon.

"My cousin has just been dismissed from the hospital and can't travel, so I'll expect Mr. Duncan at my home by four o'clock."

Regina's next task: a few moments of silence in the attic studio and some creative thinking.

She rocked in the chair, sketchpad at the ready. Sad faced children with tear stained cheeks peered back at her from several pages.

After a momentary hesitation, she tossed those sketches away. The drawing that developed next was a mixture of smiling, smudged, luminous faces. A collage of Tad, Megan, and Peggy poured from her fingers.

"This is how they should be."

The voice of Victoria Morgan echoed in her mind.

"They're ragamuffins, darling. Not the royal purple of true American society."

"The purple of society no longer exists, Mother. It's been replaced by the red, white, and blue. Or, in Belle's case the black and blue, soon to be purple, green, and yellow. She hates purple, and so do I."

"Green will always rule this country. It's power. Preserve it."

"Yes, green has power. Father made our fortune, and you taught me to protect it. But, there's an even greater responsibility, Mother, which you never understood. Wealth's worthless if it isn't used to help others."

"If I weren't already dead, I'd be ill."

"Go away."

Regina resumed her drawing with a vengeful vigor.

On the drive to the grocery store Tillie asked pointed questions of the sulky children, hoping for some insight and a bit of inspiration.

"What do you kids like best about school?"

Barely audible above the engine noise, Tad spoke. "Art and PE."

Megan pulled her thumb out of her mouth long enough to say, "Music and lunch."

Peggy sighed. "I used to like spring break."

Choosing not to look but listen, Tillie heard the despair in the preteen's voice.

"I had a great home economics teacher. She encouraged me to become a chef. Not everyone is lucky enough to be able to make a living doing what they enjoy, like I did."

Megan spoke to the back of Tillie's head.

"Do you mean people pay you to cook?"

"Well, sure, honey. I cook for the Uptown Bistro."

"I heard that place is cool," Tad said.

With a quick look in the rearview mirror, Tillie saw Megan's face scrunch in concentration.

"Can you get paid to eat?"

Tillie struggled to keep from laughing at the little girl's earnest question.

"Actually, yes. Food critics work for magazines and newspapers, and they get to write about the restaurants they visit."

"Cool," Megan said.

"How about you, Tad? What do you want to be when you grow up?"

"Why do you care?"

"Too tough a question, huh?"

"No, I'm going to be an artist," he said.

Tillie smiled into the rearview mirror. "Did you know your cousin is a successful artist? She has an exhibit at the university right now. We can go see it."

"Do we have to?" Tad said.

Choosing to ignore the bait, Tillie spoke to the passenger riding shotgun. "Peggy, what do you want to do with your life?"

"I dunno," Peggy said. "I guess I'd like to marry a rich old guy so I can inherit his money and stuff when he dies."

A snort came from the backseat. Tillie envisioned the dagger filled look Peggy must've given her little brother.

"Hmm. Well, I suppose we all need goals in life. Aren't too many single old rich guys around town. Believe me, I've looked."

They pulled into the grocery store parking lot. Grabbing a nearby cart, Tillie led them inside.

"So, what do you guys like to eat?"

"Tacos, hamburgers and pizza." Tad smiled. "What else is there?"

Megan thought for a moment before answering. "I like chocolate chip cookies and Gram's pancakes."

Tillie smiled at the chubby cheeked child.

"Me, too. What about you, Peggy?"

The girl's eyes were flat as she dragged her feet behind the cart. "I don't care."

"Well, I need to make some delicious dishes that'll help your grandmother get well."

Megan frowned up at Tillie. "You mean like cauliflower and Brussels sprouts?"

With a laugh, Tillie replied, "Not quite. I tell you what. If I make anything you think is really awful, you just tell me, and I'll order pizza."

"Deal," Tad said.

Megan covered her mouth with her hand and giggled.

Tillie caught Peggy rolling her eyes and smiled to herself.

The kids' eyes bulged when the cashier rang up $157 on the register.

Tad and Megan punched each other in the backseat while Peggy batted her eyelashes at the blond-headed boy putting the bags in the trunk.

The drive home was a quiet one. As they stopped in the drive, the three youngsters attempted to bolt from the car but came up short at Tillie's shout.

"Stop right there. If you want to eat, you'd better carry these bags inside."

Tad grabbed for the bread and chips, but Tillie was too fast for him. "You're stronger than that!"

"My arm's in a cast," Tad said.

"Use it to support the bottom of the sack."

"Geez, child labor," Tad grumbled.

"What good are children if they don't do chores?" Tillie said, leading the trio to the kitchen.

Sam Duncan pulled up fifteen minutes early in a gleaming white Crown Victoria. Regina observed him from behind the lace curtains.

Not bad. He'd better be prepared, though.

She smoothed her black cotton tunic and glided to the door, opening it before his knock.

Sam Duncan gave Regina a toothy grin as his huge brown hand engulfed her slender one as he kissed it.

"Really, Sam. This is the twenty-first century. Let's just shake hands. Come in and we'll get down to business."

He covered his chest with his hands and closed his eyes. "You pierce my heart, Regina." Smiling, he followed her into the parlor. "I guess I belong in a previous century."

"Can I get you some coffee or tea?"

"No, thank you. I'm fine."

She indicated that he should sit on the brocade loveseat.

"I'll get Annabelle and Matilda."

Annabelle asked the children to stay in their rooms until the visitor was gone.

The ladies settled around the attorney as Regina introduced them. "Sam Duncan, this is Annabelle Hubbard, my cousin, and our friend, Matilda Dawson."

He gave each a warm smile. "My assistant told me about the three packages left on your doorstep this morning. Let me tell you what I've found out, and then we'll discuss your alternatives."

"Proceed," Regina said.

Sam turned his gaze to Annabelle.

"First, I'd advise you, Mrs. Hubbard, to file for legal custody. If you don't, their mother can come back any time and take them."

At Annabelle's nod, he continued.

"Option two, we can contact Child Protective Services, who'll place them in foster care, where they will probably be split up."

"No." Annabelle shot off the chair, her face as florid as holiday wrapping.

Tillie reached out a hand to ease her back down so the gentleman could continue.

Sam gave her a reassuring smile.

"They could also go to the Children's Home and remain together."

Annabelle shook her head. "Not the orphanage." Tears

streaked down mottled cheeks as she pulled her hankie from her sleeve.

"Mrs. Hubbard, the grounds of abandonment and abuse will require their mother to go to court to request custody or visitation. Under the circumstances, she'll have a hard time proving she's fit. The courts usually try to preserve the family. As their grandmother, you have more power than a foster caregiver."

Blotting her eyes Annabelle patted her blue hair. "I see. Are there any income requirements?"

"There must be proof of income and a suitable home."

Regina watched her cousin strive to maintain her composure. "She lives here."

"And income?"

"I have my husband's social security," Annabelle said.

"The court's ultimate concern is for the children's welfare. Let's put that aside a moment."

He assessed Regina's cool countenance. "How do you feel about all this?"

"I'll be honest with you. I have mixed emotions. I've never had children in my home. Now there are three half-grown ones living here."

Annabelle gasped.

"At least she's honest," Tillie said.

Duncan returned his attention back to Regina. "You're under no legal obligation to assist them. That's what Child Protective Services was designed for."

Before the other ladies could protest, Regina held up her elegant hand.

"You're wrong, Sam. I do feel an obligation. They're family."

Regina's clear blue eyes turned to Annabelle's watery brown ones as she proceeded. "You see, there's been a history of abuse in our family, generations of it in fact. My parents didn't want to get involved, and, frankly, I think we could've helped. If we had, Liddy might not have continued the pattern. As it is, abuse is all she knows."

"It's up to you. As your attorney, it's my job to propose the options. You and Mrs. Hubbard will have to make the final decision regarding the care of these children."

Regina slid from the seat and gave him her warm hand. "We need to discuss this. I'll call you tomorrow."

Squeezing her hand, he rose and nodded. "That'll be fine. I'll make whatever arrangements you wish."

Carefully removing her hand from his, she walked him to the door.

His mane of white hair and broad shoulders bowed over her palm as he kissed it.

"You are a gallant. Thank you." Regina smiled into his bright blue eyes, level with her own. Not bad looking. She shook her head and sighed. Tillie was a bad influence.

"We'll talk tomorrow," she said.

"It'll be my genuine pleasure."

Dinner consisted of Señorita Matilda's Taco Casserole, which thrilled the kids and dismayed Regina.

If they continued to eat like this, they'd weigh more than Annabelle, and her cranky colon would mutiny.

After the table was cleared, the youngsters plunked down in front of the television to watch an old swashbuckler on the classic movie channel. Regina listened to the children's conversation from the doorway.

"It's so weird to see guys in pantyhose and ruffled shirts," Peggy said.

"But the sword fighting is cool," Tad said, slicing the air with an invisible rapier before flopping down on the sofa.

Ms. Pickles joined the littlest girl on the other end of the couch, allowing the rowdy boy plenty of space. Megan crossed her legs, Indian style, giving the silver feline a place to curl up.

With the kids occupied and out of earshot, the ladies met at the kitchen table to discuss the situation.

"Well?" Tillie demanded without preamble.

Annabelle's multicolored face couldn't hide her concern. "I'm keeping the kids."

Regina cleared her throat. "If that's what you want."

"Of course that's what I want."

Tillie's black eyes bore into Regina's icy blue ones. "This is Belle's home now, isn't it?"

With a regal lift of her chin Regina crossed her arms over her chest and met the piercing black gaze. "Yes."

A pudgy hand slapped the table. "Don't talk as if I'm not here. I told you I'd find a way to keep the kids."

"So you've said," Regina said.

"Well, daughter, as P. T. Barnum once said, 'There's a sucker born every minute.'"

Yes, Mother. And as the Jolly Old Pedagogue, George Arnold, said, 'The living need charity more than the dead.'

After a pregnant pause, Regina responded to her cousin's indignation. "You have my support. You and the youngsters can stay here. It'll be crowded, but we'll find a way to manage. Keep them out of my studio, Belle. That's all that I ask."

"Thank you."

"I'll live to regret this, I'm sure. And Mother will haunt us both." Regina stood and walked to the sink.

"Then we'll just have to deal with the old spook," Tillie said. "I learned a lot about the kids today when we were at the store. A plan's been simmering in my brain all evening. Let's turn the room over the garage into a playroom."

"A playroom?" Regina faced the curtain and the dark night beyond.

Tillie spouted her thoughts like a gurgling stream. "There's a tiny bathroom that just needs to be scoured. Tad could have his own easel. I don't know what Megan likes besides food, and Peggy's a little tough to figure out."

With a flip of her salt and pepper braid, Regina turned to face them, eyes raised heavenward and a hint of a smile on her lips.

"Lord, help me. I knew it. I'll never have another moment of peace. Matilda Jean, you're either obsessed or possessed, I'm not sure which."

Tillie's enthusiasm was contagious.

Annabelle laughed for the first time in days. "Megan loves to read, so maybe we could get a secondhand bookcase and fill it from the Paperback Swap store. And Peggy is a modern music buff, like most teenagers."

"My life is mutating right before my eyes," Regina said and exited the kitchen.

Hesitating in the darkened dining area, she listened to Tillie and her cousin plan, feeling surprised at the excitement growing inside her chest.

"We'll have to get Peggy some earphones, or the neighbors will complain. The whole house shakes with what she plays," Annabelle said.

"I know what you mean. Typical teenager. Hey, no problem," Tillie said.

Lord, help us all.

From the shadows, Regina slipped across the room to survey the kids, still lounging in the parlor.

Don't worry, little ones, you're not alone. We won't let anything happen to you. She pressed her fist into her tightening chest

191

CHAPTER 27

After Regina and the kids were in bed, Annabelle confided in Tillie, tears flowing. "I don't know if I can handle them. What if I screw them up like I did their mother?"

Seeing that the usual hankie was missing, Tillie handed her a tissue. "In the first place, you aren't responsible for Liddy's behavior. And secondly, those kids need you as much as you need them." Her voice held no room for argument.

With a sniffle, Annabelle straightened her spine. "I guess you're right."

"You'll be fine, hon. With three of us looking after those younguns, what could go wrong?"

"More than I care to imagine." Annabelle grimaced, her hand over her heart.

Giving her friend's hand a squeeze, Tillie shooed her up the stairs. "Off to bed. You need rest."

"Good night."

"Night."

Tillie woke the next morning with a serious mad-on. Annabelle's fears sat heavily on her heart. She was ticked at Regina for her aloofness, angry at Liddy's violent nature and infuriated with the disease that threatened to take her away before things were put right. She got out of bed, pissed off at the world.

Cooking had always been good medicine, so she stomped

down to the kitchen and began hacking at a pile of fresh vegetables.

The backdoor squeaked. She recognized the smell of his cologne, but Tillie jumped at the prickly feeling on her neck. "Get the hell out of my kitchen." She shook the paring knife at Joe. "Don't think you can sneak in here, put your whiskers on my skin, and expect me to melt. I could've cut off my finger. You're lucky I don't . . . ."

Joe smirked. "You're irresistible when you're angry."

"Typical, arrogant, clueless male. Go home. I'm busy." She turned back to the cutting board and laid waste to the carrots.

When the blade paused, he swatted her backside and ducked behind the table.

She spun on her heel and aimed the business end of the utensil at him. "You'd better keep something solid between us so I don't chop you up and put you in this pot."

"Something solid between us. Hmmm. Interesting thought, but I'll ignore it for now." He chuckled.

She raised her eyes heavenward. "You're obviously beyond comprehension."

"I'm tough and tenacious, too."

"That's for damned sure. Now, behave yourself or hit the road."

Cocking his head to one side like a puppy, Joe cupped his hand to his ear.

"Is it time to feed you some red meat so you'll stop chewing on my ass? By the way, it's awfully quiet around here. Where're the kids?"

"They're out back with Ms. Pickles." She pointed towards the garden.

"And the other ladies?"

"Belle's asleep, I hope. The kids are wearing her out." Tillie frowned at the ceiling. "Regina's hiding in her studio."

"You have to admit this must be a strain on Regina."

The blade flashed as Tillie whirled around. She used it to punctuate her words. "Yes, it is, but I'd dearly love to throttle her."

Joe leaned back against the wall, crossing his arms over his chest, raising a silver brow. "Why?"

"She was hateful to Belle, who stood her ground. She told Regina she'd find a place to live and get a job ironing shirts if she had to."

"Then what?" he asked.

Tillie stopped brandishing the knife in the air, gazing at nothing. "Kinda strange, really. Regina backed down. I swear, it was as if she was trying to goad Belle into taking a stand."

Sporting a smile, Joe slapped his thigh. "Her Majesty is developing a heart. It's got to be difficult since she never had any kids of her own."

From behind them, Regina cleared her throat. "You're only partially right, Joseph," she said, entering the room. "It is a challenge suddenly having three prepubescents under foot," she said.

Joe sat up in the chair, a scowl on his face. "How was I wrong, then?"

"I've had a child."

The steel pot lid hit the floor with a clatter as Tillie swung around.

"What?"

Regina slid into the chair beside Joe, flipped her braid behind her shoulder, and crossed her manicured hands on the tabletop.

"Devlin and I had a baby girl the year after I finished at the university."

Taking a towel from the stove handle, Tillie wiped her hands and sank into the chair across from Joe. Tillie could see Regina's turmoil behind the calm exterior.

Joe remained unusually silent.

"You never told me," Tillie whispered. "We've been friends for twelve years, and you never said a word. What else have you held back?"

The handsome man's green eyes clouded. "What happened to your baby?"

"She died."

He stood and briefly touched Regina's white hand with his. "I'm so sorry. Please, excuse me," he said.

Tillie stared at his retreating back. "There he goes again. Tough guy, my aunt's fanny."

The slamming of the front screen door marked his hasty exit and returned Tillie's attention to her friend. "How did it happen?"

Regina's pale jaw was set. "She died four months after we brought her home. Crib death."

"Oh, my God." Regina looked lost. Why hadn't Regina ever shared her sorrow?

Both of the ladies' eyes glistened with tears.

"Honey, I'm so sorry. Did you have anyone to talk to?" Tillie asked.

"No one. Belle and I weren't speaking. My folks and *Grandmere* were dead. Devlin and I bore the sorrow alone. That's when he started carousing. I found solace in father's wine cellar, and painting eventually helped."

"Did you try to have another child?"

"No. Our love died with our baby girl." Regina gazed into space. "Her name was Elizabeth Mae, after *Grandmere*. Peggy reminds me of her. Especially around the eyes." Tears cascaded down the slope of Regina's cheek and onto her clinched fists.

"Why didn't you tell me?" Tillie said.

"Honey, Devlin's death brought us together. I couldn't bear to talk about my losing Beth, too."

"I could've helped you grieve."

"It was too late by then. I'd dug the moat, and access was denied."

"It's about time you built a bridge. Way past time, in fact." Shaking her head, Tillie stood and leaned over to give her friend a hug. Feeling the implacable spine, she thoroughly drenched Regina's silk clad shoulder with tears in the process.

Regina crumpled in her friend's embrace. They clung to each other and sobbed for several minutes.

Tillie's voice finally rose between sniffles. "Life's too short. When you get to be our age, you start to realize just how quickly it passes. I feel a chill. How about a shot of brandy?"

With a teary nod, Regina agreed. "Sounds good."

Shoving a stepstool to the cabinet, Tillie retrieved a hundred-year-old bottle of cognac from the back of the cookbook shelf. "This is my secret stash. It's the good stuff."

She poured a half-inch of amber liquid into two snifters. Holding a glass high towards her friend, Tillie offered a toast. "To friends and family, who'll be in our hearts forever."

A delicate ping chimed when the rims touched.

Regina lifted her glass to Tillie, tipping her head. "A toast to friendship and love. You can never have too much of either, and I've heard that it's never too late for the latter."

They tossed back the liquid heat in one unified gulp.

"Don't waste any more time, Tillie," Regina said. She pointed towards Joe's escape route. "Go after your softhearted beau."

A glance at the front of the house sent Tillie's black eyes sparking fire. She tossed the last of the vegetables into the pot. "He can stew a bit longer."

After dinner, Annabelle and Regina cleared the table.

"Well, shit," Tillie said. "I guess I'll go over and console my sad knight."

196

The cousins traded winks over the dishwasher, then watched their friend head out into the night.

"It's about time," Regina said.

Tillie noticed the curtains on Joe's front window swing closed on her way across the street. The cold March wind invaded the tiny holes in her cap, tickling the short white hairs growing there. Its icy touch was invigorating, a welcome reminder that she was alive.

Watching for me, poor dolt.

With her knuckles she gave the door three quick raps. Her hand reached to pat her blazing red skullcap, tipped at a jaunty angle. As the door opened her gaze sought his.

"Hey, Little Bit." He beckoned her in with a slight bow and lopsided smile.

She crossed the threshold and walked into his arms, pressing her cheek into his warm chest.

"Joe, when are you going to realize that people in pain don't appreciate your desertion."

He wrapped himself around her and kissed the top of her cap. "Mea culpa."

The shrill ring of the phone shattered the silence. He broke from her embrace and mumbled. "Hold it, one minute. Don't move."

She didn't mind the intrusion. It'd give her time to compose herself for whatever would come next.

Tillie scanned the room, noticing the intimate arrangement of sofa, fireplace, and bearskin rug. Thoughts of running her naked toes through the fur brought erotic images tingling up from the soles of her feet.

Whoa, girl. Keep your knees together.

She snuggled into the cushions and hugged a brown suede pillow, shiny from use.

Joe slipped down beside her and laid his head on the leather she held close.

"That was short, and none too sweet. You're sure in a hurry today," she said.

"You have no idea."

"Try me," she said.

"Okay." He sat up and straightened his broad shoulders. "I think you know how I feel about you."

She giggled. "You find me stimulating company, right?"

"Something like that. You aren't making this easy." His voice rumbled like an oncoming storm. He reached out his large square hand and stroked her thigh.

An involuntary spasm washed over her. His warmth penetrated her jeans and into the depths of her marrow. Her breath caught. She stammered, feeling the bloom of embarrassment color her cheeks. Tillie grabbed his fingers and squeezed. "Why don't you start a fire?"

He leaned across her lap, pressing her into the cushions. "You already have."

Using the pillow for a shield, she pushed him to arms' length. "In the fireplace, please."

With a sigh, he pushed off the couch. "The sofa would be softer." Grabbing the newspaper off the end table, he wadded up several sheets and stuffed them under the grate. He pulled sticks of kindling from an old blue battery jar that stood beside the hearth, then reached for a self-starting log.

Tillie watched the muscles flex underneath his shirt. *Damn, this guy is a total panty damper.*

He blew on the tiny flame and watched the paper blacken and curl. Without turning to face her, he whispered, "I want all of you, Tillie."

"Honey, I think we've been this way before, and it didn't turn out like we'd hoped."

His eyes sought hers. "I know. I was afraid."

"What makes this time any different?"

"I'm not scared anymore," he said.

She broke from his gaze and twisted her hands in her lap. A tear fell on her thumb. "Maybe I am."

From his position on the rug, Joe reached out his hands and laid them firmly on her knees. Then moved them upward, pausing at the junction where molten heat was forming, then proceeded to trace a path up her sides, pausing to caress her beating heart. He gently pulled her onto his lap, stroking and kissing her wet face. "I love you, sweetheart."

"Oh, Joe. I want to rip your clothes off right here and christen this rug, but . . ."

"But, what?"

"Not only has gravity done its worst to my buns, but all that's left of my chest are ugly scars."

"Scars inside or out, you're beautiful to me."

She sniffled and looked into his brilliant green orbs.

He touched her cheek. "You're a soft hearted warrior, just like I am. We both have scars." Holding her eyes captive, he laid his hand on her chest.

Taking a cleansing breath, she closed her eyes and remembered her first date and how she'd agonized over her bust size. It would be nice to have them back, even with all their imperfections.

"Well, shit." She grabbed her sweater with shaky hands and lifted it over her head. The skullcap caught in the crew neck, charging the tiny white hairs on her head.

Joe smiled at the spiky fuzz around her face. "Punk looks good on you, darlin'. Everything does, but nothin' looks even better."

Her smile melted and her breath caught.

His gaze slid from her face to her torso. The only sound in

her ears was the pounding of her heartbeat.

Even mostly clothed, she felt more exposed than any other time in her life.

His index finger traced the scars first on one side, then the other. He bowed his head and kissed them each in turn, then kissed her pale, tear-streaked face.

CHAPTER 28

The next morning, Annabelle smiled at Tillie from across the kitchen table. "I'm relieved the kids are back in school. My thoughts are a mass of scrambles."

Tillie's cheeks were flushed as she kneaded bread dough.

"We'll get busy on their playroom today. Kids need their own space," she said.

With a nod, Annabelle blew on the coffee to cool it. Her hair was a tangle from sleep, and her faded robe looked as tired as its wearer. "Soon, before something goes wrong, or gets broken, or . . ."

"Quit being paranoid." Tillie patted Annabelle's hand, leaving a little flour behind.

"Regina gave you the key to the room over the garage, so I'd say that's the go ahead to get busy."

"I suppose. I just feel like such an interloper."

"Interloper? Where on earth did you hear that?"

Annabelle's cheeks pinked. "TV. But I looked it up. It's a Regina word if I ever heard one. And the kids and I are the definition."

"Hogwash." Tillie slapped the tabletop, sending up a puff of white.

A chuckle shook Belle from shoulders to tummy.

"That doesn't sound like a Tillie word."

"I'm trying to clean up my act." Tillie winked. "For the kids."

"Oh, please don't change. You're so perfect the way you are."

"Not to worry," Tillie laughed. "Hogwash may cross these lips, but my mind is hollering bullshit." Taking her cup to the sink she grinned. "Now, let's get dressed and go tackle the new kid corral."

Tillie looked at the clock. "It's almost time for me to pick up the kids from school."

"I sure appreciate you and Joe taking care of their transportation for right now." Annabelle smiled at her friend, wiping a smudge of dirt from Tillie's cheek with her hankie.

"No problem. Joe doesn't mind dropping them at school on his way to the gym. I don't believe in getting up early, unless someone pays me handsomely to do it or the house is on fire. I'm just hitting my stride about now."

Annabelle smiled and pointed to the message on Tillie's coffee brown t-shirt. "I can tell, Miss Allergic to Mornings."

"You just don't need as much beauty sleep as I do."

"No, it just doesn't work for me."

"Piffle." Tillie winked.

"That's Aunt Victoria's word. Are you making fun?" Annabelle looked formidable with her hands on her ample hips, blue hair a flurry around her head.

"No, I just think it's a great word. Besides, I didn't think you liked Regina's mother."

Annabelle relaxed her stance.

"Oh, no. She was beautiful, like a marble statue. I admired her. I just didn't like it when she said my momma married beneath her."

"That's not a very nice thing to say to an impressionable young girl."

"She never said it to me, just whispered about it whenever we were visiting *Grandmere.*"

"What a crock," Tillie said.

"After I grew up and married David, I realized she was right."

"Doesn't make it any nicer."

"No, it doesn't."

The vacuum whirred as Tillie prepared to give the blinds one last swipe. She watched Annabelle from the corner of her eye.

The room became instantly silent as she flicked off the switch and wound up the cord.

"You know, we need to put in a telephone or intercom up here," Annabelle said, looking around the room.

"I don't know." A belly laugh burst from Tillie's tiny frame. "I can see it now." Her arms swept circles around the room. "They'll be ordering pizza every day and charging it to Regina."

Annabelle's knees creaked as she stooped to pick up her dust rag. "Maybe, but we have to have a way to communicate with them without walking up those stairs all the time."

Mischief flashed across Tillie's face. "Two cans and a long string. No. We could re-hang the dinner bell on the back porch. Regina told me her mother thought it was an uncivilized way to communicate and hid it in the cellar."

"The neighbors might object, not to mention Regina. It'd disturb the peace and quiet." Annabelle resumed storing boxes in the cupboard.

"No doubt about that. I'll talk to Joe. He'll think of something. Let's get cleaned up."

Annabelle closed the closet door and wiped her dusty hands on her apron. "I think we've sorted out all the 'do not touch' things. The children can help with the rest."

Rubbing the white stubble on her head, Tillie grinned. "Sounds like a plan. Too bad Regina missed out on all the fun."

"What on earth has she been doing at the university all day?"

Tillie scrunched her shoulders. "Who knows? Do me a favor and make my favorite chocolate chip cookie recipe. I have a craving for a glass of cold milk and fresh cookies."

Annabelle's stomach emitted a loud growl. "That sounds yummy."

They giggled as they turned off the lights and headed back to the house.

Annabelle quickly changed out of her dirty dress and apron and grabbed a mixing bowl. The first dozen cookies were baking in the oven, the aroma just beginning to permeate the air, when she dipped her finger into the bowl and started nibbling.

Tillie had just left to pick up the kids when the phone rang.

"Hello."

"Yes, is this Mrs. Hubbard? This is the school."

"Yes, what's happened?" Annabelle listened in horror, her eyes the size of saucers. "Is Tad all right? Thank the Lord . . . Oh.

"I'll take care of it," Annabelle said with a grimace.

"Matilda Dawson—she's on the approved to pick up list. She'll be picking them up shortly. Thank you for letting me know."

Annabelle hung up the handset. The timer on the stove buzzed. Donning the faded floral mitt, Annabelle removed the cookie sheet and turned off the oven. She crossed to the cabinet and took a glob of dough and shoved it into her mouth. A tear slid off her chin.

The quartet followed their noses to the kitchen.

Peggy hooked her book bag on the back of a chair.

"What smells so good, Gram?"

"Cookies!" Megan squealed and grabbed two off the plate.

The girls flopped into chairs, exchanged glances, and started eating while Tad stood in the shadow of the doorway.

Their grandmother poured glasses of milk. She placed one before her granddaughters and called over her shoulder,

"Tad, don't you want one?"

"No."

Annabelle faced him, crossing her arms over her bosom. "The school called."

"So?" he said.

"So." Belle pointed to the blood on his shirtfront. "You've been fighting."

The girls watched the quick volleys between their brother and grandmother.

He snorted. "Yeah, so what?"

Unfolding her arms, Annabelle directed him towards the stairs. "Go to your room, Tad."

"I don't have one." His voice tightened to the brink of breaking. "This isn't my house. It's an ugly old barn."

Annabelle's cheeks colored with the struggle to maintain control. "This is our home now. Go upstairs. I'll be up later to discuss your punishment."

"Punishment!" Tad slammed his backpack on the floor. "You're not my mom. What're you gonna do, ground me? Take away my supper? That's no big deal. Mom did it all the time."

Liddy probably broke his arm, too, but I refuse spank him.

"You've got to learn that striking someone is not the answer." Taking a step towards the angry child, Annabelle firmed her shoulders and pointed once again. "Go. Upstairs. Now."

He stormed from the room, the heat of his rage lingering in his wake.

No one spoke.

Megan finished her milk.

Peggy whispered, "Excuse us," then tugged her sister out of the kitchen.

Tillie slipped into Peggy's vacated chair. "Hang in there, old girl."

"What am I going to do?" Annabelle knotted her fingers

through her hankie.

"The best you can."

They missed Tad's presence at dinner, which was punctuated by stilted conversation and long silences.

Regina helped Tillie clear the table while the girls loaded the dishwasher.

Annabelle prepared a cold plate for her grandson and proceeded up the stairs.

He's got to be hungry. He's just skin, bones, and feet. She wouldn't starve the poor child, no matter how naughty he became.

What she found at the top of the stairs was an empty room. The contents of his duffel were strewn across the floor and onto his unmade bed. She placed the plate on the bureau and looked towards the bathroom. The door was open and the room unoccupied.

Leaning over the stair rail she called, "Has anyone seen Tad?"

From the parlor, Regina hollered back. "He hasn't come down here. I would've seen him. He's probably in the bath."

"No, he's not there. Oh, my God, where can he be? What if he's run away?" Annabelle wrung her hankie.

Tillie and the girls came from the kitchen and stood at the base of the staircase.

"Let's all take a look around," Tillie said.

They explored every room on the first two floors, finding no sign of the boy.

Converging in the upper hall, the ladies turned their heads towards the attic. The door stood ajar.

Annabelle sucked in her breath and laid her hand over her heart. "He wouldn't. Regina will kill us both."

"Oh, shit," Tillie whispered.

Peggy tugged on Tillie's sleeve. "What's wrong?"

Megan popped a thumb in her mouth.

Lowering her voice, Tillie said, "Regina's studio is up these stairs."

Megan mumbled behind her digit, "We know."

"How?" her grandmother wondered aloud.

Pulling her thumb free, Megan's eyes began to tear.

"Tad said he went exploring and found a room full of ugly pictures."

Regina squared her shoulders and proceeded up the stairs, past the group of worried faces, towards the sliver of light at the top of the steep stairwell.

Her hankie in a death grip, Annabelle whispered to Tillie, "But they've only been here a week."

"I'm surprised it took 'em that long," Tillie said. She followed Regina up the narrow stairs.

Annabelle stopped the girls. "Go to bed."

"But . . ." Peggy said. She bit her lip. "Yes, ma'am." Peggy took her little sister's hand, and she and Megan slowly descended the stairs. At their bedroom door they paused, a look of fear and pleading on both of their faces.

Annabelle waited until they'd closed their bedroom door before hustling up to the attic.

Tumbling across the studio threshold, Annabelle found a room filled with canvases and shadows. Several portraits were turned towards the door, each with a shiny new orange mustache. The angel portrait of Tillie stood on the easel, sporting a pumpkin colored goatee.

Regina's face had bloomed with color, rivaling the unnatural hues on the canvases. Her chest heaved as she exploded, "You heathen, get out of my house!"

Stepping in front of her cousin, Annabelle blocked the offending pictures, holding her stare. "Tad, go to your room," she said.

He scampered from a darkened corner and hid behind his grandmother. Without turning around she said, "Go to bed, young man, right now."

He shuffled out of the room while the cousins glared at each other.

The blue-haired grandmother nearly swayed before the storm that was her cousin. If she fell apart now she'd be eaten alive. Sucking in her tummy, Annabelle faced Regina. "Calm down."

"I think the damage can be repaired." Tillie walked over to the canvas and touched it. Her finger came away with an orange smudge.

Regina didn't respond. Her color continued to rise and her eyes narrowed at Annabelle. "How dare you? Your white trash family invades my house, destroys my peace and quiet, mutilates my work, and you expect me to be calm?"

Pulling herself up to her full five-feet, four inches, Annabelle growled, putting her hand on her ample hips, "You're not the only one having to make adjustments. These kids have been abused then dumped like garbage."

"So, as usual my benevolence is taken for granted." Regina turned in place, her arms outstretched. "He soiled my creations and contaminated my space. Mother always predicted you'd suck us dry."

"Nonsense. They're frightened children. I'm sorry for what he did, but you offered us a home here, remember?" Annabelle removed her hands from her hips and tried to touch her cousin's stiff shoulder.

Moving between them, Tillie grabbed Regina's rigid hand. "The damage can be repaired. Belle gave you friendship and the chance for some happiness with these kids."

"Happiness? It was a mistake. Order and quiet make me happy, not this chaos. Those brats can't be trusted. Don't you see the carnage in this room?"

Annabelle shook her head back and forth. "Regina, it's just a little paint."

Tears streamed down Regina's cheeks. "I created these, and they're mine."

Tillie stomped on the wooden floor. "They're not living, breathing things. They won't grow or die with you, and they won't warm your old bones. These paintings aren't real."

Regina sniffed and wiped her nose on her sleeve. "They're real to me. They've helped me through all the living and the dying."

Annabelle shook Regina's arm. "Oh, stop it. You used art to help you through the tough times. Tillie cooks, and I sew. We all find our own ways to cope."

With a flip of her braid, Regina dislodged her arm from her cousin's grip. "What do you know about anything, Belle?"

"I know that sewing helps me focus and not wander the dark, painful corners of the past."

"Those children bring hope, Regina." Tillie tugged on her friend's hand. "They have so much to give. They'll let us see the world through their eyes. They'll warm us with their smudged smiles and loving little arms."

"Get real. Look at this mess. You're such a dreamer," Regina said.

Annabelle pushed her cousin back a step. "Maybe so, but better that than a lonely old witch. Without love, we're lonely and alone. I'm willing to share what I have with you, just as you're sharing home and hearth with me."

Tillie crossed between the cousins again, took a rag in her hand and began wiping the orange paint from the hanging woman portrait. "This is oil, isn't it? Oils take weeks to dry. It'll clean up."

Annabelle picked up a cloth and crossed to the angel painting.

Regina took the rag from Annabelle's hands. "I'll do it."

The surface of the canvas changed before Annabelle's eyes. "Tillie, you looked kinda cute with a goatee."

Tillie stepped back, perusing her work. "Maybe I could dye my peach fuzz orange, use gel, and punk it up."

A low chuckle rolled from Regina's chest as she continued to remove the offending paint. "I'd rather you didn't. Although the children would probably think you're cool."

Annabelle reached out her hand to her cousin. "Truce?"

Regina tentatively touched her hand. "For now. Tillie's right. No permanent damage was done."

Annabelle pressed her ear to the girls' door, then tapped and waited. Shuffling sounds reached her from behind the wooden barrier. The knob turned, and Peggy peeked around the jam. "Gram?"

"May I come in?" Annabelle asked.

"Just a minute," Peggy said and turned her head. The whispering stopped, and she opened the door.

Megan, clad in white flannel pajamas with yellow kittens, sat on a wad of covers, her eyes wide, thumb hidden in her mouth.

Annabelle stood by the door and watched Peggy dash to the bed and scoot her bare legs under the blanket with her sister. "You can come out now, Tad," Peggy said. "It's Gram."

Behind the bed, the tips of his spiked blond hair preceded Tad's pale face.

"Did she kick us out?"

Stepping closer, Annabelle shook her head. "No. Did you eat the dinner I brought up for you?"

Tad emerged from behind the bed. "No. Will I be punished?"

"Yes." Annabelle took a step nearer, her hankie twisted in her hand. "Are you hungry?"

Tad's eyes glistened with tears as his head bobbed up and

down. "I'm starved."

"Come on then, I'll fix you a fresh sandwich. Say your good-nights. Oh, and Tad . . ."

"Yes, Gram."

"There'll be no TV for you for two weeks, young man."

He nodded his understanding and scrambled up to follow her. His stomach emitted a loud growl, causing his ears to pinken.

Peggy sat up on her heels, pulling her jalapeno colored sleep shirt over her feet. "Gram, will Cousin Regina throw us out like Mom did?"

Shrugging her round shoulders, Annabelle's face looked glum. "No, we don't have to leave."

Tad whispered, "Guess we could sleep in the park. I'm sorry, Gram."

"I know. Girls, go to bed. Tad, let's go get a snack."

CHAPTER 29

Dipping the last of her scone in her coffee cup, Regina sighed and pictured her mother's porcelain face. "What a mess."

"I know, dear. Don't blame yourself."

"I don't, really. It was bound to happen sooner or later."

"You just can't trust poor relations."

"That's not what I mean, Mother. That boy's justified in his anger."

"Oh, please, don't tell me you feel sorry for the ragamuffin?"

"As a matter of fact, I do."

"You're hopeless, Regina. Have you forgotten everything I taught you?"

"No. But, at my age I think I know which parts to keep and which to toss out with the garbage."

"Don't be disrespectful."

"Just stating the facts. Now go haunt the neighbors. I need some quiet."

The phone rang three times before she decided to answer. "Hello."

"Regina?"

"Yes."

"Sam Duncan here."

"Oh, hello, Sam." Regina patted her hair, a smile finding its way to her lips.

"I'd like to bring some documents by for Mrs. Hubbard to sign this afternoon. Is she feeling up to it?"

Regina answered, "That would be fine."

"Say about four?"

"We'll see you then."

Grinning, she replaced the receiver and wrapped her arms around her chest. She went to the refrigerator where she found a huge beef roast and plenty of potatoes. Perfect. There must be a crock-pot around here somewhere.

Arms loaded with grocery bags, Tillie and Annabelle arrived home just before noon.

"Hello, anybody home?" Tillie hollered as they came through the front entry.

"I'm in the parlor," Regina said. *Ready and waiting for whatever you two can dish out.*

Lifting her nose in the air, Annabelle sniffed. "What's that smell?"

"Supper," Regina said.

Tillie quickened her step to the kitchen. "Holy cow. Did someone deliver? Are you sick?"

With a regal sway of her skirts, Regina entered the kitchen to find her friend with the glass lid in her hand and a grin stretched from ear-to-ear.

"I'm not ill. I just felt like fixing a pot roast, that's all."

"Why?" Annabelle asked. "Is this our last meal?"

"Too bad I hadn't thought of that. No, Sam's coming by, and I thought we might invite him to dine with us." The stately woman flipped her braid and sat down.

With a whoosh, Annabelle landed in the chair beside her. "Is something wrong with the custody case?"

"I don't think so. He has some papers for you to sign."

Tillie returned the lid to the pot. "Where did you find this? You haven't used anything besides the coffee maker in this kitchen for ten years!"

"It was in the pantry. What's the big deal? I know how to cook." Regina lifted her nose to the air. "As everyone can attest from that delicious aroma."

"Agreed, but I'm not buying your voluntary return to domesticity as anything but a play for the hunky lawyer."

"Pshaw, you have an active imagination, my friend."

And you're too right by half.

"Yeah, whatever." Tillie chuckled. "How about dessert? Death by Chocolate? Crème Brule? I have a wonderful recipe with champagne and strawberries, which according to Richard Gere and Julia Roberts, is great for the libido."

Regina barely stifled a smile. "Matilda Jean, they need to check your medication. You're hallucinating."

"Men prefer chocolate, don't they?"

"Men will eat anything that doesn't eat them first." Annabelle covered her mouth with her hankie, unsuccessfully hiding her grin.

Regina stood and smoothed her skirt. "Excuse me. I think I'll leave you two old biddies to your groceries."

As soon as Regina was out of sight, but not out of hearing, Tillie and Belle burst into giggles.

To his credit, Sam arrived promptly. Regina ushered him to the parlor sofa before Tillie and Annabelle had a chance to pounce.

"How are you, Regina?" He smiled and captured her hand.

This man could melt kneecaps. Regina returned an equally brilliant smile and allowed him to hold her fingers for a moment longer than courtesy demanded. "I'm fine, Sam, just fine."

She liked the fact that they could see eye-to-eye. And his broad shoulders and muscular body reminded her of a well dressed mountain man.

"Getting on with the kids okay?"

"We have our moments, but we're finding creative ways to survive."

"I've no doubt you could manage anything, Regina," he said.

She felt her cheeks infuse with color as she led him to the formal dining room.

Annabelle joined them while Tillie worked in the kitchen. When their business was concluded Sam took Annabelle's hand. "I'll get these filed right away."

He turned to Regina, captured her fingers again, and kissed the back of her hand.

Blushing twice in one day was totally unlike her. She pulled away, holding her hands behind her back. "Would you like to stay for dinner?"

"Thank you. I'd be delighted," he said.

Sounding like herds of rogue elephants, the children descended the stairs, stopped short and stared at the candles, china, linen tablecloth, and napkins.

Megan's eyes widened as she approached the setting.

"How come we're eating in here instead of the kitchen?" Her brow furrowed as she touched the row of utensils.

Sam chuckled as Regina seated him to the right of the head of the table.

"What's he doing here?" Tad asked.

"Mind your manners, young man. Sam is our dinner guest." Regina punctuated her response by flipping her braid over her shoulder.

Peggy poked Tad in the ribs with a whispered "shush."

Annabelle and Tillie set the bowls and platters of roast and vegetables on the table, Ms. Pickles close on their heels.

"Would anyone like some wine?" Regina said, proceeding without waiting for an answer. She uncorked the merlot with ease and poured a tiny sip in Sam's glass.

Smiling, he held it up to his nose, inhaling the rich fragrance, then he tasted. "Excellent choice." Holding out his glass to be filled, he winked at his hostess.

Regina noticed that Tillie's sharp black eyes didn't miss the exchange. A quick glance around the table confirmed that no one else had either. Annabelle's face was aglow with pink. Tad crossed his arms over his chest and scowled. Megan grinned.

Peggy turned a pale countenance towards Sam. "Mr. Duncan, have you heard from our mom?"

He slowly shook his head. "Not yet, I'm afraid."

Tad's snort sounded harsh following the attorney's soft-spoken response.

"You should be afraid. Mom's mean."

His older sister smacked his knee. "Shut up, Tad. Mr. Duncan can take care of himself."

"Yeah, I suppose. He's a lot bigger than Mom, but what about Gram?"

Everyone turned to look at Sam, who seemed totally unaffected by the scrutiny. "I'll do my best to protect all of you, including your grandmother."

After dinner, Regina walked Sam to the door.

With a bow and kiss to her palm he left.

Megan giggled from behind the staircase. "Didn't that tickle?"

Seeing no malice in those chocolate brown eyes, Regina smiled. "As a matter of fact, it did."

The little girl bounced around the corner. "Way, cool. He reminds me of a big teddy bear. Is he your boyfriend?"

"No. I'm too old for that sort of nonsense."

"I was just wondering, 'cuz he didn't kiss Tillie or Gram's hand. He acts like a boyfriend."

The regal woman looked down into the shining face and wondered aloud. "He did, didn't he?"

Megan grabbed Regina's hand, her brow furrowed beneath

her bangs. "You're not really too old for boys, are you, Cousin Regina?"

"Boys, yes, but not men my age." Regina squeezed Megan's hand as Ms. Pickles step-hopped into the foyer.

The little girl scooped her up and plopped down on the step, settling the cat into her lap for some serious stroking. The feline's contented purring was the signal to proceed. "Do old people fall in love?"

"If they're very lucky," Regina said. "Now, I have something to show you children."

"What?"

"Follow me."

Waltzing into the kitchen, Regina announced, "I think it's time to show the children the carriage house."

Tillie's grin filled her face. "That's a great idea, but I have something I need to do. You and Belle go ahead." She left the kids standing with puzzled frowns on their faces.

Regina clapped her hands. "All right, this way please."

Like the Pied Piper, she led them out the back door to the carriage house and the outside stairway to the second floor.

"I thought this was a garage," Tad said.

Annabelle smiled. "It is now, but in the old days, before there were cars, carriages were kept here."

"What's up there?" Megan said, pointing to the door at the top of the stairs.

"That's where the groundskeeper used to live when our grandmother was small," Regina said.

"But what's up there, now?" Tad said.

Regina looked back over their heads at Annabelle.

The cousins shared a smile and spoke in unison. "You'll see."

Removing three keys from a black silk cord around her neck, Regina inserted one, unlocked the door, and stepped in, flipping on the light.

Peggy, Tad, and Megan hurried through the doorway, stumbling over each other.

"Cool," Peggy said, and crossed the room to the stereo. She slipped on the headphones and flipped the switch. Her head bobbed to the beat that only she could hear.

Megan walked to the matching pair of shelves that flanked the window. "Look at all the books," she said, sliding her fingers over the spines. She looked at Regina, who smiled and nodded before choosing a book and settling into the rocker.

Annabelle stood in the doorway, her hands on Tad's bony shoulders.

His stare was directed towards an adjustable easel in the corner. Beside it, a small table stood with paints and brushes lined at attention. A pure white canvas stood at the ready.

Tears filled his eyes as he looked up at his grandmother, then across the room at Regina.

Peggy pulled off the headphones and laughed. "This is so cool."

Regina smiled. "We figured you children needed your own space."

Tad turned and buried his face into his grandmother's bountiful body. "Thanks."

Peggy and Megan gave Regina a group hug. "Thank you."

Regina didn't bother to wipe the tear that fell.

"This is your home now."

CHAPTER 30

The clock struck a dozen times. Everyone had gone to bed except Annabelle, who'd stayed up to finish crocheting an afghan for the girls. She held the rows of yellow sunshine up to the light thinking how lovely it would look on the end of their four-poster bed.

A banging on the front door rattled the window. Startled, Annabelle went to the door and switched on the porch light. When she peeked around the lace curtain, she saw Liddy glaring back, looking more haggard than ever.

Hands shoved deep in her pockets, hair a straggly mess, she shouted at the glass. "Open up, Mother!"

"Hush. You're making too much noise. Someone will call the police." Annabelle removed the chain and opened the door a crack. "Liddy, it's late."

"I don't give a crap. Let me in!" Her voice rose like a pressure cooker ready to spew.

Stepping back, Annabelle allowed her daughter entry, catching a potent whiff of liquor as she passed.

"Please be quiet," Annabelle whispered, "you'll wake the whole neighborhood."

Liddy lowered her voice as she stomped across the threshold. "Then quit screwing around." She stopped just inside the door, waving crumpled papers under her mother's nose. "Subpoena? What is this shit?"

"I've requested legal guardianship of the children."

"Yeah, right. You? That'll be the day." Spittle dotted the corners of Liddy's thin lips. "Where're my kids?"

Putting her hands on her ample hips, Annabelle responded. "In bed, asleep, of course." In a perfect imitation of her cousin, she stiffened her spine.

Peeling her lips back in a feral smile, Liddy stepped closer to her mother. "Get 'em up. We're going home. Vacation's over."

Crossing her arms over her bosom, Belle stood her ground. "This is their home now."

Liddy leaned into her mother's face, her hot breath reeking of booze and stale cigarettes. "What'd you say?"

Annabelle wrinkled her nose but didn't step back. "You're not taking those children anywhere."

"Where do you get off? They're mine. I'll do as I please. No legal bullshit is going to change that." Liddy hauled back her fist.

Anticipating the blow, Annabelle caught her daughter's bony wrist before it could strike. "Not anymore. You abandoned them, and they're going to stay with me."

Yanking her arm from her mother's grasp, Liddy hissed. "You'll pay for that. They're my kids, not yours." She rubbed her wrist a moment, then the corner of her narrow lips turned up. "Hoping for a second chance? Don't bother. You'll screw 'em up, just like you did me."

Annabelle shook her head, her shoulders sagging, but no less formidable. "Go home, Liddy. I'm getting legal custody. Your bullying days are over."

Her thin face purple with rage, Liddy spat, "What do you mean? They belong to me!"

"You gave them to me. They're mine now. I have witnesses that you deserted them weeks ago."

"You bitch. You can't stop me." Liddy's face was pinched, splotches of red on her cheeks and chin matching the roadmaps covering what used to be the whites of her eyes.

Crossing her arms, Annabelle hugged them close to her chest. "The kids need me, and I need them."

"Give me a break. What've you got that anyone needs?"

"Love." Annabelle reached out a hand and stroked her daughter's shoulder. "Go home and sleep it off. The kids have a chance here. Don't blow it for them. Find your own way. It's past time. Use this for your own second chance."

Liddy tipped her head like a confused puppy, then turned on her heel and slogged down the porch steps. "I'll be back, Mother."

Annabelle snicked the door closed on her retreating daughter and turned off the porch light. She watched through the dark as Liddy crossed the lawn to her car and slipped behind the wheel. She sat there for several minutes before starting the engine and driving away.

Turning off the lights in the parlor, Annabelle emitted a heavy sigh and went up to bed. "Lord, please help my poor daughter."

The morning broke cloudy and gray, a good Kansas storm in the making. Joe pulled up in his SUV to give the kids a ride to school.

Hurrying down the hall, Annabelle knocked on the girls' door. "Peggy, Megan. Joe's here."

Silence hollered louder than the usual bustle from behind the door. She opened it. The tidy room and neatly made bed showed no sign of anyone ever having been there. Even Megan's ragged doll was missing.

She rushed to Tad's room. "Tad, are you up?"

Again she found the same sterile scene. There were no books, toys, or dirty clothes anywhere.

"Oh, God, no. She's taken them. Liddy must've sneaked in and stolen them like a thief."

221

B. D. Tharp

Annabelle clutched the front of her housedress, feeling her heart jumping from her chest.

Joe's second honk propelled her down the stairs, through the childless parlor, and into the empty kitchen.

She screamed, "Children, where are you?"

Dashing to the front of the house she threw open the door to meet Joe coming up the steps.

"Good morning. Did everyone oversleep?"

At the sight of Annabelle's watery eyes and trembling chin, the smile faded from his lips. "What happened?"

The dam broke and Annabelle sobbed. "I can't find them anywhere. Liddy's made good on last night's threat."

"Can't find who, the kids? What threat? Slow down, Belle."

Tears streaming down her chin, she clutched her dress.

Taking her elbow, he led her back inside. "Are you sure they're gone? Maybe they're just hiding. Let's take another quick look, shall we?" Joe said.

As soon as Tillie and Regina joined them, Annabelle explained the late night scene with her daughter.

And although they searched everywhere, the results were the same: the children were missing.

Pulling on her sweats, Tillie slid into her mules and jumped in the car with Joe to search the neighborhood.

Regina tied her shoes while Annabelle sat on the window seat, staring at the empty street.

Her sodden hankie held tight in her fist, Annabelle railed against the fates. "Where can they be? Lord, where did I go wrong this time?"

"You didn't do anything wrong, Annabelle," Regina said. "We don't know what's happened yet, so don't assume the worst. You stay here in case they come back."

"Okay." Annabelle sniffled and wiped her nose.

Regina slipped out the back door to join in the search. When she and Devlin were fighting, she used to visit Riverside Park. There were plenty of places to hide, the little house, the old zoo, the witches' cauldron, even the stone bridge by the park entrance off the boulevard along the river.

Heading to the closest place on her list, Regina slid down the grass to look under the bridge. The creek splashed with raindrops, but it hadn't flooded the sandy shelf along the bank.

Huddled in the shadows, she saw what resembled a three-headed creature covered by a yellow rain slicker. An assortment of bags and backpacks were tucked in amongst several pairs of jean-covered legs. Their whispering masked Regina's approach.

"It's not a very good day for exploring," she said.

Leaping up in unison, the trio squealed when she spoke.

Megan's thumb was held firmly in her mouth.

Tad's fist was clenched at his side.

Peggy, pale in the gloom, chewed her bottom lip before she spoke. "We're not going back, Cousin Regina."

"And why not?"

Tad took a step forward. "Because we heard Mom threaten Gram."

"I see. And how will running away help this situation?"

"We don't want to live with Mom anymore." Peggy put her arms around her siblings.

"And what about your grandmother?"

"Mom would beat her up again if we stayed," Tad said.

Regina sighed. "You still haven't told me how running away is going to make anything better."

It's sad these kids have been driven to this kind of desperation.

Clearing her throat, Peggy said, "If we aren't there, then no one gets hurt."

"Little ones, you're wrong. Your leaving won't solve anything. It'll only cause more trouble. Your grandmother will suffer most of all because she loves you and wants you to be with her."

223

Tad's chin came up as he confronted the older woman. "What about you? Are you sure you want us in your old house? We're noisy and messy, and we touch your stuff."

"That's very true, but I've come to realize something of equal importance," Regina said.

Megan pulled her thumb free with a wet pop. "What?"

"That love is more important than *stuff*."

Tears filled Peggy's eyes. "But you don't love us. You don't love anybody."

"She does, too," Megan said. "She loves Tillie and Mr. Duncan. And I think she likes me."

"Ahem." Regina paused before replying. "The fact of the matter is this. You three are my family. I *do* love you. I'm just not very good at showing it yet."

Regina watched as shock registered on the faces of all three children before realizing they weren't reacting to her declaration. Their eyes were wide as saucers and focused over her left shoulder.

"What kind of bull are you feeding my kids?" Liddy said.

The anger in that voice made Regina's spine snap to Victorian attention. Drawing up to her full height, she stepped in front of the children, shielding them from their mother's gaze, and turned with a flip of her braid.

Tad whispered to his sisters, "Uh-oh, when her hair flies, someone's gonna get it!"

Suppressing a smile at his words, Regina raised an eyebrow and placed her elegant hands on her slender hips. "What are you doing here?"

Liddy's teeth looked pointed in the morning haze as her lips curled back. "My stupid mother called, blubbering that she'd lost my kids."

"She was mistaken. The kids are with me, and they're fine."

A good three inches taller than her cousin, Regina set her

jaw, looked down her nose and took a firm step towards Liddy. "Go home. Our lawyer will be in touch."

"No doubt, the best money can buy, eh, cuz? Aren't you sick of my brats by now? They aren't exactly the cream of the family crop, now are they?"

"Don't you have a sleazy beau somewhere you can exchange punches with?" Regina asked.

"Bitch." Liddy stood up on her toes to try and glimpse the children over her cousin's shoulder. "You kids get your butts over here."

All three kids burrowed closer beneath Regina's imaginary wing, the one she thought she'd lost years ago.

"No. They're staying with their grandmother and me. At least with us they'll be well cared for, educated, and loved," Regina said.

"And what would you know about love? Where were you and your money when my husband took off? You'll display them like dolls behind locked glass. Trophies. Mother told me that was your parents' idea of raising kids. Oh, and by the way, where was the family support when Dad used to beat my mother?"

"Perhaps my mother did have difficulty showing affection, but child-rearing did not include punching," Regina said.

A small warm hand with a wet thumb slid into hers and squeezed.

"You can't have everything. It's not fair." Liddy stomped her foot only to splatter mud on her shoes from the soggy bank. "They're either in my car in thirty seconds, or I'm calling the cops."

"If you keep screeching this way, the park patrol will be here shortly, and I doubt they'll let you take anyone anywhere."

Peggy clasped Regina's right hand and stepped around her. The young girl's face was chalky but stern, her eyes dry. "We don't want to leave Gram and Cousin Regina. They love us."

225

"You ungrateful brat. All they're doing is buying you kids off."

Sticking out her chin Peggy shouted back at her mother. "You don't want us. Don't forget you made Megan sleep in the closet, and you broke Tad's arm. We're just an inconvenience unless you want free labor or a punching bag. Let us go, Mom."

Her eyes narrowed to slits and Liddy's hands curled into claws.

Pulling Peggy back, Regina lifted her chin another notch.

"Leave, or we'll just see who the police take to jail."

"Fine. You send your legal shyster over, and I'll kick his fat butt."

Throwing back the greasy strings of her hair that had fallen across her brow, Liddy struggled to climb back up the creek bank.

Tad peeked around Regina's elbow, wiping his nose on his sleeve. "She doesn't know how big Mr. Duncan is, does she?"

With her big doe eyes brimmed with tears, Megan looked up at Regina. "She didn't want us. She said so. She said it was our fault Daddy left."

Regina squatted on her haunches to face the little girl. "It wasn't you children's fault that your daddy left. She shouldn't have said that. Sometimes when people are angry or hurt, they say mean things."

Regina held her close while Megan wrapped her arms around her neck and sniffled. "Let's go home, kids, before your grandmother works herself into a tizzy."

"What's a tizzy?" Megan asked.

"I think it's when your face turns purple and you throw up," Tad offered.

"Something like that," Regina said. She winked at Peggy, and they struggled not to laugh.

CHAPTER 31

Regina led the way up the steep bank to the street. Liddy's car was gone, so they proceeded to the boulevard and home. As they rounded the corner, Megan pulled on Regina's hand. "You should put some gargoyles on the front of our house like they did at the castle."

"That's not a bad idea, young lady. Or maybe a lion or two."

Shaking his head, Tad smiled and puffed out his chest. "Griffins would be better."

"What's a griffin?" Megan asked her big brother.

"They're really cool. They have the body of a lion, the head of an eagle, huge claws, and wings." He lifted his arms, curving his fingers to illustrate.

"You may have something there. What do you think, Peggy?"

Peggy shuffled. "I don't think it'll matter much."

"Will they scare Ms. Pickles?" Megan's eyes were bright.

"Oh, no." Regina smiled at the concern in the little girl's face. "Ms. Pickles isn't afraid of anything."

Joe's SUV was the only vehicle in evidence as they approached the wraparound porch.

Tad ran up the steps and met his grandmother as she threw open the door. Fierce hugs were given all around, and tears fell in torrents as she led the children inside.

Congregating around the kitchen table, Joe began preparing a fresh pot of coffee, and Tillie started frying bacon.

Annabelle wiped her eyes one final time and sat ramrod

straight in her chair. "Why did you leave?"

The oldest children exchanged glances before Peggy proceeded.

"We heard Mom screaming at you last night. We were scared you'd get hurt again." Her voice lowered. "Or you'd give us back."

"I have no plans to give you to anyone, and I won't let anyone hurt you, even your mother," Annabelle said.

"We didn't know," Peggy said. "And we didn't want you to be in the hospital again." She looked down at her lap. "You've never stopped her before, Gram."

Their grandmother nodded. "I see. Well, I never had an important enough reason before."

"Then why did you call her this morning?" Tad's voice snapped with anger. "She came looking for us, and Regina told her to go away. Mom said you told her you lost us."

"What?" Annabelle jumped up, toppling her chair. "That's not what I said at all. I thought she might've taken you."

"I knew Gram wouldn't squeal." Megan smiled.

Joe righted Annabelle's chair and set a cup of hot coffee on the table in front of her.

Tillie brought bacon, eggs, and a basket of sliced banana bread to the table while Joe doled out plates and silverware.

The clock chimed eight. Peggy looked at her siblings and sighed. "We're late for school."

Annabelle smiled at her grandchildren. "Don't worry. I'll go with you and explain to the principal. No matter how upset we are, we do what's necessary. You need to focus on school. Let me worry about the rest."

Tillie and Joe wedged chairs in at the corners of the small table and helped themselves.

"I just have one question, Regina Louise." Tillie's black eyes sparkled.

Regina turned to her friend. "What's that, Matilda Jean?"

"How did you find the kids so fast?"

Tad spoke through a mouthful of scrambled eggs. "She knows all the good hiding places in the park, don't you?"

Regina gave him a wink and a nod.

"I'll phone Sam and see what's holding things up."

Regina picked up the phone and dialed Sam's number. She identified herself to his receptionist and asked to be put through immediately.

A scant minute later, he picked up the line.

"Regina. What can I do for the woman who's stolen my heart?"

She hesitated, swallowed, and then replied. "What's holding up the guardianship of the children?"

"There's no hold up. I just received a call from Judge Tuttle's office. We're to meet him in chambers tomorrow afternoon."

"All of us?"

"Not exactly. Counsel for both sides will meet with him privately. Then he'll want to speak with Annabelle and Lydia."

"I want to be there, Sam."

"That shouldn't be a problem. Meet me at the courthouse at three-thirty."

"Very well," she said.

"Don't worry."

"It's hard not to."

"Hang in there, woman. Sam Duncan will slam dunk this one."

She chuckled. "My hero."

The kids had arrived home from school the next day just as their grandmother and cousin were leaving for the courthouse.

All three children stood in front of the door, hands clasped to bar any exit.

"We're going, too. You might need our help," Peggy said in a clear, crisp, grown-up voice.

Annabelle looked to Regina. "I don't think that's a good idea."

Tad's words, however, were the clincher. "It's our lives they're deciding."

Once again, Regina felt saddened that the children had had to grow up so fast. "Well then, comb your hair, wash your face and hands, and be quick about it. It wouldn't do to be late for the judge."

With great haste they complied and piled into the Cadillac.

It didn't take long to drive to the courthouse, and no one felt very talkative.

Annabelle sat down beside Regina in the courtroom, facing the door that separated them from the person with the power to change their lives.

They'd been waiting for over an hour while counsel for both sides met with the judge, and then individual interviews were held with Liddy, Annabelle, and finally thirteen-year-old Peggy.

She exited the judge's chambers and joined her siblings, who sat squirming behind the wooden rail, flanked by Tillie and Joe, who had arrived separately.

"All rise," the bailiff said, as Judge Tuttle entered the courtroom.

Even in chambers, Judge Tuttle wore the requisite flowing black robe. The starched white cuffs of his shirt protruded from the sleeves as he clasped his fingers on top of the desk. Everything about him appeared stiff. His long face perched on a turtle-like neck that floated in his collar. He had elongated fingers, and his ghostly pallor made it obvious he didn't get out in the sun much.

A bald, fireplug of a man sat beside Liddy. His flushed cheeks and pate were in high contrast to the complexion of his client and the judge.

"After reviewing the testimony of all concerned, the court believes it is in the best interest of the children to grant guardianship to their grandmother, Mrs. Annabelle Hubbard. This arrangement will be reviewed six months from today."

Regina squeezed Annabelle's hand.

From behind them, Peggy sighed, and Tad expelled the breath he'd been holding. Megan's thumb was firmly planted in her mouth.

"This is bullshit," Liddy said, her teeth clinched.

Pointing a narrow finger in Liddy's direction, the skinny judge roared. "Silence. The court further recommends that you, Lydia Malone, obtain counseling and attend anger management classes. As the children's mother you will have limited, supervised visitation until you have fully complied with this order."

Punching the squat lawyer in the arm, Liddy said, "Do something!"

Judge Tuttle smacked his desk with the gavel. "You, young woman, will remain quiet or find yourself in contempt."

Clamping her narrow lips together, Liddy slumped in her chair.

Mr. Fireplug's right eye began to twitch as he stood. "I'm sorry, Your Honor. This is very hard on my client."

Pointing the business end of the gavel in Liddy's direction, the judge said, "If full compliance is not met or an adequate attempt to do so is not shown in twelve months' time, maternal rights will be severed."

Liddy's head came up with a snap. "What?"

"You're lucky you haven't been charged with assault or child endangerment. Court is adjourned."

The final slam of the gavel made Liddy jump.

The bailiff ordered them to rise as the judge left the courtroom.

Before the door shut on his chambers, Liddy stomped down the aisle to the exit. "This isn't over yet."

Annabelle took Sam's bear-sized hand in hers and smiled through her tears. "Thank you, Mr. Duncan."

"You're most welcome, and please call me Sam."

Through the cacophony of cheering children and slapping high fives, Regina leaned up to Sam's ear and whispered, "Nice slam dunk."

Before she could pull away, he slipped his arm around her waist and pulled her close. Their faces were a mere three inches apart.

"That was just the warm up. I've been waiting until this was concluded. I didn't want there to be any questions regarding my interest in the outcome of this case. Now, my dear lady, I think it's time I mounted a full court press."

Regina felt her face warm and her knees weaken.

With a wink, he let her go and joined the children in their revelry.

CHAPTER 32

Tillie smiled across the table. "Thanks for inviting me over."

A chuckle rumbled from deep in Joe's chest.

"You invited yourself, remember? Was it the desire to get me alone and defenseless or the need for a little peace and quiet?"

"Both," she said.

"So tell me, Little Bit, are things just a mite intense at the royal manse these days?"

"You know they are. Between the kids, Belle and Regina, then court today . . . I need a break."

He circled the table, stopping behind her chair. Resting his hands on Tillie's shoulders, he began to knead and stroke the tight muscles.

"Your touch feels nice."

The bass tones of his voice penetrated her trance. "It's been so long, I was afraid you'd forgotten."

"Not likely," she said.

"That's good to hear."

His hands played her like a well-strung instrument.

Tillie's body thrummed to the tune he invoked.

"Come upstairs and let me finish rubbing your troubles away."

"Mmmmm. Sounds like an offer I can't refuse."

Bending down, he whispered, "That's the general idea."

Goosebumps raced down her back and arms, tantalizing her insides.

Taking her small hand in his, he led her up the stairs to his bedroom.

Concentrating on the rise and fall of their combined breathing, Tillie rested her cheek on his warm chest. Her short white curls mingled with the salt and pepper ones that covered his torso. "I love the way you smell," she said.

Joe wrapped his arm around her shoulders, snuggling close. "Stay with me."

"I have no plans to run just yet. Too comfortable."

"Good, but I was thinking of a more permanent arrangement."

Her eyes popped open.

"With or without the benefit or clergy?"

He expelled the breath he held. "You do cut to the crux, darlin'."

She smiled and closed her eyes. "Scared?"

"Not anymore."

Pushing up on her elbow, Tillie looked deep into his eyes. "Me neither."

He lifted her chin. "You wouldn't be messing with me now, would ya?"

With an impish grin, Tillie kissed his nose. "Did I make it too easy for you?"

He whooped and rolled her onto her back.

"Way too easy. Damn, I love you, woman. Will you marry me?"

Tillie bit his shoulder. "I'll answer as soon as you get your big hunky body off me."

He gave her a toe-curling smooch and pushed up on his hands and toes above her. "Impressed?"

"Very."

"Well?"

"Well, what?" she asked.

"What's your answer?"

"Yes, yes, yes," she said, kissing him three times for emphasis.

His face broke in a brilliant smile before he collapsed on top of her.

"At least . . . have the decency . . . not to crush me . . . before it's legal."

Sliding his arms beneath her, he pulled her close and rolled until she was safely on top of him. "Better?"

Tillie wiggled her bottom, molding against his loins. "Much, thanks."

He moaned with pleasure, swatting her behind.

"Brute."

Pulling her down on his chest, he kissed the top of her head. "Forgive me?"

She giggled and pressed her lips to his collarbone. "On one condition."

"What's that?"

"That you impress me again."

"With a push-up?" He flexed his bicep.

"Not exactly," Tillie said, with a shake of her head.

"I think I can rise to the challenge."

"Hot damn."

CHAPTER 33

"Matilda Jean, what do you mean, give you away?" Regina sent her braid flying.

"Just that. Will you and Annabelle give me away?"

Annabelle's cheeks flushed and her smile bloomed.

"Does this mean . . . ?" she asked.

A giggle escaped before Tillie could continue. "Joe and I are getting married."

Regina sat ramrod straight on the sofa, her chin dropping to her chest. It took her a full minute and two hands to put everything back in place. "Congratulations. But why?"

"Why, what? Why am I getting married?" Her black eyes danced as she sparred with her best friend. "Because I love the old fool and he asked?"

"No, no. Why do you want us to give you away?"

"Don't stick your royal nose in the air. You two are my family. I want the older kids to stand up with us, too. Megan can be the ring bearer."

Tears streaming from her eyes, Annabelle popped out of the chair. "I'd be honored. How wonderful. Congratulations. Oh, my stars . . ." She wrung her hankie then unfurled it like a flag.

Regina's jaw was set, but her eyes glistened. "I'd rather give you to the gypsies."

"Joe is rather swarthy. We could pretend he's a gypsy if it'll make you feel better."

Rising from the seat and with a slow smile, Regina engulfed

Tillie in her arms. "I'd be honored, too."

Joe came over and helped Tillie fix seven-layered lasagna, tossed salad, and homemade foccacia bread—guaranteed to make them all comatose from overindulgence. Everyone was seated in the formal dining room and wine was poured.

Megan sniffed and wrinkled her nose.

"This isn't grape juice."

"Yes, it is kiddo," Tillie said. "It's the juice of grapes, only fermented."

"It smells old," Tad said.

"That's what fermented means, stupid," Peggy said.

Shaking her head, Regina stood. "That's the point, young man. Like women, it's aged to perfection." She raised her glass. "Everyone, a toast. We're celebrating the union of two wonderful individuals who deserve much love, happiness, and good fortune."

The children exchanged puzzled looks then took small sips.

"It tastes funny, too," Megan said. "And I don't see any toast."

Annabelle leaned closer to her grandchildren and whispered. "Joe and Tillie are getting married, and when you give good wishes, that's called a toast."

Flashing a grin, Megan announced, "Oh, I knew that."

Everyone laughed, took another sip, and saluted with glasses raised.

Clearing his throat, Joe turned to Tad. "Would you be my best man?"

Sitting up straighter in the chair, he nodded. "Sure, but do I have to wear a tie?"

Joe winked. "We can negotiate."

Tillie stood and leaned over the table. "Peg, would you be my maid of honor?"

Her cheeks infused with pink. "Me?" She turned towards her

cousin and frowned. "But what about Regina? She's your best friend."

Touched by the young woman's concern, Tillie squeezed her hand and smiled. "Your grandmother and Regina are my very best friends, and they are going to give me away."

Megan's brow furrowed at the exchange. "Why would you give her away? And what do I do?"

Joe stood, walked around the table, and knelt beside the little girl and kissed the back of her hand. "Regina and your grandmother have given their permission for me to marry Tillie. And we would like it very much if you would carry our rings for us."

"Okay, I'll try not to lose them," Megan said, and she kissed the back of Joe's hand.

With a smile, Joe hugged the little girl.

Whipping out her hankie, Annabelle blew her nose. "I'll make you girls the most beautiful dresses."

Tad looked stricken. "What about me?"

"You'll look very dashing in a tuxedo, young man." Regina gave him a wink.

Crossing his arms, Tad glared toward Joe. "Thought we were going to negotiate."

"Yes, well, we'll figure something out." Joe patted Tad's shoulder as he circled the table to resume his seat.

"Shit," Tillie said. "I don't have a thing to wear."

Rubbing her hands together, Annabelle beamed. "Not to worry. I'll have four dresses whipped up in no time."

Looking at the ceiling, Regina sent up a silent prayer.

Hang on to your pointed hat, Mother. There's going to be a wedding in the house.

CHAPTER 34

"No you don't!" Annabelle put a hand out to stop Liddy from pushing her way into the house, her nose quivering from the whiskey fumes she emitted.

"I got a right to be here." Liddy shoved her mother's shoulder. "I wanna see my kids."

Standing her ground, Annabelle said, "No. The wedding is only a few hours away. We've got tons to do. It's still morning, and you've been drinking. Please leave. Now."

Liddy's face fused with red, but her lips were thin and white at the corners. "Bullshit, Mother," she said. "Megan called to tell me about her pretty new dress."

"Not now, Liddy. This is Tillie's day, and you weren't invited."

Annabelle forced her daughter back and shut the door in Liddy's angry face. Her heart slammed in her chest as she held her breath and threw the bolt.

Tillie stood at the top of the stairs, remembering her conversation with Joe the week previous.

"I love the fragrance of roses, and daisies are such happy flowers." And here she was, surrounded by them. She smelled their perfume all through the house.

The sight of the elegant young lady slowly descending the staircase in front of her brought Tillie back to the present. "My wedding day," she whispered.

They all looked gorgeous, due to Annabelle's dawn till

midnight labors over the past month.

Tillie couldn't help but admire the first in line, Megan, who wore a seashell pink satin dress. The little girl looked adorable holding the silk pillow where the two wedding rings were tied with tiny white ribbons.

Behind her younger sister, Peggy looked very grown up in her sleeveless, v-neck dress of the same fabric. The dropped waist was trimmed in Belgian lace and hung to midcalf.

Regina had offered the lace trim, a keepsake from *Grandmere* Morgan's cedar chest.

"It needs to be worn to be appreciated," she said.

Tillie fluffed her short white curls and smoothed the front of her straight sheath. It was the color of Irish Crème. A Battenberg lace bolero jacket added the spice. Lifting her head high, she wiped a wayward tear from her cheek and started down the stairs.

"I feel like a queen," Tillie said. "Victoria, move over."

Annabelle and Regina waited at the bottom of the stairs to perform their duty as surrogate parents. Tillie studied them, standing there decked to the nines.

Looking smashing in her ultramarine gown, Annabelle wore her grandmother's pearls with grace. She'd told them about the graduation gift and the note in her grandmother's spidery script: *"Everything goes with pearls, my dear."*

As stand-in parent, Regina opted for a gray tux that matched those worn by the guys. Her throat was adorned with silk ruffles, a black cameo brooch, and her requisite braid wound around her head like a silver crown.

"You two look wonderful." Tillie beamed.

Bobbing a curtsy, Annabelle sniffed and pulled out a new lace hankie for the occasion.

Regina offered her arm to Tillie. "You look grand."

Tillie took it with a squeeze, unable to speak.

When the ladies rounded the corner, the bride's eyes filled with watery pride as she admired her dashing, green-eyed mate. Giving Regina's arm a tug, Tillie whispered, "He looks good enough to eat."

Both Joe and Tad looked rather rakish in their tailcoats, white vests, and ascots. Neither could abide the patent leather shoes, so they had opted instead on flamboyant gray high-tops with black swirls on the sides.

Ms. Pickles led the way, sporting her new royal blue rhinestone collar, her nose and tail skyward as she pranced with as much grace as a three-legged cat could muster. She positioned herself beside Megan and Peggy.

Pastor Paul, bald and robed, stood in the homey parlor, surrounded by hundreds of red and white flowers.

"Who gives this woman in marriage?"

Annabelle and Regina responded in unison, "We do."

Tillie's toes curled inside her slippers, and she mumbled to herself, "I wish my Mom and Dad were here."

Regina took her place beside Sam, invited as a friend, advisor, and future possibility.

He winked and spoke loud enough for all to hear. "I never thought I'd go for a body in a tux, but Regina, my dear, you're making me re-think my position."

With a nonchalant glance over her shoulder, Tillie saw Regina's cheeks suffused with color.

The ceremony began.

The couple faced the minister, who stood before the bay window seat blooming with flowers. Sunbeams shone on the Bible and illuminated the room.

The reverend spoke. "A joyous occasion . . . in sickness and health, until death do you part . . ."

There wasn't a dry eye in the house, except for Ms. Pickles. Her tail didn't twitch and her chin was raised, as if she were lording over the proceedings.

"I now pronounce you husband and wife. You may kiss the . . ."

"*Meow.*"

After the untimely but amusing interruption, the cat, ears at attention, sped from the room as fast as her three legs could carry her. Megan was right on her tail.

Tillie and Joe burst out laughing.

Pastor Paul cleared his throat, trying to disguise his chuckle. "I believe your feline wanted the last word. You are husband and wife."

Regina's eyes rolled. "Damn cat."

A squeal of tires, the crunch of metal, and Megan's shrill scream cut the moment short.

Sam and Regina dashed out the front door. Descending the steps two at a time, they found Megan on her knees at the curb beside the twisted body of the cat. The ring pillow she'd tucked under its tiny head was now crimson with blood.

Tillie and Joe were there in seconds.

Kneeling beside the little girl, Regina wrapped her arms around the quaking shoulders. "Megan, are you hurt?"

"Ms. Pickles is dead. She jumped at Mommy's car."

Regina looked up in time to see her beau running into the street. "Sam?"

He shouted over his shoulder, "Regina, call 9-1-1."

The young man next door stepped out on the porch, cellular phone in one hand. "They're already on their way."

Regina's eyes widened at the sight of the mangled sedan three doors down. "Oh, Lord, that wreck belongs to Liddy."

Tillie clutched her bouquet against her heart, watching Joe.

He was forced to look in the back window of the car that now lay on its side.

Sam and Joe had circled the car a second time when Sam

called out, "Lydia, can you hear me?"

The only response was the blare of the sirens.

Minutes later the emergency team arrived with lights flashing.

Megan laid a hand on the gray fur, but her eyes were fixed on the twisted metal that was once their family car. "Is she dead?"

Regina leaned forward and took the feline into her arms, covered the tiny snout with her mouth, and attempted to resuscitate the cat. Ms. Pickles answered with a tiny sneeze and squeezed her eyes to slits, her labored breaths shaking her body.

Standing, Regina looked at Megan's flooded eyes. "She's alive, but she'll have to go to the hospital."

"Can I go?" Megan asked, her doe eyes filled to overflowing.

"No, sweetheart. You need to be with your grandmother right now."

Regina helped the little girl from the ground. Her knees and the front of her pretty dress were soiled with mud and blood.

Sticking her thumb in her mouth, Megan nodded.

Regina gave Tillie's hand a squeeze. "I'm taking Ms. Pickles to the vet. Call when you know something about Lydia."

Sam walked over and leaned down to Megan's eye level. "Don't you worry." He took her by the hand. "I'll stay and take care of things here."

A tear slid down the little girl's cheek. Her thumb remained implanted between her pale lips.

Sam rose to face Regina, never letting go of Megan's icy fingers. "I'll call."

With a weak smile, Regina whispered, "My hero," then climbed into the Cadillac and pulled away.

Standing alone now at the curb, Tillie heaved a sigh before joining Joe and the others.

Silent tears fell from the red and swollen faces of the older children.

Annabelle's new hankie was in shreds.

They watched the emergency medical technicians extract Liddy's ruined body through the shattered windshield. Her face and hands were covered with tiny cuts, but the bleeding had stopped. They strapped her to a collapsible gurney and began CPR.

Annabelle followed them to the waiting ambulance, but before stepping inside, she turned to her family and friends.

"Sam, would you and Joe please bring Tillie and the children to the hospital. I'm riding with my daughter."

CHAPTER 35

The doors to the vehicle shut. The EMT continued to administer CPR and oxygen. Liddy's chest rose and fell with the paramedic's efforts. The monitor had blipped once, then gone flat.

Annabelle saw no signs of life in her only child. The fog cleared from the plastic mask over the still face. Silent tears slid from Annabelle's chin, drops of darkness marred the shining fabric over her heart.

They arrived at the nearest hospital emergency entrance within minutes. Annabelle joined her family as the technicians wheeled Liddy's lifeless form into the building.

Following in silence, Sam took the children to the waiting area. Joe and Tillie accompanied Annabelle and the gurney into the exam room.

A doctor took the technician's staccato report while examining Liddy's pupils and checking for a pulse. Removing his stethoscope, he spoke for the first time.

"Are you her family?"

"I'm her mother," Annabelle said.

"I'm sorry." He reached down and covered Liddy's empty eyes with the sheet. "We did everything we could," the doctor said.

"I know."

"I understand that she was in an automobile accident?" he asked.

"Yes."

"Was she drinking?"

Annabelle's shoulders drooped with resignation. "I believe so."

"We'll have to run blood alcohol tests and verify the cause of death."

"Very well," Annabelle said.

"I'm sorry. I'll send someone from patient services to help you with the arrangements."

"Thank you," Annabelle said.

The doctor left them alone with the lifeless body.

Joe helped Annabelle to a chair and grabbed Tillie's hand. "What about the kids?" he said.

Raising her chin, Annabelle sniffed. "I'll tell them." She stiffened her spine and walked from behind the curtain. Tillie and Joe shadowed her as she moved down the hall to inform the children their mother was dead.

Tad stepped closer to his sister. "Is Mom okay?"

Their grandmother's grim countenance gave them their answer.

Dry-eyed, Peggy gathered her siblings to face the news.

Annabelle squeezed in beside them on the couch and pulled them into her arms.

"I'm sorry. Your mother's gone. She was too badly hurt."

How much had she contributed to the damage? She forced the picture of her child's bloodless face from her mind. God had given her a second chance, so Annabelle made a vow to do better for her grandchildren.

Peggy jerked away from her grandmother's embrace.

Stomping his foot, Tad shouted, "No. She's too mean to die. She was supposed to quit drinking and hitting and be our mom again."

"I know. I wish you'd known her when she was young and

happy. We have choices, kids. Let's choose to stay together and help each other." Annabelle reached her hand out to her eldest grandchild.

Peggy buried her face in her grandmother's bosom, shaking them both with her screams.

In that instant, Tad's anger crumbled, and he fell to his knees. Covering his face with his hands, he laid his head in his grandmother's lap and let the tears flow, his body wracked with sobs.

Megan continued to suck her thumb, her face a stone mask.

Tillie and Joe sat on the sofa across from their friends. Their happy day had turned into tragedy.

Regina took Sam's call at the vet's office.

"I know Bob at Foster Funeral Home. He can help, Sam. We'll bury her next to her father."

"I'll make the arrangements," Sam said.

Regina's voice broke. "Thank you."

His soft tones caressed her. "I'd do anything for you, my dear."

Not trusting her response, Regina remained silent.

"What about the cat?" he said.

"Oh, she's a tough critter. If she lives through the night, she'll make it."

"I'm glad. Megan needs that cat," Sam said.

"How are Belle and the kids holding up?"

"The older ones are crying in their grandmother's arms. The littlest is too quiet."

Straightening her shoulders, Regina tugged her braid. "They're not alone. They've got Belle and me, and each other."

Regina heard a smile in Sam's voice. "Then I'm sure they'll be fine. I'll bring them home as soon as we've finished here."

"Oh, Lord, what about Tillie and Joe?"

"They look pretty tuckered out, but I don't think they're going anywhere until everyone is safely back home."

Tillie's voice carried across the line. "Is that Regina?"

Regina listened to the sound of the receiver changing hands. "How's Ms. Pickles?"

"Honey, she's hanging in there. Dr. Kincaid is planning on sleeping on the office couch so he can check on her tonight."

"Bless his heart. Is she that bad?"

"She's got two broken ribs and suffered some trauma to her lungs. That's what caused the bleeding. He thinks she'll be fine by morning."

"Good."

"Tillie?" Regina spoke in a whisper.

"Yes?"

"Please don't postpone your honeymoon."

A sigh was barely audible. "We'll talk about that later, okay?"

"Could you put Sam back on?"

"Sure."

Regina hesitated a moment, listening for his breathing. "Sam?"

"I'm here."

"Thanks, for . . . being there."

His voice eased through the lines. "Not to worry. Your servant, always."

CHAPTER 36

Under the shadows of the green tent, Annabelle took a seat beside Tad, glancing to the other end of the row of dreary, cloth-covered folding chairs. Regina's stalwart presence bolstered her flagging strength. Her gaze touched on the two older children who bracketed Megan. The flood of tears they shed threatened to wash them all away.

Pastor Paul stood beside the open grave and said a prayer of blessing. His words were nearly swallowed up by the Kansas wind. "Please join me in the first verse of 'Amazing Grace.' "

Less than a dozen voices strained to fill the air with song. No one could remember the second verse, so they repeated the first verse and then their voices petered out.

The kids fidgeted as the minister read from the book of Psalms.

"God is our refuge and strength, a very present help in trouble. Therefore we will not fear though the earth should change . . ."

The children stared at the stark white surface of the closed casket. It loomed large above the dark hole in the ground.

"Please join me in reciting the Lord's Prayer."

"Our Father, who art in heaven . . . forgive us our trespasses . . ."

During the pause, Annabelle's voice stabbed the silence. "Everyone deserves a second chance in life, but my daughter didn't get hers."

Silence. There was nothing left to say.

A prayer of benediction was offered. Then everyone took their turn to speak with the family.

The minister moved quickly and efficiently down the line, touching everyone's hands, blessing each in turn, and then moving on.

The children's eyes were red and swollen.

Annabelle presented a solemn figure. She shook hands with Liddy's two co-workers.

Accepting a comforting bear hug from Sam, her voice broke as she whispered in his ear, "Thank you for coming."

He stepped back and gave her a wink before squatting down in front of the children. Taking their small, cold hands in his huge paws, he looked into their tear streaked faces. "You're going to be all right. Your grandmother and Cousin Regina will see to it."

Tad nodded and Peggy gave him a peck on the cheek. Megan stared at nothing.

Sam took his place beside Regina and laid his arm around her shoulders.

Annabelle approached the casket. She rested her hand on the cold surface. "Lord, I vow to do better this time." She took a pink rose from the spray and motioned for the children to do the same.

Each took a blossom from the arrangement and walked away.

As Regina approached, Annabelle spoke in undertones. "I had hoped Tom would attend. He's a sorry excuse for a man, but he is their father."

"He probably doesn't even know," Regina said. "The kids weren't even sure he still lives around here."

"I suppose." Annabelle wrung her hankie. "I think it would've meant a lot to them if he'd managed to come."

Regina flipped her braid over her shoulder. "We'll deal with

Tom Malone when and if the time arrives."

The family and Liddy's few friends converged at the house in Riverside. Tillie had cooked up a platter of finger food ahead of time, and the neighbors had brought cakes and cookies for the kids.

Murmurs of conversation filled the parlor, as did the wedding daisies and the peace lilies from the funeral. Such a sad contrast, Annabelle thought, sunny flowers of promise and stoic representatives of death.

Megan sat on the window seat stroking Ms. Pickles with one hand. She stared at the white bandage that swathed the cat's thin chest and sucked on her thumb.

Annabelle couldn't help but notice that, unlike normal, Megan hadn't touched the sweets.

"You doing okay, honey?"

Megan shook her head.

Annabelle wiped the tear from her granddaughter's pale cheek. "Want to talk about it?"

Removing her thumb, Megan looked at her lap. "It was my fault, Gram."

"What?"

"If I hadn't called, Momma wouldn't have come."

"It was not your fault. Her car turned over."

"It is, too. I chased Ms. Pickles, and Momma swerved as we jumped off the curb."

She swerved to miss her baby.

"If Momma hadn't turned her car like that, Ms. Pickles would've been smashed."

"Oh, my, you could've been killed."

Lord, thank you. My daughter was there to protect her child when it mattered most.

"If it wasn't for me, Momma wouldn't be dead."

Wrapping her arms around Megan, Annabelle kissed her

tears. "It was an accident, honey. You didn't do anything wrong."

Regina glided over and knelt beside the little girl. "Every-thing's going to be all right. I promise."

"But, I never got to tell her I love her." Megan sobbed.

"She knows," Annabelle said, giving her granddaughter a squeeze. "I promise you, she knows."

Regina encouraged Annabelle to settle the kids into bed early and was thankful Sam stayed to help clean up.

She watched him through her lashes as they moved in tandem. He seemed to know what needed to be done without being asked. It felt comfortable and frightening at the same time.

The atonal symphony of Victoria Morgan's voice invaded her mind.

"Why is he still here? What does he want from you?"

Sam reached out and touched her arm. "A quarter for your thoughts."

Her eyebrow rose in question.

"Inflation," he answered, though she hadn't spoken aloud.

Raising her chin, Regina squared her shoulders. "Okay, why are you still here?"

He gave her a crooked grin. "I'm just here to help."

"Do you always go so far beyond the call of duty?"

He scowled. "Excuse me?"

"You're my lawyer. You don't have to do dishes or hold our hands."

She could see the angry storm beginning to build in his brown eyes. "No. I thought you knew by now how much more you mean to me."

Regina had the good sense to blush but continued to fall over the precipice of her own making. "You're here for my family."

"Only because they are a part of you."

"That's very flattering, but unnecessary," Regina said.

Flexing his hands at his sides, he took a calming breath. "Are you deliberately trying to be insulting?"

"Hardly," she said. "You're a very good attorney, and I appreciate all you've done for us." She crossed her arms in either defiance or protection; she hadn't decided which.

The muscle in his jaw twitched, his eyes narrowed, and his cheeks flushed. Sam gripped her forearms and dragged her up against his massive chest. "I don't know what you're up to, Regina Morgan-Smith. It's just the two of us now, and we've only just begun." His lips took hers in a searing kiss.

Conscious thought was impossible as Regina melted under the onslaught. She stumbled back against the cabinet when he released his grip.

"Regina Louise Morgan."

Oh, shut up, Mother.

The day had been way too long. She could no longer shield herself against the deep feelings Sam invoked. Her heart ached in her chest, and her knees felt like jelly.

"We'll talk about us soon. That's a fact as well as a promise, Rags." Without waiting for a response, Sam departed.

Regina stood alone in the kitchen, feeling the brand of his mouth on hers. *Rags?* She gave in to her desire to collapse into a puddle on the floor.

Her mother's discordant voice screeched.

"Now you've done it. You've tempted the man beyond his station. He's a solicitor, for pity sake. First the lovelorn cook, then a gaggle of poor relations, now this. Where will it end?"

"I'm not sure, Mother, so just stow the sarcasm." Regina stood, dusted herself off, and dug in the junk drawer for a cigarette. Finding none, she took out Tillie's brandy and poured two fingers in a water glass. Tossing it down in one gulp, she shook the image of her mother from her mind.

Maybe that will drown the bitch.

CHAPTER 37

Two days later, Annabelle answered the phone. The newlyweds related tales of New Orleans Cajun cuisine and the jazz festival.

"We'll bring the kids back a bucket of mud bugs," Tillie said.

Wrinkling her nose, Annabelle asked, "Whatever for?"

"They're crawfish. You eat 'em!"

Shaking her blue coif, Annabelle smiled into the telephone. "Oh? Well, you could make anything taste good."

Tillie laughed. "You'll love them, I promise."

"When will you be back?"

"That's part of the reason I called. I think we're going to stay an extra two or three weeks. Do you think you and Regina can manage without me for that long?"

"Of course. We're adults, and besides, there's always pizza delivery and take-out Chinese."

"Good point. I doubt you'll starve. It's intoxicating here. All lush and decadent, steamy and spicy, old world and new, teaming in the streets and bayous. It's really awesome. Definitely a great place for a honeymoon."

"You two must be enjoying yourselves."

"You better believe it. We have a balcony suite on Bourbon Street, although we haven't made it out on the balcony, yet."

Annabelle's cheeks warmed. "We'll see you when you get back."

"With the mud bugs."

She chuckled, "If you say so."

When she replaced the receiver on the cradle, it began to ring again.

"What did you forget?"

A warm, male voice coughed.

"Oh, excuse me. I mean, hello . . ." Annabelle said.

"Hello, Annabelle. This is Sam."

"I'm sorry, Sam, I thought you were Tillie calling back."

"How are the newlyweds?"

"They're having such a fine time they plan on staying another couple of weeks."

"Excellent. Is Regina home?"

"Sure. I'll get her."

Annabelle laid the handset across the top of the wall phone. The parlor was empty, so she stepped into the foyer and called up the stairs.

"Regina, telephone."

The door opened to Regina's bedroom. Her hair hung unfettered in black and silver waves around her shoulders.

"Who is it?"

"Sam."

She wrapped her robe around her body and cinched the belt tight.

"Tell him I'm not home."

"I will not. Stop acting like a ninny and pick up the extension."

"Damn." Regina slammed her bedroom door.

Annabelle went back to the kitchen and listened for Regina to answer. She heard a click and Regina's shaky voice.

"Yes?"

Wanting to eavesdrop but knowing she shouldn't, Annabelle hung up the phone and fussed with the dishes. It wasn't long before a disheveled Regina appeared.

"Is there any coffee?"

"In the pot." Annabelle turned to face her cousin. "Why didn't you want to talk to Sam?"

"I just didn't, that's all."

"Pish-tosh, you know you two like each other. Why pretend you don't?"

Regina grabbed for her braid and tangled her fingers in her unbound locks. With a minor struggle, she managed to flip a handful of hair over one shoulder. "That's utter fantasy, and you know it."

Crossing her arms, Annabelle scowled at her cousin. "I know no such thing. You're being ridiculous."

"Bullshit," Regina said. She slammed her half-empty cup on the cabinet. Ignoring the splattered brown mess, she exited in a flurry of velvet and bare feet.

A smile crept across Annabelle's face as she wiped up the spill. She giggled and began to hum the melody of "Do You Want to Know a Secret?" while Regina banged around upstairs.

When the doorbell rang promptly at six that evening, Regina glided down the stairs to open it. She wore an azure blue silk skirt with an embroidered long sleeve tunic. She gave her braid one last stroke before opening the door.

Sam's brown eyes bulged at the sight of her. His Adam's apple bobbed as he swallowed and offered her his arm.

"You look delicious. Are you ready to be wined and dined?"

She gave him a cool smile and took his elbow. "I suppose."

Sam escorted Regina to his car, opened the door, and assisted her into the passenger seat. He climbed behind the wheel and simply stared at her for a moment.

"What is it?" she asked.

He grinned and started the ignition. "Change of plans."

"Oh? No dinner? No wine?"

No seduction?

Pulling out of the drive, he headed north. "There's something I want you to see, then we'll have dinner. All right?"

"Fine." Regina felt herself losing control, and she didn't know what to do about it.

In silence they drove out of the city. Society manners had deserted her. Unable to think of anything to say, Regina stared at the red prairie grasses and yellow flax growing wild along the fencerow, trying to keep her hands from shaking. She rolled down her window and sniffed. "I love the scent of spring."

Smiling, Sam turned east onto a gravel access road that led into a grove of elm trees.

The car emerged from the sudden shade, revealing a three-story house, reminiscent of a Frank Lloyd Wright design.

"Why are we here?"

"It's not a hundred years old like your place, but I'm comfortable."

"It's yours?" she asked.

"Uh-huh."

Regina didn't wait for him to open her door. She slipped out onto the stone walk, admiring the manicured lawn and the lovely house.

"What a wonderful place to live."

Taking her arm, Sam led her to the double oak doors. With a smile and a bow, he opened one. "After you, my dearest Rags."

"I'm not taking another step until you tell me where you came up with that ridiculous name."

Placing his hand on the small of her back, he maneuvered her into the entry. "Because you're its antithesis. I've never met anyone more polished than you, and yet I have the feeling you'd be just as regal if you were penniless."

"Nonsense." The heat of his fingers made her stomach flop and her knees wobble.

"Regina is much too formal. Reggie isn't feminine enough,

257

and Rags is silly. That's why Rags fits."

Trying not to show how much his words pleased her, Regina's eyes feasted on the ordered chaos. He'd furnished the house with a mix of antique wood with modern glass and chrome. Ceramic tiles filled the entry, a subtle blend of every color and hue. The furniture was Arts and Crafts period, simple yet elegant.

He let out a low whistle that startled her but resulted in a loud "Woof" from upstairs. The biggest yellow Labrador retriever she'd ever seen came bounding toward her, its tongue lolling to one side.

Regina took a step back, closer to Sam. "Is it vicious?"

With a chuckle, Sam hunkered down and held his stance as the mammoth canine leapt towards his arms. "This is Sugar Bear. She might lick you to death, and she'll certainly shed on you, but that's about as dangerous as she gets."

Regina watched in fascination as the dog slurped and slobbered Sam's face.

"Am I to be a new friend or its next meal?"

"Don't be afraid. Just hold your hand palm up. Then after she sniffs you, stroke her head and tell her your name."

With a mix of curiosity and terror, Regina reached out. "I've never been around dogs. Mother said they were dirty and mean."

Sugar Bear gave Regina's hand the Hoover treatment with her nose, then licked the palm.

Regina giggled. "Nice dog. I'm Regina." Petting the soft golden fur, she admired the animal's liquid brown eyes, and realized her mother had been wrong, again.

Stepping back, Regina smiled. "She's delightful. If I weren't afraid of being eaten, I think I'd be in love."

"My sentiments exactly," Sam said.

She turned, and he winked.

"Let me show you the rest of the house."

Regina toyed with her braid as he led her through the living room, then the formal dining room, and into the kitchen. She'd admired the floor to ceiling fireplace constructed of stone. The kitchen was charming with its brick oven, copper pots, and steel appliances.

"Sam, do you cook?" she asked.

"I will tonight. Do you want to finish the tour on your own while I get things started?"

"If you wouldn't mind."

"Not in the least," he said. He opened the side-by-side refrigerator and began loading his arms with fresh vegetables.

Taking her cue, Regina walked to the window above the sink and looked out back.

The deck ran the length of the back of the house, and the yard sloped down to a creek that ran amongst the trees. "What a wonderful view."

He continued to chop. "Sometimes at dusk, deer will come down to drink. In the early morning, if Sugar is still inside, there's a red fox that brings her kits to visit."

It was hard to tear her mind away from the images his words invoked, but curiosity won out, and she decided to explore.

Sugar Bear led Regina up the stairs. She found a small, sparse guest room, an office piled with books and papers, and an immaculate bathroom with a basket of magazines close at hand. The master bedroom was huge, decorated in cherry oak Mission furniture. Across from the bed, a landscape hung. She recognized it as her own work.

Her heart thudded in her chest as her eyes began to tear. The picture had hung in a gallery in Kansas City. She'd wondered for ten years who'd bought it, and now she knew. It fit the room, and no matter where you stood you could admire it.

Woof.

She wiped her eyes and followed the dog to the stairs leading up to the third floor. The staircase was wide and sturdy, so unlike the narrow, squeaky one at her home. Anticipating a dark attic room, Regina opened the door and gasped. There were windows on every wall, and the room was filled with light. In its center sat a worn, leather recliner, table and lamp, with a stack of books beneath it.

The dog ran circles around the room, then settled on the rug in front of the table and watched Regina cross to the windows. She saw fields of wheat just beginning to turn golden, a pasture of blue stem with cows grazing around tiny evergreens, no doubt planted by passing flocks of birds.

"Oh, my," she said, clutching her arms around herself. "This would make a great studio." She watched the lazy bovines. The sky began to glow, pink and orange, painted by the setting sun.

Enough time passed that the dog fell asleep, her chin on her paws. Regina stroked the animal's silky head. "We'd better go check on the cook."

Sugar Bear jumped up and bounded down the stairs. Regina rose to follow, then froze. On the walls adjacent to the door were two more of her paintings: one of a little girl, dandelions and daisies in her hand, barefoot, standing in a puddle; the other, the same little girl, dirty feet in the sky, black hair flying behind her, on a swing, laughing.

Sam cleared his throat and wiped his hands on a dishtowel. "Hi."

"Where did you get these?"

"Here and there. They make me think of what you must've been like when you were a kid," he said.

"Those aren't me. I was never allowed to run barefoot in puddles or pick weeds. The paintings are . . . who I wanted to be."

He crossed the room in two long strides and gave her a hug. "You know what you need?"

"Yes, food."

"And wine, but more than that, you need loving, Rags, and I'm here to give it to you."

"My hero." But was she brave enough to take what he offered?

CHAPTER 38

After a fine dinner of grilled salmon, rice pilaf, and salad, Sam refilled their wine. "Let's go out on the back deck," he said.

"All right."

Sugar Bear preceded them and headed for the creek.

Regina watched the animal's easy lope and smiled. "I always wanted a dog. She's so tidy and sweet."

"She's a very good house dog, now that she's matured. As a pup I debated changing her name to Bulldozer or Destructo."

Regina laughed.

"I'm not kidding. She dismantled my furniture, chewed a hole in the rug, and ate more shoes than I'll ever admit I owned. She's grown out of that stage, thank goodness, and takes good care of things now."

"It's a very nice home. Thank you for showing it to me. And dinner was superb."

His cheeks pinked as his smile grew.

She shivered. "It's a bit chilly."

He rose and helped Regina from her chair. "Let's go upstairs. We can watch the night begin."

The dog romped up the deck stairs to join them.

Sam patted her head. "You stay here, girl, and stand guard."

The yellow Lab barked, circled in place, then settled down to keep an eye on things.

Hands clasped, Regina and Sam walked up the stairs without speaking. From their vantage point on the third floor, she saw the fading glow of the sun sliding behind the horizon. Sam slipped up beside her.

"It's beautiful. I love this room."

He placed an arm around her waist. "It'd make a great artist's studio, don't you think?"

Tingles tripped up her spine. "Yes, I do."

"I can see an easel just over there, turned so it can catch the sunlight," he said.

"Yes," she said. And Regina could see it perfectly, and him in the chair reading while she painted.

He encircled her with both arms and kissed her cheek, her forehead, and her mouth. "I was hoping you'd like it."

"How could I not?" The contents of her stomach churned. She clutched a fist and held it against her middle. The warmth of his embrace melted into her bones and seeped into every fiber of her being.

Sam turned her to face him. "I'm going to kiss you, Rags."

Speech had flown with the light, so she nodded and hoped she wouldn't embarrass herself by swooning. She wanted this man. More than anything else, she wanted Sam. Her mother would have a coronary if the she weren't already dead. Unfortunately, she wouldn't stay buried.

He brushed her lips with his, then went back for more— sampling, tasting. Their bodies molded together.

Stars burst in Regina's mind, singed her lips, and flowed down her back. Her body filled with a glorious heat that she'd never felt before. She was greedy and wanted more.

Their lips parted as they gasped for air.

Sam winked. "I see the fire in you, burning beneath the ice. I've wanted you for so very long. Let me show you how much."

Her eyes danced. Regina took his hand and led him down the stairs to the master bedroom. Although shocked by her boldness, it felt right somehow. She'd wasted enough time.

They helped each other undress, folded their garments, laying them on the back of the chair. Regina enjoyed the slow and tender process.

Her heart thudded in her chest. She thought she saw appreciation and acceptance written on his face, while she hid her anxiety as they came together.

Oh, lord. What if I can't . . .

But they found the rhythm and harmony only two people in love could experience.

Reaching their peak and soaring beyond, they held on to each other, clinging to the explosions they shared.

Sam wiped the damp tendrils from Regina's forehead. "I love you, Rags. Will you marry me?"

"Oh, Sam. I've never felt so cherished, and, frankly, it scares the hell out of me. I have to think, and right now, in this position, all I can do is feel."

He kissed her swollen lips and smiled. "You were worth waiting for. We can talk tomorrow. For now, let's enjoy each other."

Wrapping her arms around his neck, she kissed him with desperation and need. She'd think later.

Regina woke with a start as the grandfather clock struck three and penetrated her dreams. Sam was spooned behind her, his big body keeping her warm under the sheet. She felt content and sated. She'd never experienced such feelings or been loved so thoroughly.

"Sam."

"Hum."

"It's time I went home."

"Huh? You are home."

She turned in his arms to face him. "Please. Besides, that poor dog has been out all night."

He opened his eyes to slits. "She's fine. She has a fur coat and very sharp teeth."

"Please, Sam."

"Oh, all right." He rose from the bed, and they dressed in silence.

Regina scooted to the edge to braid her hair while Sam went to let in the dog.

Sugar Bear dashed into the room and sailed into the bed beside her, landing in a flurry of fur and sheets.

With a laugh, Regina patted the canine and stood. "You're a funny thing. I'll see you later."

When they pulled into the drive at four A.M. they found the porch light on, but every window was dark.

Regina leaned toward Sam and kissed his cheek.

"Thank you for the most wonderful night of my life," she said.

"I told you. We've just gotten started." He gave her a hokey grin.

She smiled and opened the car door. "Good morning."

"You, too, love."

Thinking her heart would burst, Regina sauntered up the steps and slipped inside the sleeping house.

She turned and waved before heading up the stairs to her own room, hoping her dreams would be glorious replays of the night she'd just spent.

CHAPTER 39

Regina luxuriated in bed late—against all childhood dictates. The sound of loud whispers in the hallway forced her to rise. She turned the knob and eased the door open, hoping to catch the children unaware.

Peggy, hands on hips, hissed a warning. "Shhhh. You'll wake Regina."

Tad crossed his eyes and scowled. "Will not."

"Will, too," Regina said, causing them both to jump. "Good morning."

The teenager sneered at her little brother. "See?"

He poked his sister in the arm then frowned up at Regina. "Sorry."

She patted his head and smiled. "Not to worry, young man."

She felt his eyes on her back as she proceeded down the steps to the kitchen and fresh coffee, she hoped.

"Good morning," Annabelle said, eyeing Regina from the top of her disheveled head to the bottom of her bare feet. "You look bright and shining this morning."

"Why, thank you. I'll feel even better when I've had my java." She poured herself a cup and strolled to the window. "What's on the agenda for today?"

"It's Saturday, so I thought I'd get groceries. The kids can come along and help."

"Sounds like fun."

Annabelle's mouth fell open. "Do you want to come with us?"

With a chuckle, Regina took her finger and lifted Annabelle's chin back in place. "No, I have some things to think about, and a quiet house is probably the best place."

Her cheeks flushed and a smile split Annabelle's face. "Oh? Care to tell me what this is all about?"

"No, but thanks for the offer." Regina drained her cup and waltzed out of the room.

Before she was finished dressing, the kids and Annabelle left for Wally World. She decided to do her thinking in her attic studio. The creaking and the narrowness of the stairs irritated her.

She opened the door to what had always been her sanctuary and felt hemmed in by the darkness. Pulling the cord on the bulb did little to brighten the dingy, coffin-like space. Paintings were stacked all along the walls, hidden, one behind the other, buried in shadow and dust. No wonder her work had become so depressing, she thought. She exited the room with a slam.

Regina slid her hand down the smooth banister, darkened by time and touch. Reaching the second floor, she paused to scan the hallway with its dark framed photographs and paintings. Everything looked worn and stale.

Annabelle's favorite painting, the farm scene, caught her eye. She lifted it from its hanger, ignoring the contrast between the bright wallpaper beneath it and the faded pattern surrounding its vacated spot.

She crossed the landing to Annabelle's room. She scanned the tidy but lived in space and smiled, then laid the painting on the bedspread.

Regina marched down the stairs to the parlor and stood in the middle of the room. Her mother's bric-a-brac lay on every surface. The doilies that had protected the tables and sofa arms were yellowed with age.

Walking to the bookshelves, she ran her long fingers over the spines and sighed. Some of the books were her father's, but most were her own. Taking one of her favorites, she crossed to the window seat, her favored spot in the house. Gazing out the window, she could feel her mother's presence chill the room.

"Lollygagging about, Regina?"

"I suppose you could say that, Mother."

"And where were you all night?"

"In the arms of a lusty man."

"How crass. I see the poor relations have affected your judgment."

"Perhaps, but you want to know something?"

"I don't believe you have anything to say that I want to hear. You are definitely in a mood."

"Oh, well, that's too bad. You see, I've decided to move."

And go where, might I ask?"

"I'm tired of this stodgy old place."

"You wouldn't dare sell this house. It's your legacy."

"I'm giving it to Annabelle and the kids."

"Have you lost your mind?"

"No, everything about me now is working fine. This was your house, Mother. Never mine. It's old fashioned and fits Grandmother Annabelle perfectly. She and the kids will enjoy it."

"Oh, my God. You're serious. You'd leave my house to them? They don't deserve it."

"I think they do. They need this place more than I do. I've been overshadowed by you and this house long enough. It's past time I did something for myself."

"You selfish child. What will you do?"

"I'm not a child. Haven't been one for forty years." She closed the book with a snap. "I'm moving in with Sam, in his sunny house in the country."

"Marry an attorney?"

"Who said anything about marriage?"

"You'd live in sin?"

"Give it a rest, you old spook. The only time you set foot in the church was your wedding day and Grandfather's funeral. I'm not buying this holy attitude from you." Regina smiled. "Good Lord, I sound just like Tillie."

"What has happened to you, Regina?"

"I've fallen in love."

"Malarkey."

Regina laughed at the cluster of dust motes resembling a woman's form flitting through a sunbeam. She swiped an elegant hand through them and watched as they dissipated.

"I think I'll go call Sam, then pack. Good-bye, Mother. From now on, you're on your own."

ABOUT THE AUTHOR

A lifetime resident of Kansas, **B. D. Tharp** graduated magna cum laude with a Bachelor of Arts in Communications, Women/Minority Studies, and Fine Arts. She has published a short story in the *Sheridan Edwards Review,* an essay in *A Waist Is a Terrible Thing to Mind, an Anthology,* and more than a hundred articles for various magazines and newsletters. She's received awards on a local, state, and national level for short stories, children's picture books, playwriting, and novels. B. D. is married with one grown son, two grandsons, and two very spoiled dogs.